To Frank,
The fittest of us all!
with best wishes,
Freda Hansburg

Shrink Rapt

Freda Hansburg

Shrink Rapt
Freda Hansburg

First Printing:
ISBN 978-0-9905604-0-1

Copyright © 2014 by Freda Hansburg
All rights reserved.

This book or any portion thereof may
not be reproduced or used in any manner
whatsoever without the express written
permission of the publisher except for the
use of brief quotations in a book review.

Poos Press
www.fredahansburg.com
freda@fredahansburg.com

This book is a work of fiction.
Names, characters, organizations, events
and incidents either are the product
of the author's imagination
or are used fictitiously.

Back cover Author photo by Hannah Forman
Cover photo, design & layout by Bradley Knox (SUBATOMIC)

To Muriel, Leon and Michael.

Wish you were here.

Philadelphia
Thursday, August 26

Prologue

One more subject, that's all he needed for the project. He intended to make sure the woman sitting across from him signed on.

"So, Carla." Lowell Morgenstern, MD sat back in his comfortable leather chair and regarded the young woman sitting stiffly on the couch. "What did Dr. Simon explain to you about the study you'll be participating in?"

"It's Carlee. She said you'd be trying me on a new medication to help with my anxiety and mood swings."

"Correct. And did you have any questions about your involvement?" The psychiatrist reflected that this young woman – Carlee, not Carla – looked like an easy sell. If she would just pull that damned stringy hair out of her face, he could get a good look at her and be better able to gauge her reactions. But she was a mental patient, he reminded himself. An obvious case of low self esteem.

"Dr. Morgenstern?"

He'd been caught up in his thoughts, anticipating the next stage of his project. "Yes?" He put enough bite into the syllable to assert his authority.

The young woman flinched. "I was wondering about any possible side effects from the, you know, that drug. The Paso –"

"Pacifil," he corrected her. "It will be used in low doses that won't cause any discernable side effects."

"I know, Doctor, but I mean, have you used it before? With other patients? I read that it's a type of antidepressant that's rarely used anymore, and I wondered–"

He raised his hand in a "stop" signal. As she stared, he closed his hand into a fist, except for his index finger. This he lowered until it pointed directly at Carlee's face. He fixed his gaze on her with a penetrating stare.

"You," he said. She gaped, speechless. "You," he repeated, "are always afraid. Are you not?"

Carlee nodded.

He nodded back. "It is time for you to change. Yes?"

She nodded once again.

"Time," he whispered.

In the silence that followed, a clock ticked.

Tick, tock. He saw the muscles of Carlee's face go slack.

Tick, tock. He could see her body relaxing, going limp. Excellent response, he thought. She'd make a perfect subject.

Morgenstern had been delighted when his old fraternity brother, Freddy Kurtz, had recruited him to submit a research proposal. Freddy was now the development officer for the international pharmaceutical giant, Basel Aniline Farbenfabri (BAFF). He had come up with the brilliant idea of a Phase Two study of their outdated antidepressant Pacifil to treat borderline personality disorder – a diagnosis Morgenstern treated. BAFF, Freddy explained, hoped the drug would find new life as a treatment for the impulsivity and frantic emotional swings these patients suffered. But Morgenstern added his own bright idea to the project. Why not capitalize on Pacifil's sedative-hypnotic properties? He persuaded Freddy that the study was a perfect opportunity to test his own protocol – the use of hypnosis to eliminate cutting and other forms of self-injury practiced by borderlines. He would use hypnosis on the subjects to suggest a better way to release their pent-up rage.

Morgenstern was about to ensure that Carlee signed on as one of those subjects. He began speaking to her, explaining things in a quiet tone of voice he'd found effective in the recruitment process – especially when he'd already put the person into a trance state.

Morgenstern and Freddy had agreed to keep the hypnosis part out of the formal proposal to BAFF. It would remain their private understanding. They'd shaken on it, using the Tau Omega secret handshake. Morgenstern assured Freddy of better outcomes from the combination of Pacifil and hypnosis. Freddy would deliver a sure thing to his employers. BAFF would be happy, and no doubt fund an expanded trial. Morgenstern would get his funds and publications, and the chance to perfect his hypnosis protocols on someone else's dollar. Everybody wins. Even the subjects might benefit. Including this one. Morgenstern clapped his hands. "Carlee?"

The girl blinked. "Uh – what were you saying, Doctor?"

"Now, if there are no further questions…?"

She gave a slight shake of her head, regarding him sleepily through the curtain of her dark hair.

"Good! Then I'll have Dana bring in the consent form for you to sign."

Done! He pressed the intercom to summon his administrative assistant. The fourth, and final, subject was on board.

Sunday, September 26

1

April couldn't believe she'd ventured this far.

At least the dating website, Go Cupid, was a freebie, so all she'd invested was time she should have spent on her long overdue research proposal. Instead, she'd devoted the afternoon to working her way through a bunch of inane screening questions. How much did astrological sign matter to her in a potential match? Not at all. Had she had even one puff on a cigarette in the last month? No How long did she hope her next relationship would last? She wondered if anyone actually selected the "Just One Night" option.

April wasn't crazy about providing her e-mail address, but it was required. She wondered whether strange men would start stalking her inbox.

Next Go Cupid wanted her profile: April Simon, Ph.D., 34, divorced, 5'4", 112 lbs. Green-eyed redhead. She wrinkled her nose, deliberating. Should she say "attractive?"

Go Cupid demanded more. A Self-Summary. If she wrote: "I'm a psychologist," that might scare men away or attract the neediest freaks. What I'm Doing With My Life. How about: "Directing a treatment program in Philadelphia for the seriously mentally ill, by day; sitting at home with my cats, Boris and Natasha, by night"? Yeah, right. What I'm Looking For: "A strong, sensitive man, who can make me laugh." And he'll have his work cut out for him.

A new column appeared on the left side of the page. "Men! Matches!" Already listed, before she'd even posted her personal details. Merely by answering Go Cupid's dumb screening questions, Brian (36), Scott (38) and Marty (42). 42? Wasn't that a little old? had been chosen for her. Feeling a ripple of excitement, she clicked and read about fun-loving, outdoorsy Brian. As soon as she did, two more matches appeared on the left. "Women who liked Brian also liked…" It reminded her of buying shoes on-line. "Customers who viewed this product also considered…" She wondered if Brian came with a pre-paid return envelope.

Now Go Cupid invited her to post a photo – better yet, several. April froze. Putting her face out there into cyberspace meant passing the point of no return. Suppose her colleagues saw her up there, like merchandise? What if her patients did?

She clicked off the site. Lonely as she was, April wasn't ready for this. She looked up and noticed the shadows in her bedroom office. The late afternoon sun was getting low outside. She decided it was too late to start on her research proposal. Especially after the two glasses of wine she'd had. She powered down her laptop.

More like her hypothetical research proposal, April thought to herself. In the fifteen months she'd been at Franklin University Medical Center, she had some accomplishments she was proud of. She'd passed the exam for her psychology license and launched a successful day treatment program. Praxis was already developing a reputation in Philadelphia as a dynamic, state-of-the-art psychiatric rehabilitation center. Referrals, initially a trickle, were now coming in a steady flow. Quite a respectable achievement for a newly-minted Ph.D. However, there remained the unresolved matter of her faculty appointment.

When Lowell Morgenstern, chairman of the Department of Behavioral Health Sciences, hired April they had made an understanding. April would spend her first year at Franklin getting Praxis up and running and Morgenstern would consider appointing her to a tenure track position of assistant professor – if she produced an acceptable research proposal to measure patient outcomes.

April couldn't get her brain in focus on outcome studies. She was a skilled clinician, but had little interest in research. The coveted title of assistant professor seemed beyond her grasp. In an academic medical center like Franklin, that reduced her to pretty much a second-class citizen, a wanna-be.

Enough. She needed another glass of wine to wash away her sour feelings. Before she even stood, Boris and Natasha sensed her motion. They stirred and separated themselves from a single ball of fur on the nearby bed into two tabby cats, one grey and one orange. They hopped to the floor, meowing for their dinner and, like little shadows, trailed April to her small, spotless kitchen.

Six months ago, after her divorce was finalized, April signed the lease on her one-bedroom apartment. Briar Hill was a quiet, mid-rise development and a convenient commute to work. She could drive down Broad Street or take the train from the nearby SEPTA station. Owners of the condo units were a mix of empty-nesters and young couples. Renters, like April, were transients, the divorced or relocated. As she surveyed her living room through the pass-through kitchen window, she congratulated herself on having cobbled together such a presentable space. The colors were soft shades of mauve and olive green, with a fluffy beige area rug and patterned throw pillows adding texture to the room. A room with a decidedly feminine vibe.

She fed the cats and poured her third glass of white wine. As she raised it in a silent toast to her empty, girlish apartment, a little wine sloshed over the rim. She wiped the spill off the countertop with a paper towel, then carefully made her way to the living room couch.

She picked up the remote and flicked on the television. That was one good thing about living alone, you never had to fight over the remote. Also, the place was always neat, and you could eat whatever you were in the mood to cook or call out for. The downside was that it was so damned quiet. But tomorrow was Monday. She'd have plenty of company. Including at least twenty people with serious mental illnesses.

As April scrolled through the cable menu to see what movies might be on, she noticed the date listed at the top of the screen.

"Shit!" She slammed her wine glass onto the table, nearly spilling its contents. She hadn't realized what day it was. If she and Mark hadn't divorced, today would have been their fifth wedding anniversary.

She threw the remote across the room and the cats scurried for safety.

Ψ

He was twenty five minutes in. Detective Sam Perone intended to continue sweating for another twenty. It was his decompression ritual, challenging his body enough to allow his mind to wind down. It helped him avoid feeling too much.

Sam pushed back a lock of shaggy, brown hair from his sweaty forehead. His leg muscles strained as the dots on the Stairmaster display climbed to the maximum level.

At thirty eight, he was in peak physical condition. A handsome man with dark eyes and strong features. Emotionally however, he felt about eighty.

Sam finished up his cycle on the machine and headed to the locker room to shower. The gym was in Andorra, minutes away from his small house in Roxborough. He planned to stop at Rocco's for a cheese steak with sauce and onions. Say what you would about South Philly, Sam believed the best cheese steaks were to be had in Roxborough. A six-pack was already cooling in the fridge.

Before he could repress it, he was hit with a memory – coming home to Toni at the end of the day. The way she looked in her last trimester – body rounded, face glowing – as she set the dinner table. The aromas of the meal she prepared, her favorite music playing in the background, her smile of greeting. He had not heard her voice in three years.

No, he told himself. Don't go there. He'd had plenty of practice slamming a lid on such thoughts without taking the meds the department's psychiatrist tried to press on him. He'd only seen the guy once, because it was mandatory after what happened. Sam accepted the prescription and tore it up as soon as he left the doctor's office. Damn pills. Goddamned shrinks.

He turned the shower water as hot as he could stand it and finished with a blast of cold. Toweling off, he dressed in khakis and a polo shirt and left. As he pulled his car out onto Henry Avenue, his cellphone rang. He answered the call.

"Hey!" It was his young rookie partner, Justin O'Malley.

"Hi. Could you turn down that God-awful, so-called music so I can hear you?"

"Man, get into this century already will you?" The volume on the hip-hop was mercifully lowered. "You doing anything this evening?"

Sam shrugged. "The usual."

"Great, that means you can help me out," Justin said.

"What is it this time?"

"My sister has a new sofa coming tomorrow."

"Uh-huh." Sam waited for the other shoe to fall.

"She said I can have the old one if I come by and get it tonight. No way can I haul that thing alone. I need you to come and help me out. Beer and pizza's on me afterwards."

"No." Sam's tone was adamant.

"No?" Justin echoed.

"No pizza," Sam said. "I want cheese steaks."

"Sure, cheese steaks," Justin agreed. "When can you get here?"

Sam sighed, "I'll be at your place in twenty." He ended the call, smiling to himself. Justin came up with these projects all the time. Sam knew perfectly well that his partner's real purpose was to keep him engaged and busy without either of them acknowledging what was really going on.

It was good to know his partner had his back.

2

At 6:15 on a Sunday evening, the only fifth floor office with its lights on was Lowell Morgenstern's. Even the senior faculty spent part of their weekends at home. Morgenstern worked hard, but he played hard, too. Right now, he was eagerly awaiting a visitor.

Da da da DAH da. Da da da *DAH* da.

Instead of the hoped-for footfalls outside his door, Morgenstern heard the sound of his cellphone. Not just any ringtone, but the Wagnerian strains that signaled an incoming call from his wife. He was tempted to ignore it. Then again, why not get the conversation over with before he became otherwise engaged?

"Hello, Miranda." His tone was neutral, revealing neither pleasure nor annoyance at her intrusion. Psychiatrists were trained to do that.

"Where are you, Lowell? Will you be home for dinner?"

"At the office," he replied, "and, no."

"Don't tell me you're still working at this hour?" Miranda sounded skeptical. "Are you really at your office?"

Now she sounded incredulous.

"The answer to both your questions is, I am," he replied evenly. "If you like, you can hang up and call back on my office line. Will that satisfy you?"

She muttered a response.

"What was that you said, Miranda? Do you want to call me here?"

He heard her sigh. "No, Lowell, that won't be necessary. Any idea what time you'll be home?"

Her sigh was audible. "No, Lowell, that won't be necessary. Any idea what time you'll be home?"

"Not late. I'll get a bite when I finish up these papers." At last he heard footsteps coming down the corridor. "See you later." He ended the call and turned to the doorway with a smile of anticipation.

Ψ

Miranda Morgenstern stirred her vodka martini. She could feel the tension in her clenched jaws, and knew it wasn't good for her teeth or mouth. There was no point in getting injections to plump your lips if you were going to scrunch them. But who could be married to Lowell without grinding their teeth hard enough to crack walnuts?

He couldn't fool her. Not after all these years. She knew perfectly well he was fooling around with someone – probably some junior faculty member or psychiatric resident. As a psychiatrist who had counseled many a couple on the rocks, Lowell was an expert on the pitfalls posed by modern technology. He knew better than to leave histories of calls, texts or e-mails for her to discover. Miranda herself wasn't half as scrupulous about her own phone and computer. But then, Lowell didn't care enough to check them.

For the thousandth time, she thought about leaving him. Emotionally, she'd be okay, at least no worse than she was now. But divorce would be a financial nightmare for her. Miranda had no wish to resume her career in real estate. These days, a realtor needed the survival instincts of a junkyard dog. Nearing sixty, she should be long past hard work or sacrifice. She was an attractive woman and worked damned hard at it. Still in good shape and, thanks to minor plastic surgical enhancements and regular Botox injections, her face was smooth and youthful.

Despite her efforts, her husband rarely looked at her. It was infuriating. Humiliating.

Men had no inkling of the suffering endured by aging women who'd been beauties in their youth. Feeling your own power and self-assurance erode, year by year. Watching men stare through you, instead of at you.

Miranda swallowed a generous sip of her martini. Why had she ever agreed to their pre-nup? She should have fought him on it, but Lowell was adamant. Miranda had some money she'd inherited from her mother and figured she'd be all right. Who knew the stock market would crater, taking a chunk of her nest egg with it? If they divorced, her lifestyle would become unthinkable.

She drained the martini. It would be different if Lowell died. There would be a generous life insurance policy and she'd have the house in Lower Merion. She could let her lover move in. Or find a better lover. With any justice, that's how the story would end. Miranda knew better. You had to make your own justice in this world.

Ψ

"I was afraid you wouldn't come." Morgenstern closed and locked his office door before embracing Sandra Chang.

"I really shouldn't have." The petite psychiatric resident stood only as high as his chest, and his shirt muffled her words. "My case presentation is tomorrow, and – "

"Nonsense!" Morgenstern began unbuttoning her blouse. "You have plenty of time." He slipped the blouse off her shoulders and kissed her bare throat. "But if you're worried, we can make it a quickie," he teased.

Sandra smiled uncertainly. She should be home finishing her presentation, but she found the sexual attentions of her department chairman both exciting and flattering. Planting a kiss on his lips, she reached back to unfasten her bra.

"Let me get it." Morgenstern turned her around. He unhooked the bra and reached under it to cup Sandra's small breasts. He groaned, nuzzling her ear. "I should forbid you to even wear a bra, with these perky girls."

Sandra pushed back, feeling his erection against her. "It's unprofessional to go braless." Her breathing was growing faster. Morgenstern's hands were now pushing up her skirt, pulling down her pantyhose. He caressed her and she moaned with pleasure.

"Ohhh, Lowell, I really should be preparing for tomorrow."

"Shhh. I am preparing you. Don't you feel ready?"

She did.

Turning Sandra around, Morgenstern picked her up and sat her on his desk. He tugged off her pantyhose and tossed them aside. Sandra surrendered all thoughts of tomorrow's presentation – a decision she would later regret.

Monday, September 27

3

The start of the work week was a time for making promises to yourself. Resolutions to try harder, produce more, screw up less. En route to Franklin, April vowed to do all three. She wanted to have more self-discipline, produce a decent research proposal, and drink less

It wasn't the first time she'd set those goals. She was about to cross Vine Street when a hand closed around the back of her neck, startling her. The grip released as she whirled around.

"Damn it, Chris, you scared me!" The tall, dark-haired man smirked at her. "Are things so quiet at the psychiatric emergency service that you have time to accost women on the street, Dr. Willis?"

He gave her a mock bow. "Dr. Simon, for you I make the time."

April frowned. "You know, one of these days you'll do that to someone and wind up with a face full of mace."

"Nah, I'm a good judge of character – very selective about the women I sneak up on." He winked and gave a finger wave as he walked away.

Chuckling and waving him off, April made her way across Vine, wondering, as she had many times, why Chris Willis flirted with her, but never asked her out. The question perplexed and frustrated her. Was it because they were colleagues? Perhaps he was simply a player, with no real interest in a relationship. She found him attractive and enjoyed his off-beat sense of humor, but he could be – mercurial. Yes, that was the word.

She was following this train of thought as she headed for the storefront that housed Praxis. Her program was part of the outpatient mental health services at Franklin University Medical Center or FU, as it was more familiarly known among faculty and staff.

She reached the entrance to Praxis and saw two men standing off to the side, deep in conversation. Their heads were almost touching, as if they were conspirators. Felipe and Mickey, two Praxis members. She was about to call out a greeting, when she saw Mickey back away from Felipe, furiously shaking his head. Felipe stepped toward him, hand extended, offering something and pressing Mickey to take it from him.

April approached them, not liking the look of it. Felipe had his back to her, but Mickey looked up her approach, wide-eyed.

"I wasn't buying! I swear!" His voice was an octave higher than usual.

"Buying?" She caught a glimpse of a plastic baggie, as Felipe's hand moved swiftly into his pants pocket.

"He tried to sell me meth!" Mickey was close to tears.

"He's lying!" Felipe protested. His angular features were pinched with indignation, but April didn't buy it. She knew what was going down.

"Mickey." She kept her voice level. "Go inside, please." The tension drained from his face. Flashing her a grateful smile, Mickey raced for the Praxis entrance. April turned to Felipe. "What's in your pocket?"

"Nothing." He backed away.

Her voice was tight with outrage. "Mickey's been clean for months, and you're selling him that – that poison! I'll call the police! You –"

James Duvall, the Praxis program coordinator, came out of the building and joined them. "Mickey told me what happened," he said.

"Nothin' happened, man!" Felipe insisted.

"I interrupted the transaction." April glanced at James, then turned to face Felipe again. "You're suspended. Go clean up your act before you come back here." She stopped, too angry to say more. Praxis wasn't a rehab program, but many of their members struggled with drugs and alcohol, along with mental health problems. Keeping the environment free of temptation was a high priority.

"James," April asked. "Will you please arrange a referral to Freedom House for Felipe?" She headed for the entrance, as James nodded.

"You'll pay for this!"

She turned at Felipe's loud shout, feeling the hairs prickling on the back of her neck. She stared him down, willing herself to keep her expression impassive. "Are you threatening me?"

Wordlessly, Felipe looked at the sidewalk.

April went inside. Her hands were icy and her eyelid was twitching. She hated confrontations, but her role as director gave her the backbone to handle them when required. As she walked past the reception desk, Cynthia, the program secretary, greeted her and April mumbled a response.

She continued down the hall to her office. What a way to start the week. April put away her purse, hung her jacket on the hook behind her door, and retraced her steps to the front of the facility to look for James.

He was waiting for her in his office, which was in its usual state of disarray. Papers and charts were piled on his desk and filled the corners of the floor. Empty cardboard cups attested to his fondness for Starbucks.

Plants dangled their leaves and tendrils from the shelf above his desk. James was an avid gardener. Even his stocky build made him appear rooted in the earth. After a really good weekend, he still had dirt under his fingernails. April trusted him more than anyone she knew.

"I gave him the contact information for Freedom House." James lifted a stack of charts from the chair next to his desk, so April could sit. He looked around for an empty space before giving up and adding them to the collection on his desk. A cup of coffee sat perilously close to the edge. He picked it up and took a sip.

April sank into the chair. "You think he'll actually call them?"

James sighed, "we can hope."

April shook her head, already anticipating the chairman's displeasure at her decision. "I hope I didn't overreact, suspending him on the spot like that. He's already got two strikes against him for coming in high a couple of times. It's not fair to the people trying to stay sober here." Hearing her own arguments, April admitted to herself that James wasn't the one she'd need to convince.

"The rules are clear," James agreed. "No dealing. Felipe needs rehab before he'll be ready for us."

"You and I know that," she said. "But Dr. Morgenstern might have another take on the situation."

James nodded. "I don't think he'll like the idea of losing one of his research subjects." He made air quotation marks. "The Great Borderline Medication Project." Felipe was one of the chairman's four Pacifil subjects.

April chewed her lip. In her head, she was still arguing with the chairman. "If we made an exception for Felipe, we'd be setting a terrible precedent," she said. A good point, she thought, but still didn't imagine winning the debate.

She sighed. "I'll talk to Lowell and see if we can reach some kind of agreement. Maybe he could see Felipe for med visits while he does a stint at Freedom House."

The door to James' office opened and Cynthia appeared.

"April? The new psychology student is here. Ready to meet with her?"

4

Lowell Morgenstern closed the blinds to darken the office against the morning light. He appraised his research subject with a smile of satisfaction. Tyrell Johnson reclined comfortably in the leather lounge chair. Like the other patients in Morgenstern's Pacifil study, the young man was a good hypnosis subject – highly suggestible. Well, like two of the other three subjects, anyway. Felipe Diaz was a bit of a challenge. Resistant, but he'd come around. All in all, the first three weeks of the project had gone extremely well.

"Are you ready, Tyrell?" Morgenstern asked, keeping his voice soft.

"Yes, doctor."

Morgenstern let the silence build and create its soothing effect. The only audible sound in the office was the ticking of the small clock on his desk.

"Concentrate on the sound of my voice," Morgenstern commanded. "The ticking of the clock – you find it's growing louder. The louder it becomes, the more you relax."

He observed Tyrell's loose limbs and steady, even breathing.

"Your body is growing heavy," he continued. "Your right arm is so heavy that you can barely lift it. Try now, and see what happens."

Tyrell raised his right arm – slowly.

"As you raise your arm, you find it falls back down." It did.

Morgenstern studied Tyrell's face. The young man's eyelids fluttered, a sign that he had entered the REM state. Droplets in the corners of his eyes indicated that the muscles around his tear ducts had relaxed.

Tyrell was in a deep trance. Time for his instructions.

First, Morgenstern gave him a few suggestions about treatment compliance, to ensure that Tyrell would take his Pacifil faithfully and show up for his appointments. Then, he delivered the most important posthypnotic suggestion – a carefully chosen alternative behavior Tyrell would use from now on, whenever he felt the urge to hurt himself. The suggested behavior wasn't one Morgenstern would want to share with his psychiatry colleagues. He figured he could always replace the suggestion with something more politically correct in the Phase Two study later on.

Now Morgenstern concluded his directions to Tyrell. "You will follow my instructions, even though you will not remember them when you awake. The more you try to remember, the more you will forget. Do you understand?"

"Yes." Tyrell's voice was distant, dreamlike.

"All right. I will count backwards from five," Morgenstern said. "When I reach one, your eyes will open and you will be fully awake.

"Five." Tyrell remained calm and still

"Four." He exhaled deeply.

"Three." A slight twitch rippled through his eyelids.

"Two." Tyrell blinked.

"One. You are fully awake. Eyes open. Take a deep breath, stretch and look around the room when you are ready."

Tyrell opened his eyes. Doctor and patient smiled at each other. Everything was going fine.

What Morgenstern didn't know was that he wouldn't live to reverse the post-hypnotic suggestion he'd just given.

5

April was torn. Although she felt an urgent need to break the news of Felipe's suspension to Morgenstern, the sight of the fledgling psychology student fidgeting in the reception area stirred her compassion. The young woman looked so anxious. April couldn't bring herself to leave her in that state, and Morgenstern was never an easy man to reach. Maybe a brief orientation would be enough to settle the student's nerves, allowing April time to call the chairman before other duties engulfed her.

"Welcome to Praxis." April extended her hand and the young woman rose to clasp it in a moist handshake. April had to look up to make eye contact with the willowy blonde.

"Kristin Lawrence. A pleasure to meet you." A tense smile flickered across her All-American features.

She looked like a model. Some of the male patients would be following this one around like puppies. April gave her a smile. "Let's go to my office and talk for five minutes." Mentally, she underscored the five minutes part.

Leading Kristin down the corridor, April gave a quick tour of the facility. "This will be your office," she said. "You'll share it with the psychiatric residents. They're mostly here on different days than you."

"Dr. April?" An obese, disheveled man appeared out of nowhere.

Oh no, April silently lamented. "What, Brendan?" She hoped her voice hadn't revealed her impatience.

"Where are we going for the next Friday trip? The older ladies said we're going to the Art Museum again, and we did that, like two weeks ago. Can't we go to a movie?" His voice carried an insistent whine.

"We'll talk about it in community meeting." April turned to Kristin. "This is Brendan, one of our members. Brendan, Kristin Lawrence, the new psychology student."

He eyed Kristin with the scrutiny of an entomologist studying a new species of moth. "Are you a psychologist?"

"Not yet," Kristin admitted. "I'm in the doctoral program here."

"You know anything about MPD?"

"Multiple personality disorder?"

"Right. That's my diagnosis. I have 26 alters."

"Alters?" Kristin echoed. "You mean – personalities?"

"Yup." He glowed with pride.

April sighed. "Brendan, see you in community meeting."

She led Kristin to her office, sat at the desk and offered her the spare chair. April's office was small, but homey. She'd brought in a floor lamp, rather than rely on the harsh overhead fluorescent lighting. A wicker bookcase and a little table she'd assembled, with a thin stone slab mounted on two translucent blocks from a gardening store, added a natural touch.

April glanced unobtrusively at her watch. She'd already gone past her five-minute limit. The monthly outpatient case conference was scheduled for later that morning. Maybe she could catch Morgenstern before then.

"What exactly does 'Praxis' stand for?" Kristin asked, interrupting April's thoughts.

"It's a Greek word that means 'the practical application of learning.'" She really had to wrap this up.

"And it's a partial hospital program, right?" Kristin continued. "For the chronically mentally ill?"

"Individuals with major mental illnesses, yes. Like schizophrenia or bipolar disorder." One more minute, that's all, April promised herself.

"We help them develop skills and supports to succeed at home, at work, or in school." She rattled this off, having had plenty of practice. Her mind was on what to tell the chairman. Should she phone? Or e-mail him? "I know you must have questions," April concluded, "and we'll talk more later. Okay?"

"Uh, sure." Kristin stood and hesitated for a moment before walking out of the office. April reached for the phone, but froze as she heard a familiar voice booming down the corridor – on a collision course with Kristin.

"I knew it! See, I knew it. I can't help but be late walkin', but can't get no bus pass if you all don't let me come to no program full time." The sounds stopped in front of April's office, then resumed. "Who're you? I ain't seen you here before."

"Kristin Lawrence, the new psychology student."

"Yeah? How you get to be a psychologist? Think I could go to school for that? Say, can you get me a bus pass?"

"I – uh – I don't think…"

At the sound of Kristin's quavering voice, April reluctantly hung up the phone. She got up from her desk and stepped into the hall.

"Morning," she said to a tall, gangly black man, who radiated nervous energy. Kristin shot her a look of gratitude.

"Hey, Doc," he said.

"Want to go sit in the community room? We'll start the meeting in a minute."

"Nah, I'm standin'." He fidgeted from foot to foot.

"Okay, but in the community room, please."

He moved on, his voice reverberating off the walls. "Don't know if I can be sitting through no community meeting today. Ten minutes. Don't know if I can do more'n ten minutes, Doc…"

April turned to Kristin. "Community meeting starts in five minutes. Maybe you'd like to go put your things away in your office. I'll come and get you."

Kristin nodded. "Thank you, Dr. Simon."

April ducked back into her office and closed the door. Taking a deep breath, she picked up the phone and dialed the chairman's extension.

6

"What is it?" Lowell Morgenstern barked from his desk, in response to the light rap on his closed office door. He massaged his temples, wincing. His sinuses were flaring up again.

The door opened and his assistant, Dana, peered in. "Doctor Simon is on the phone. She'd like an appointment with you today."

Morgenstern waved her off. "No time today or tomorrow. Fit her in Wednesday."

"But she said it was –"

Morgenstern's glare stopped Dana in mid-sentence.

"Very well, Doctor. Wednesday."

"And Dana?" He held up a vial of saline nasal spray. "Get me another one of these at the pharmacy during your lunch break. This one's almost empty."

"   Of course, Doctor."

His assistant closed the door behind her. Morgenstern stood and removed his suit jacket. He exchanged it for a white lab coat, his name embroidered on the pocket. He didn't actually need to wear it. As a psychiatrist, he had no hands-on contact with lab medicine – thankfully, as even the sight of blood in a tube made him queasy. But he regarded the lab coat as his chairman's mantle of authority and wore it whenever he was on site at Franklin. Besides the dignity it conferred, Morgenstern liked the way the crisp, white garment set off his blue eyes and mane of salt-and-pepper hair. At 6'1" and now down to 185 pounds, he looked great for a man of 61 years. He worked at it with tennis on weekends and laps at the pool during lunch breaks.

His intercom buzzed. "Yes, Dana?"

"Dr. Hartman is here for his meeting with you, Doctor."

"Good. Send him in."

Moments later, Stuart Hartman, Ph.D., Director of Franklin's Doctor of Psychology program, entered. Morgenstern regarded the small, slight man in his early fifties. He had a chin that came to a decisive point, which, the chairman reflected, Hartman himself rarely did. He noted that the psychologist was wearing one of his signature nondescript suits. Who the hell picked his ties?

"Morning, Lowell."

"Morning, Stuart." Morgenstern pointed him towards the sofa, table and leather chairs that served as the conversation pit in his spacious office. "Coffee?"

A last meal before the execution?

Hartman shook his head. "Thanks, no."

They sat. Morgenstern, on the sofa, crossed his legs and extended his arms along the sofa back, claiming his territory. He watched Hartman position himself stiffly in a chair. Did he realize a duel was about to begin?

Morgenstern made his first thrust. "Stuart, your Psy.D. program trains capable clinicians, but the research component isn't cutting it." He had the satisfaction of seeing Hartman's jaw drop. *Touché!* Before the psychologist could respond, Morgenstern struck again. "I've decided to start a Ph.D. program here at Franklin – with faculty who'll bring research grants and students who'll want to work alongside them. That's going to be our new direction."

Hartman gaped. "But – but what about my program? I mean, the Psy.D. program?"

The doctor of psychology program had been Stuart's fief for over ten years. Morgenstern found it gratifying to serve him with an eviction notice. He'd probably like to punch me in the mouth, Morgenstern reflected. But you can't hit the department chairman. Not even if you had tenure.

Stuart cleared his throat, making a painful rasping sound. "Lowell, I understand your concerns about the research. When you wanted to bring in Larissa Lewis, I was happy to have her on my faculty." Lewis, a recent hire, was a psychologist with a strong research track record.

"Larissa is great. We're lucky to have her," Morgenstern said bluntly. His faculty? Hah! "In the year she's been here, how many of your students have asked to work with her?"

Hartman shifted in his chair. "Well..."

"Not one," Morgenstern cut in. "Larissa is the beginning, Stuart, not the solution. When we have Ph.D. students, they'll do their clinical coursework in your Psy.D. program. But their research courses and dissertation guidance will come from new faculty."

Stuart looked confused. "You want me to hire new faculty, Lowell?"

"No." This was going to be the fun part. Morgenstern uncrossed his legs and sat up straight. "The new director I hire for the Ph.D. program will recruit the faculty." He smiled. "With your consultation of course." The concession was a crumb, and both men knew it.

Hartman recoiled as if he'd been slapped. "You're making this sound like a fait accompli. How can you do this without consulting me? Without allowing me to discuss this with my faculty? This is encroaching on the autonomy of the psychology profession here. It's – frankly, Lowell, I'd say it's unethical."

Morgenstern leaned forward, moving in for the kill. "This decision is well within my mandate as chairman of the department of behavioral sciences." He smoothed back his shock of gray hair. "We've had our consultation, Stuart."

The psychologist's face turned beet red. "What exactly is the timeline for all this?" he croaked.

Best for last. "I've talked with Michael Giametti about taking the director position," Morgenstern announced. "He's open to relocating and likes the idea of launching a program from the ground floor."

Stuart was seized with a paroxysm of coughing. Giametti was a psychologist of real stature, known and respected for the clinical assessment instruments he'd developed. They were standards in the field. Hartman's humiliation was complete.

"Do you need some water?" Morgenstern asked pleasantly. "I can have Dana bring you some." And she'd better remember to get that nasal spray, he added to himself. His sinuses were killing him.

Hartman shook his head, his coughs subsiding to a wheeze. Slowly, he stood on unsteady legs and turned to walk out. He turned back at the door.

"Is this confidential," he began. "Or – ?" He stopped and stared, dumbfounded.

Morgenstern pulled the small plastic bottle from his lab coat pocket, thrust the tip into each nostril and inhaled deeply. Still a little saline left, after all. He sighed with relief.

The sweet smell of success!

7

"I think you made a mistake." Clarence McKay, MD, director of outpatient psychiatric services at Franklin, frowned at April. They sat in his office, one flight up from Praxis, for her weekly supervision meeting. McKay was a portly man, whose white beard made a striking contrast with his cocoa brown skin. April thought of him as a teddy bear because of his ursine appearance and friendly demeanor. Still, she knew that, faced with incompetence, laziness or disrespect, this teddy could turn into a grizzly.

"Lowell won't like it that you suspended Felipe before consulting him," Clarence said.

"But, Clarence! He was selling drugs on the premises."

Her supervisor raised his hands in a gesture of surrender. "Hey, don't shoot the messenger. I'm only warning you that the chairman won't be happy."

April's stomach sank. Her decision to suspend Felipe had seemed like a no-brainer at the time. Now her dread of Morgenstern's reaction was steadily mounting.

"I did call him right away, Clarence," she explained. "But Dana said he was too busy to see me until Wednesday. Then I sent him an e-mail explaining the situation. He hasn't responded."

"Are you surprised?" Clarence asked. "How many e-mails do you suppose the man gets?"

April sat back and folded her arms across her chest. She longed for a shell to pull into, like a turtle. "It pisses me off that I don't have the authority to call the shots in my own program," she complained.

"It's not about authority, April. It's politics. You have to give the chairman his due. Hail to the Chief, and all that." Clarence tried to soothe her ruffled feathers. She knew he was right, but didn't like it.

A sharp rap on the door interrupted them. It flew open a nanosecond later. Morgenstern stood in the doorway, scowling. "I need to speak with you, Dr. McKay," he announced.

Clarence pursed his lips, as if tasting something bitter. He nodded at April. "Thank you for the update, Dr. Simon."

Awkwardly, she rose. "Dr. Morgenstern," she began."

"Get out, April," he said, striding into Clarence's office as if he owned it.

"But did you get the e-mail I – ?" She stopped, as Morgenstern pointed at the open door. Her face growing hot, April stalked out. Seething and humiliated, she felt like a child banished so the grownups could talk.

April walked to the elevator, fuming. It wasn't enough that Morgenstern was too busy for her. Now he'd thrown her out of her regular meeting with Clarence. She punched the button for the elevator, wishing it were Morgenstern's eye. Politics, right. The eight-hundred-pound gorilla sat wherever he wanted.

The elevator arrived, but April ignored the open doors. She'd given up too easily. Eventually, Morgenstern had to come out of there. She decided to go back and wait for him. She strode down the corridor and took up a post outside Clarence's office. Immediately, she heard loud, angry voices inside.

" – can recheck my data. It's possible there were some mistakes," she heard Clarence say.

"Not mistakes!" Morgenstern's voice thundered. "Those numbers are too damned good to be believable. Nothing in the literature supports outcomes like that."

April froze. Her better judgment warned her to get out of there, but she felt compelled to keep listening.

"You will not submit that data to the National Institute of Mental Health on my watch," Morgenstern continued. "I intend to inform the NIMH what you've done and recommend they transfer the project to someone else."

"My God, Lowell!" Clarence sounded stricken. "You'd disgrace me like that? Ruin my career?" The sound of salsa music made April look down. Her cellphone, in her hand, was ringing.

"Oh, shit!" she exploded. She silenced the phone and stepped away from the office, colliding with Sandra Chang.

"Whoa!" The psychiatric resident laughed. "Where's the fire?"

In there, April thought. "I, ah, was just on my way downstairs," she muttered, feeling ridiculous.

Before she could escape, the door opened and she found herself staring into the chairman's scowling face. She opened her mouth to speak.

"Not now," he barked, before turning to smile at Sandra. "Case conference in fifteen minutes." He cuffed her chin playfully. "You should be primed to give a first-class presentation, after all that good preparation we did."

Sandra blushed. He winked at her and walked away, whistling.

Ψ

The last thing April wanted to do was show up late for the case conference. She fled to her office anyway, desperate for sanctuary where she could try to make sense of what she'd heard. The very idea of Clarence committing research fraud was like learning there was no Santa Claus. Why would Morgenstern accuse him? She'd never noticed any particular friction between the two. Of course, everyone endured the pressure of Morgenstern's mission to augment Franklin's research programs. The mere thought of facing him with the non-existent status of her own research made April queasy.

But – Clarence? He was a distinguished scholar, a reviewer for important professional journals. What was going on? And that little pas de deux between Morgenstern and Sandra Chang – what was that about? This whole place was crazy. What chance did she have to survive here?

Her cellphone beeped, letting her know she had a voice-mail..

"Hey, April, it's Mark. There's something I need to talk with you about. Give me a call, okay?"

She stared into space, her mind reeling. Following months of silence, her ex was back in touch.

8

PACIFIL SUBJECT: **Felipe Diaz**

Felipe kicked an empty soda can down the sidewalk, blowing off the dirty looks aimed in his direction. Stupid Anglos. Who cared what they thought? His real problem was what the fuck he was going to do now that he'd been kicked out of Praxis. He liked it there. He'd started to feel at home. He had *amigos*. More than that, he felt as if he had to be there, or… Or what? Felipe didn't know. When he tried to figure it out, it was like his mind got all foggy. Fuck that Dr. Simon, throwing him out like that.

He walked down 15th Street, toward his mother's apartment in North Philly. Although there was probably no point in going there. She'd already threatened to put him out the last time she caught him stealing from her purse. If she knew he'd been kicked out of his program – worse, if she knew why – he'd be on the street for sure.

So he couldn't tell her.

That meant he would have to disappear for most of the day, as if he were still going to Praxis. Which sucked, because what would he do with himself for all those hours? Felipe kicked the can clear off the sidewalk and it rolled under a passing car. They couldn't get away with this. When he got to his mother's place, he'd call Dr. Morgenstern. His psychiatrist would take care of this. He was the guy in charge.

Spotting a drug store on the corner, Felipe considered buying some rolling papers. The meth was for selling, not personal consumption, but he still had a little weed at home and needed something to help him chill. He checked his pockets and found only coins, no bills. Not enough for papers. *Mierdo.* His mood darkened another degree.

The sound of excited barking caught his attention. A golden retriever was tied to a parking meter outside the drug store. The animal must be lonely for its master. An old man, passing by, stopped and reached out to pet the dog. The golden's tail wagged with excitement as it licked the friendly hand. Felipe grinned, in spite of his sour mood. He liked dogs, and this one was a beauty, blond and silky, with that doggy smile golden retrievers always seemed to wear.

Without warning Felipe's impulse to pet the dog gave way to another urge.

He glanced around. Some pebbles lay in the street, next to the curb. He strolled over, picked up a few, and stationed himself about three yards from the dog. Leaning against a parked car, he scanned the immediate surroundings. *Bueno.* No one watching. Taking a pebble, Felipe tossed it, aiming the stone so it landed just behind the golden retriever. The dog snorted and turned, but there was nothing for it to see. Felipe chuckled.

He waited a few seconds for the animal to sit back down on the sidewalk, then took aim. This time the pebble hit the dog's flank. It yelped in pain. Target practice. Felipe was starting to enjoy himself.

Now the dog was agitated, shifting around and whimpering, tail tucked between its hind legs. Felipe grinned. Time to go for the bull's eye. He drew back his arm, aiming for a head shot.

"Hey you!" A deep, angry voice boomed from behind him. Felipe lowered his arm and glanced over his shoulder. A man and woman were coming down the block and the guy was pointing at him. "Leave that dog alone and get the hell out of here before I call a cop! You hear me?"

Felipe dropped the stone, flipped his middle finger at the guy, and took off at a run. He thought he heard the golden retriever growl as he went past. A block up the street, he slowed to a walk, panting, then came to a stop.

Why had he done that to the poor dog? What the fuck was happening to his head?

9

"Have you finally flipped your lid?" Justin gaped at Sam, who sat behind the desk in his office at the Philadelphia P.D. on Race Street.

"I know it sounds weird," Sam acknowledged.

"No, crazy," Justin said. "In a city awash in homicides, you've decided to start investigating animal abductions? Gimme a break."

"I didn't say I was investigating anything, yet. I said I found it suspicious that over twice the average number of missing pets were reported in the last month."

"How the fuck you even get those numbers?" Justin asked.

Sam shrugged. "A couple of the officers were talking about it. Comparing notes. I got curious and checked the data."

Justin gave him a skeptical look. "Even if the numbers are up, so what? It's probably just a, you know, a statistical whaddayacallit."

"Anomaly. A statistical anomaly. But it isn't."

"How do you know? You a mathematician now?"

"Because," Sam replied, "almost all of the reports are coming from the same two areas. That means something is going on in those neighborhoods."

Justin opened his mouth to say something, then shut it again. He reached for the printout Sam held. "Let me see that."

Sam passed him the sheet and leaned back in his chair while Justin reviewed it.

"Huh!" Justin looked up from the paper. "Looks like most of the complaints came in from West and North Philly."

"Uh-huh," Sam agreed.

"And it's really double the usual amount?"

Sam gave a quick nod. "Twice the usual number of missing pets in the past month. Mostly dogs."

Justin passed the printout back to him. "You think most people even bother to tell the police when their pets go missing?"

"No. They generally ask around the neighborhood and put up posters." Sam's dark eyebrows drew into a furrow. "Which makes me believe the actual number is a lot higher."

Justin swiped a hand through his buzz-cut hair. "So what does it mean?"

Sam shook his head. "Maybe nothing. Or…" He paused. "I can think of a couple of ugly scenarios. One would be a dog fighting ring stealing animals off the street."

"Ugh!" Justin wrinkled his mouth in disgust.

"Yeah," Sam agreed. He found the notion revolting. A memory of Quark, the beagle they'd had when he was a kid, suddenly popped into Sam's mind. Maybe all hounds were quirky, but Quark had a thing for the dumb, fuzzy slippers Sam's sister used to wear. The dog would pounce on her feet when she walked by. He'd hold onto a slipper with his teeth and trail along for her next few steps. Sam hadn't thought of it for a long time, and the image amused him.

"What's the other one?" Justin asked.

"Huh?" Sam snapped out of his nostalgic reverie.

"You said 'scenarios.' Plural."

"Yeah." Sam's thoughts darkened. "If there is someone out there stealing pets, he could be a baby psychopath, sharpening his teeth."

"You mean, torturing or killing animals before – "

"Before he works his way up to bigger prey."

10

Distracted by Mark's message, April was the last to arrive at the outpatient conference room. Technically, she wasn't late, but Morgenstern glared at her as she took her seat. April's eyes canvassed the room, taking in the other faculty and four residents assembled for the monthly case conference. The residents took turns as presenters, as part of their training. Sandra Chang's ashen face and shaking hands, as she shuffled through her notes, made it obvious that today was her turn in the rotation. April mentally wished her luck. The chairman was a tough audience.

At precisely 11:00 AM, Morgenstern cleared his throat. On cue, the residency director spoke, "Dr. Chang, you have the floor."

"Thank you." Sandra's voice quavered and she paused to sip from her water glass before continuing. "The patient, Mr. C., is a 73-year-old widowed white male, who presented at the clinic with the chief complaint, 'I need something to help me sleep.' He recently completed radiation treatment for prostate cancer and said he'd been feeling low."

Sandra described the patient's symptoms of insomnia and weight loss, then his medical history. He'd seen a social worker previously at Franklin after his wife died eight years ago.

Garden variety depression, April thought.

"Mr. C. denied any history of drug or alcohol abuse, but admitted he drinks a couple of beers in the evening," Sandra continued.

Morgenstern interrupted. "How many beers? How many evenings?" His voice grated harshly, nearly making April jump.

"Uh – he said, 'a couple.' Beers, that is," Sandra said. "I think he meant every evening."

"You're not sure?"

"Uh, no."

Morgenstern nodded, tight lipped. "Please continue."

April watched Sandra leafing through her papers. The resident's voice wavered again as she reviewed the patient's family and occupational history – a blue-collar Korean War vet. Youngest of three, with a surviving older sister he talked to on the phone every few weeks. A son who'd moved to the Midwest.

"He denied any significant problems growing up," Sandra added. "He described his father as 'strict' and his mother as 'nice.'"

Not the most articulate guy, April thought.

"Mr. C. said his dad used to go out drinking with his buddies a few nights a week," Sandra continued, "and Mom looked down in the dumps a lot. He used to have friends at work, but they drifted apart after Mr. C. retired. He still plays cards every week with one pal."

April stifled a yawn. Pretty boring case. She wondered why Sandra had chosen it.

Sandra plodded through the patient's mental status, concluding with her diagnosis of major depression. Her voice was firmer, more confident.

April gave a small sigh of relief, and realized her own breathing had been constricted by her concern for Sandra. It could be damned hard to be the presenter here.

"Of course, I asked about suicide," Sandra said. "He said he sometimes wished he didn't wake up in the morning, but denied any plans to harm himself.

He admitted taking an overdose of pills after his wife died, but his son got him to the ER right away." Sandra rifled through her notes. "That was before the son moved out west," she added. She cleared her throat. "Anyway, the ER released Mr. C. after his son made him promise to go for therapy. He came to the clinic voluntarily this time. I don't believe he's a suicide risk." She took a sip of water and surveyed the room with a tentative smile. "Any questions, so far?"

"I have one," Morgenstern said. He paused, letting the tension build for dramatic effect. "How can you claim you've done a remotely adequate suicide assessment with this patient?"

April caught her breath. Her eyes darted to Sandra, who recoiled as if she'd been slapped.

"What are the risk factors for suicide in this case?" Morgenstern barked, eyeing each of the residents in turn. Like the other faculty, April remained silent, understanding who was meant to be in the hot seat.

Mort Abrams was the first resident to speak up, his stammer evident under stress. Something about the man's vulnerability appealed to April. "A w-w-white, elderly, w-widowed male. I think that m-makes him high risk."

"Exactly how high risk?" Morgenstern's stare encompassed the entire table. He expected the faculty to weigh in. His eyes bored into Chris Willis'. "Dr. Willis? You're the emergency specialist."

April exhaled, glad he hadn't focused his laser vision on her.

"Elderly, Caucasian widowers are the highest risk group for suicide," Chris replied calmly.

Morgenstern gave him a barely perceptible nod. "Other risk factors present?" He eyed the residents, one by one.

A heavy-set African American woman volunteered. "His previous suicide attempt. His drinking."

April nodded in agreement.

"Anything else?" Morgenstern pressed. There was a long silence. April's mouth went dry. "What does the family history suggest?" he asked.

"Uh, his father drank?" another resident ventured.

"And he described his mother as 'down in the dumps,'" Morgenstern added, "suggesting a possible family history of depression." He pinned Sandra in his gaze. "Did you explore that, Dr. Chang?"

"Yes," she answered quickly. "He denied any family history of mental illness."

Morgenstern removed a container of saline nasal spray from his lab jacket and tapped it on the tabletop. The gesture struck April as ominous.

"You were expecting him to make the diagnosis?" Sarcasm laced the chairman's voice. "Dr. Chang, it's your job to ask probing questions, then draw conclusions. You're not there to chat with the patient!"

Sandra's face flamed.

"We are here to learn from our mistakes," the residency director said gently.

April flashed him a look of gratitude for the rescue attempt. Education shouldn't have to be a trial by fire. Sandra was too shell-shocked to react at all.

Morgenstern continued relentlessly. "Fine, let's learn about suicide assessment, then. The point is to ask specific, behavioral questions. For example, Dr. Chang, did you ask whether he kept a weapon in his apartment?"

"No."

"Did you ask what kind of pills he took when he overdosed? How many?"

"No," she murmured.

"Speak up! 'No' which? The kind of pills or the number?"

April's hands felt icy. What would she do when it was her turn to face his wrath over Felipe?

Sandra shook her head, tears filling her eyes. "Neither."

"What happened right before he took the pills? Was he drinking? Did he store up the pills? For how long?" Morgenstern fired questions like machine gun blasts. "Does he regret that he survived his previous suicide attempt? Specific questions, Dr. Chang!"

Sandra covered her eyes with a trembling hand. April looked around the room. The other three residents stared down at the table to avoid witnessing their colleague's humiliation. Clarence McKay's eyes shot daggers at Morgenstern.

The residency director cleared his throat. "Uh – perhaps we should move on to discuss Dr. Chang's treatment plan."

Choking back a sob, Sandra abruptly stood, her chair rattling as she pushed it back. She ran from the room.

Clarence McKay broke the awkward silence. "April, would you please go see if she's okay?"

Nodding, April got up to go after Sandra, grateful for an excuse to get out of there. On her way to the door, she heard the residency director tell one of the other residents, "you are the presenter next time."

"Looking forward to it," she muttered.

"Well then," he concluded, "meeting adjourned."

The last sound April heard, as she closed the conference room door behind her, was the loud ping of Morgenstern throwing his empty nasal spray container into a wastebasket in the corner of the room.

The sound of sobbing coming from the ladies room made it easy to find Sandra. The crying grew more intense as April entered. One of the three stalls was closed and April tapped lightly on the door.

"Sandra? Are you okay?" The sobs became louder. April ached for the woman. "How about some water?" she asked. "I'll bring you a cup." To April's relief, the crying quieted. "Be right back," she said.

April filled a cup from the water cooler outside and returned to find Sandra rinsing her swollen eyes at one of the sinks.

"Here you go." April offered her the cup.

Sandra dried her eyes with a paper towel and accepted the water. She took a sip, swallowed, and drew a deep breath. "I feel like such a jerk." Her voice trembled and April braced for another round of tears.

"Being a resident or intern has some shitty moments," she told Sandra. "It's not really about you."

"But I screwed up!" Sandra wailed. "And maybe I risked that poor man's life."

April squeezed her shoulder. "You'll have other chances to help him. Call the guy to check on him, if you're worried."

Sandra took another sip of her water.

"You know," April continued, "suicide assessment isn't hard science. Dr. Morgenstern shouldn't have put you in the hot seat like that. It was incredibly insensitive."

Sandra shook her head vehemently. "No! It's me. I'm the one who was wrong. I should have reviewed the literature. I should have been better prepared. I don't deserve to be a psychiatrist!"

To April's distress, she burst into a fresh torrent of tears.

Five minutes later, leaving Sandra in a semblance of recovery, April returned to the conference room. She found the Psychiatric Emergency Director, Chris Willis, and two residents conducting a post mortem of the presentation. They fell silent as she entered.

"She okay?" the black woman who'd been designated the next presenter asked.

April sighed. "She blames herself for the whole thing."

"Shit," she commented.

The other resident snorted. "Man, if this is how he treats his lovers, imagine what he does to his enemies!"

Chris Willis cocked his head. "They're having an affair?"

The woman shrugged. "It's pretty common knowledge." Her mouth twisted in a wry grin. "Guess you don't get out of the ER much, Dr. Willis."

Chris faced April, frowning. "Did you know about this?"

"Not exactly," she replied, "but I'm not surprised. He flirted with her in front of me earlier today." She curled her lip with disdain. "Then he goes and treats her like dirt."

Chris's dark eyes glowered. "The guy's a predator. Somebody ought to file a charge against him."

"Can you do that anonymously?" the male resident asked, grimacing.

Chris shrugged. "In theory. But you never know what might get passed along the old boy network."

Probably Chris was making an idle threat, but the intensity of his anger surprised April. Most people at Franklin chose their words carefully, where the chairman was concerned. Chris's candor struck her as refreshing. April asked the female resident, "It's your turn to present next, isn't it?"

She nodded.

Her companion patted her on the back. "Don't forget your bullet-proof vest."

11

This was shaping up as one of the all-time worst Mondays, April reflected as she returned to Praxis after the case conference. At least it was lunchtime.

Cynthia the receptionist looked up from her work as April walked in. "How was the case conference?" she asked.

April grimaced. "Nightmare on Vine Street."

Cynthia gave her a knowing nod.

In her office April plopped into her desk chair, blew out a long breath, and quickly checked her voicemail. No new messages. Her anxiety felt like a low-level electrical current buzzing through her veins. She needed two things right away: moral support and food. Fortunately, she knew where to find both.

She phoned her colleague and frequent lunch companion, Larissa Lewis. Morgenstern had recruited Larissa, who'd known him for years. If anyone at Franklin was an authority on the chairman's idiosyncracies, she was.

"You free for lunch?" April asked when Larissa picked up.

"You bet."

"Great," April said. "Chuckwagon in ten minutes?"

"On my way."

April grabbed her purse and jacket and headed down the corridor.

James greeted her as she passed his office. "How was the case conference?"

"Like a leisurely cruise on the Titanic," she replied.

An early lunch crowd was already filling the Chuckwagon when April and Larissa collected their trays and silverware. They joined the queue moving slowly past stations for hot entrees, soup, salads, and sandwiches made to order. Its reliable deli fare was far superior to that of the hospital cafeteria and made the Chuckwagon the default lunch venue among denizens of Franklin.

April ordered her favorite sandwich – tuna on a roll with lettuce, tomato and bacon – along with iced tea. Larissa chose a garden salad with low-fat dressing and Diet Coke. They paid at the register and found one of the few remaining empty tables. Dine early or settle for take-out was the rule of thumb at the Chuckwagon.

Larissa gazed with envy at April's overstuffed sandwich. "I'd love to know how you can eat those and still stay so thin." At 5'2", Larissa weighed about thirty pounds more than April. She favored businesslike skirted suits and heels, but her oversized red eyeglasses added some edginess to her look.

"I take after my mother," April said. "So far, she's still thin. If she suddenly porks up, I'll reevaluate my relationship with mayonnaise and bacon." She took a bite of her large sandwich, a maneuver that required angling her head to go after the corner of the roll.

"No one in my family was thin after the age of two." Larissa lamented, drizzling yellowish dressing over her salad. "I'm no Freudian, but he had a point about anatomy being destiny." She stirred dressing onto lettuce leaves with her fork, not appearing very enthusiastic about the meal in front of her. "So what's up?" she asked. "How's your research proposal coming along?"

"It's coming," April replied vaguely. Not, she mentally added. "Actually, I wanted to tell you what happened this morning."

Larissa's eyebrows shot up in anticipation. "Bring it on!" She thrived on gossip, and Franklin was definitely the place to find it.

April rested her sandwich on the plate and looked around the deli before leaning in closer to Larissa. "Morgenstern ate a resident for breakfast at case conference," she confided.

Larissa shrugged. "So what else is new?"

"But there's a punch line," April said. "Apparently, she's his lover."

"Oh." Larissa nodded. "Sandra Chang, huh?"

"You knew about them?"

"Not really," Larissa said. "But she's been hanging around his office a lot, so I put two and two together." Larissa's office was down the hall from Morgenstern's.

April shook her head. "Sleeping with residents. What an abuse of power!"

"Well…" Larissa hesitated.

"You're going to defend him?" April demanded incredulously.

"I'm not condoning his sexual behavior," Larissa protested.

"Then, what? You sound like you're gearing up to make excuses for him."

"No," Larissa said. "But you have to understand him."

April sniffed derisively. "I understand that he struts around like a tom cat," she muttered.

"April, do you want to be able to work with him, or what?" Larissa asked.

April's gaze dropped to her plate. "I have to," she murmured, "if I want to keep my job."

Larissa nodded. "Lowell is brilliant and narcissistic, like a lot of men who rise to his level of prominence," she said. "Respect his abilities and achievements. Believe me, there's a lot to learn from him." She sighed. "He always needs to be the smartest person in the room."

April crumpled up her napkin. "If Lowell's the smartest one in the room, you should run the hell out of there."

Larissa chuckled. "I admit he has a powerful sense of entitlement." Now it was her turn to look around and make sure no one was listening to their conversation. "Do you know about the Botox?"

"He gets Botox injections?" April asked.

"No, his wife does."

"So?"

"I forget – were you at the faculty reception last spring when Lowell was bragging about how he gets the stuff for free?" Larissa asked.

"No." April had been in no mood for parties back then. The memory of that time, when she'd just learned of her husband's infidelity, killed her appetite for the rest of her sandwich. She forced her attention to the present moment. "So, Morgenstern gets free Botox?" she asked.

Larissa nodded. "From the dermatology department. Chad Klein, the chairman, is Lowell's tennis partner. Klein owed him a favor, so he's been supplying Lowell with vials of Botox that Miranda Morgenstern takes to her plastic surgeon for her injections. Lowell even bragged that Chad lets him come in and help himself to the Botox from the dermatology department fridge." She frowned. "Or was it a cabinet? Anyway, he joked about it being a candy store."

Larissa sighed. "So, all right. I acknowledge that Lowell's not perfect. Sometimes there's a disconnect between his professional ethics and his sense of entitlement."

"I believe that's called hypocrisy," April said dryly. She regarded the remains of her sandwich with regret. "At least we know where to get Botox samples. Maybe in, say, ten years, I'll stroll over and look in the dermatology fridge."

"Yeah. Maybe I'll go look after lunch," Larissa said. "So now that we've covered Sandra's love life, what about yours?"

"The lack of it, you mean." April hesitated. "Although Mark left me a voicemail this morning. He wants to talk about something."

"Swell. Just when you're starting to get over the guy, he's back in touch."

"What makes you say I'm getting over him?" April asked.

"Aren't you?"

April leaned back, reflecting. "Maybe. I don't know. I mean, it's not like I've dated anyone since we split."

"But you're ready to."

April looked at Larissa in surprise. "How do you know?"

"For one thing, I've seen the way you look at Chris Willis."

April face suddenly felt hot. "I do not! Oh God, do I?"

Larissa gave her a half smile. "Not so obviously that anyone would notice, except me."

"But that doesn't mean I'm over my divorce," April protested. "I still feel like damaged goods. I'm not ready to trust my feelings yet."

"Then don't rush into anything with Mark," Larissa said.

"I assure you, I'm not about to."

"Good. Anyway, since you obviously need something to take your mind off all this, if I tell you some hot news, will you promise to keep it between us?" Larissa's grin was conspiratorial.

"I swear on my cats," April vowed.

Larissa scanned the restaurant again, then leaned forward. "Stuart Hartman is toast," she whispered. She explained Morgenstern's plan to launch a new Ph.D. program.

"How do you know about all this?" April asked.

"Lowell told me last week. And I saw Stuart coming out of his office this morning looking like a train wreck."

"So what happens to Stuart? Do you think he'll leave Franklin?"

Before Larissa could answer, an angry shout interrupted.

"Damnit! Does everyone in this lousy place have to know my personal business?"

Both women's heads whirled to the side of their table, in time to see Stuart Hartman hurl his lunch tray, scattering silverware, paper plates and a half-empty plastic bottle of water across the floor.

All conversation in the Chuckwagon fell silent. A roomful of eyes stared at Stuart. He froze, opened his mouth as if to say something, then started to retrieve his tray. Apparently changing his mind, he left it on the floor and raced out the rear door.

Speechless, April whirled to stare at Larissa as the door closed behind Stuart. Her friend looked back at her, wide-eyed. She swallowed before she spoke.

"You think it was something we said?"

12

After the incident with Stuart, even Larissa lost her appetite for gossip, at least for the moment, and April felt the beginnings of a headache. Their lunch break was over. As soon as the buzz of conversation resumed, they bussed their trays and left.

The bright sunlight outside the Chuckwagon didn't help April's headache any. Nor did the realization that she'd forgotten to replenish the supply of acetaminophen she kept in her desk. Which prospect was worse, she debated – trekking across Vine Street to the Franklin Pharmacy or facilitating a therapy group for trauma survivors while battling a headache?

She made a beeline for the pharmacy.

In a rush to make it back to Praxis, April was grateful for once that the hospital drug store didn't have a make-up section to distract her. She snatched a plastic container of acetaminophen from the shelf and went straight to the register. Of course, there was a line, this being lunchtime. Reluctantly, she took her place behind a plumpish woman whose lacquered, faux blond hair looked familiar, even from the back.

"Dana?"

Dana Costelli, Morgenstern's assistant, turned to face her. "Oh, hi," she said coolly.

April never could figure out why the woman treated her in such a consistently chilly manner. Her hunch was that Dana, who obviously worshipped her boss no matter how badly he treated her, was jealous of any younger women in his vicinity. Still, Dana represented access to Morgenstern and April didn't let the opportunity pass.

"I know you said that Dr. Morgenstern couldn't see me until Wednesday," she began.

"That's right," Dana said crisply.

"But I just wondered whether I mean, if something opens up in his schedule today or tomorrow, you might be able to slip me in?" April grimaced at her deferential tone. Dana was really a glorified secretary, but April couldn't help seeing her as an extension of the chairman. Before Dana could reply, a voice spoke up from behind them in the line.

"Hello, ladies!" Chris Willis greeted them.

"Hi, Chris." April smiled, then felt suddenly self-conscious. Had she just exposed the feelings of attraction Larissa claimed to read on her face?

"Hello, Dr. Willis." Dana's tone was considerably warmer as she addressed the tall psychiatrist. "How are you?"

"Fine," Chris replied. "Attending to my grooming needs." He held up a basket containing shampoo and men's deodorant, then made a show of surveying their intended purchases.

Must be in one of his teasing moods, April thought.

Chris pointed at the bottle of nasal spray Dana was clutching. "That's the same stuff your boss uses," he commented. "You guys inhaling coke over there in the administrative wing?"

"Of course not!" Dana sniffed, obviously offended at the suggestion that anything could be amiss on the chairman's watch. "I'm picking this up for the Doctor."

It always irritated April when Dana referred to Morgenstern that way, as if he were the only doctor on the planet.

"His sinuses are bothering him," Dana added, moving up to become first in line.

"Dana " April reached for her elbow before she could step up to the register. "Please don't forget. If he has any openings – "

She yanked her arm from April's grasp. "I certainly wouldn't count on it, Dr. Simon." She raised her chin imperiously. "Doctor is a very busy man."

Fuming, April stifled a retort, busy screwing residents and making people's lives miserable.

As Dana marched to the register, Chris leaned down to murmur into April's ear. "So there, Dr. Simon!" Giving her a playful poke in the ribs, he chuckled and whispered, "You hussy!"

13

April hurried back to Praxis. She swallowed two acetomenephen tablets at the water fountain, her headache intensified by the encounter with Dana. On the other hand, the byplay with Chris had given her spirits a boost. With group scheduled to start in a few minutes, she had no time to indulge in daydreams. She took a minute to check her messages. No word from Morgenstern. April wanted to believe that no news was good news, but doubted it applied in her case.

She turned at a knock on her open door. Kristin Lawrence, the new psych student asked, "Is it time for the Survivors' Group?"

"Almost," April replied. "Come in and I'll brief you before we start." She felt relieved to have something to focus on besides her dread of Morgenstern.

Kristin pulled up a chair. "So what exactly are they survivors of?"

"Different types of trauma. Physical or sexual abuse."

"Huh. I didn't know you could do group work with trauma victims," Kristin said. "Do you try to recover repressed memories?"

April winced. "Oh, no! I can give you a dozen good reasons not to go there. We're not looking to stir things up with these women. We try to help them live safely and develop coping skills. I'm sure you know that trauma victims are often filled with rage and turn it against themselves. They blame themselves for the abuse they experienced. They may reenact it by becoming victims in future relationships."

"And they often self mutilate, right?"

"Yes, they may cut or burn themselves. The physical pain gives them a sense of release from their emotional anguish."

"How many are in the group?" Kristin asked.

"Four," April replied. "I'll give you a brief rundown. There's Carlee, who has dissociative episodes, panic attacks, and borderline personality disorder. She's hinted at some kind of abuse by her half brother, but never in any detail. Either she doesn't want to talk about it or doesn't remember. And there's Angela who was physically abused by her schizophrenic mother."

Kristin shook her head in sympathy.

April continued, "Danielle is bipolar, quite high-functioning, has a Masters in urban planning from the University of Pennsylvania. An uncle sexually abused her. And finally, there's Denise, also borderline personality disorder. She was date raped. I wouldn't be surprised if there was some earlier sexual abuse as well. Oh," April added, "and about Carlee – she's one of the subjects in the research project Dr. Morgenstern is conducting. He's testing a new medication to treat borderline personality disorder." Somehow the man kept claiming real estate in April's head.

"Quite a cast of characters," Kristin commented.

"It can get pretty intense," April agreed. "And it could have been worse. Brendan wanted to be in the group."

"That fat, uh, big guy?"

April smiled. "A real piece of work. Claims he was a victim of ritual satanic abuse in Cherry Hill and insists he has multiple personality disorder."

"Does he really have 26 alters?" Kristin asked.

"I honestly don't know," April answered. "Brendan is very manipulative and thrives on the attention he gets from flaunting the diagnosis."

"I noticed," Kristin said. "So is there anything particular you want me to do, or not do, while I'm sitting in on the group?"

"Mostly just listen and observe, for now. Show empathy. You okay with that, Kristin?"

She nodded. "I think so. Should we agree on some kind of signal you can use in case I do something really inappropriate? You know, like pull your ear or something?"

April laughed. "You'll do fine."

"I had another dream about him yesterday," Carlee Randall murmured. She picked at the cuticle of her left thumb, her long, dark hair hanging over her face. The group fell silent.

"C'mon, girl, you got to talk about it." Denise spoke, a light-skinned African American woman with large gold earrings.

"About your brother?" April asked.

"Half brother." Carlee folded her arms and crossed her feet, her gaze fixed on the floor.

"Do you often dream about him?" April asked.

"Yeah. Sometimes."

April waited a few beats. "Want to talk about it?"

Carlee shook her head.

"Dreams are one of the ways that people relive traumatic events," April said. "They can seem frighteningly real."

"I just hate being reminded – having to think about him!" Carlee blurted out. "That's why I end up cutting myself. To get him out of my head."

"Does it work?" Danielle, a short stocky woman with wavy hair, asked Carlee.

She nodded, keeping her eyes on the floor. "Better than the other things I've tried," she muttered, her lips curling into a frown.

"Like what?" April asked.

"Just…stuff." Carlee appeared to shrink into herself. "But it doesn't matter, cutting's the only thing that helps."

"Like fighting fire with fire?" April suggested.

"I suppose." Carlee shrugged, her expression noncommittal. But Angela and Denise nodded in agreement.

"So when you feel that bad, it's like you have to do something really drastic," Kristin ventured.

April flashed her a smile, appreciating her empathic response to Carlee. "Okay, but let's talk about some other ways you could do that," she said. "When you're in so much pain that you need to do something drastic, how can you do it without inflicting physical damage on yourself? Any ideas?"

"Cut the person who hurt you!" Denise suggested.

Danielle chuckled grimly.

"I can understand that impulse, but it's not one I'd recommend acting on," April said. "Besides, it's not always possible, is it? Carlee, do you even know where your half brother is these days?"

"Uh-uh. And I don't want to know. Last I heard, he went off to school in New York."

"Right. So you can't always vent the rage directly at the person," April said. "But maybe you can let it out indirectly. For instance, you could write a letter to the person, even if you never send it."

"Sometimes it helps me to draw pictures," Danielle offered. "Really gory stuff, like knives stabbing into eyeballs."

Kristin shuddered.

"That wouldn't work for me," Carlee protested. "It only works if I hurt myself. Except – " She seemed to bite back the words.

"Except what?" April pressed.

Carlee shook her head. "Nothing." She folded her arms back across her chest.

Before April could pursue the matter, Angela, a pale, heavy-set woman, chimed in. "It's the same for me. It only works if I hurt myself"

"All right. So what might be some ways to hurt yourself without causing real damage?" April asked.

Denise looked at her, eyes wide. "Can you do that?"

"Sure," April replied. "Who can think of an example?"

Danielle said, "I guess you could run up and down the stairs until you're ready to puke." The group laughed.

"Exactly!" April said. "What else?"

"You could cut all your hair off," Angela said.

"Well, that's better than cutting your skin, but it's still a kind of damage," April said.

"Yeah, and then you're stuck looking like a freak until it grows back," Denise pointed out.

"How about this?" April asked. "Put a rubber band around your wrist and snap it. It'll sting, but won't cut or scar."

Danielle nodded. Carlee rolled her eyes.

April continued, "You could also bite into a hot chili pepper."

"Whoa!" Denise said.

"I'm only saying, if your goal is to inflict pain, there are safe ways to do it." April paused. "Or you could take the opposite approach and put an ice cube on the back of your neck."

"Or on your nipple," Denise suggested.

"Oh, gross!" Danielle grimaced.

"Carlee, what do you think? Could you try one of those methods the next time you feel like cutting yourself?" April asked.

"I don't know. Cutting is automatic," she said.

"Uh-huh. So maybe you should try out one or two techniques ahead of time," April said. "You know, rehearse. That way you could pick the one that works best and have the materials ready in case you need them."

"Oh, that is cool," Denise said. "Hey, could we do that here in group? You know, try out the rubber bands and ice and peppers?"

April smiled. "Denise, I think that's a great idea."

14

"Congratulations, Kristin." James smiled at the psychology student. "You not only got through your first day at Praxis, you survived the Survivors Group."

At 3:30 in the afternoon, the Praxis members had gone for the day. The staff had gathered in the reception area to write their daily progress notes.

"Thanks," Kristin said, beaming. "The group was neat. April was amazing with those women."

"There you go, butter up the boss," one of the therapists teased her. Kristin blushed.

"I'm glad you found group so interesting," April intervened. "We were a little leery about trying it, but it seems to be working out."

"I was especially interested in Carlee," Kristin said. "She seems so fragile."

"She is," April agreed. She found herself wondering what Carlee might have been holding back during group. How was the young woman really responding to Morgenstern's experimental drug? She could be so difficult to read.

"Carlee's very defended," James said, as if echoing April's thoughts. "She doesn't let people in easily." He retrieved a stack of papers piled under his chair. "Speaking of letting people in," he segued, "it's going to get more crowded around here. We already got five new referrals this week. If this keeps up, we're going to need to hire more staff."

"You know how that works," April sighed. "First we have to show Morgenstern that we're operating at capacity and carrying a waiting list. Then he might let us recruit someone."

"Yeah, and by that time, the people on the waiting list will either decompensate or go elsewhere," James said. "It's a Catch-22."

Cynthia called out from the reception desk, "Speak of the Devil, April, Dr. Morgenstern is on the phone. He wants to talk to you. Now. Said you didn't return the voicemail message he left you."

"What voicemail?" April cried. Her mouth went bone dry. "Shit! He must have called while I was in group and I haven't checked my messages since."

She jogged down the hall to her office and picked up the phone receiver as if it were molten lava. "Dr. Morgenstern? Sorry, I just came out of group and didn't get a chance to – "

"You terminated Felipe Diaz from Praxis!" The chairman's voice thundered in her ear.

"No! No, he was selling drugs, so we just suspended him for a day or two, until we could – "

"How dare you change his treatment plan without my approval?"

"I wasn't really – "

"We will discuss it on Wednesday in my office. Two o'clock. In the meantime, I want you to know that I am completely dissatisfied with the way you handled this."

He hung up before April could utter another syllable. As she lowered the receiver, she felt her lip tremble. How could she go back and face her staff?

15

Lowell Morgenstern was clearing off his desk around 6:00 PM when his phone rang. He looked at the caller ID and groaned. He considered letting it go to voicemail, but decided he'd only be postponing the inevitable. He picked up the receiver.

"What is it Sandra?"

"Can we talk?"

He put her on speakerphone, so he could finish sorting through the papers on his desk. "Better make it brief," he said, trying to decide which to leave and which to take home with him. "I'm on my way out."

"Could I meet you? I'm on my way across Vine Street. I'll be there in two – "

"It's not a good time," he interrupted, hastily throwing some of the papers into his attaché case. The last thing he needed tonight was a scene with Sandra Chang.

"I'm sorry I messed up this morning," she said miserably. "I should have prepared better."

"Forget it, Sandra." He could hear the sound of traffic coming from her end. "Go read up on suicide assessment."

"I will. But, Lowell, what about us?"

How could the woman be shameless enough to have this conversation right out on the street? Morgenstern rummaged through his lab coat pocket, locating his new vial of nasal spray. He rolled it in his palm, soothing his irritation.

"Sandra, I think I've done you a disservice by taking up so much of your time. I can see it's interfering with your training."

"Oh, no, Lowell! I've learned so much from you!"

"I think a time out would be for the best. Focus on your studies and we'll see how it goes."

"But –"

"I have to go now, Sandra. Take care."

"I'm pregnant!" she blurted out.

Morgenstern felt like he'd been punched in the gut. Stupid, irresponsible woman! And she called herself a doctor! He bit back an angry response. This situation had to be handled carefully. He had too much to lose. Of course, he'd offer to pay for the abortion. God knows, it was better than getting stuck with child support.

"Sandra," he said haltingly. "Are you sure?" Stall, he told himself. Don't let her put the pressure on.

"I'm positive. I'm downstairs, Lowell. Should I come up or are you coming down?"

"I really can't tonight, sweetheart." He felt nauseated by his own honeyed tone. "Why don't we talk about it over dinner tomorrow? We'll have more time. I'll make a reservation someplace special."

"You promise?" Her voice quavered, like a little girl's.

"I promise. Tomorrow." He hung up before she could say anything else. He rubbed his temples. His sinuses were killing him. Breaking the seal on his new vial of nasal spray, Morgenstern opened it and squirted a hit into each nostril. He replaced the container in the pocket of his lab coat, took it off, and switched it with the jacket on his coat tree.

He had to get out of there. Sandra might still change her mind.

Snatching his attaché case, Morgenstern hurried out into the hallway, leaving the door ajar for the cleaning service. He glanced around the corridor anxiously. He didn't see anyone, but a cold trickle down his spine told him there was a presence there in the dimness, watching him.

The elevator dinged.

Panic clutched at his stomach. He rushed off in the opposite direction toward the stairway. Pulling the exit door closed behind him to avoid letting it slam, Morgenstern raced down the stairs.

16

Sprawled across the sofa in jeans and a faded, oversized red tee shirt, April contemplated her bare feet and considered a second glass of wine. She knew it would intensify her miserable mood, but the urge was powerful. Perched by her side, the cats stared at her reproachfully. Or maybe that was just her projection.

"What the hell!" April sprang up and went to the kitchen for a re-fill. Since Morgenstern's call that afternoon, she'd envisioned countless scenes of disaster awaiting her at their meeting on Wednesday – screams, insults, maybe even being fired. The worst thing was being forced to wait and worry for another thirty six hours before she could get the meeting over with. She cursed herself for feeling so intimidated by Morgenstern. Then again, he could probably intimidate an Amazon.

She was no Amazon.

She slumped into the corner of the couch, as if inviting it to swallow her. With a sigh, she reached for her cellphone and keyed in a number she still had on speed dial. Her call went to voicemail.

"Hey, it's me. Call me when you get this," she said.

Dejected, she went back to her wine and dark thoughts. Before her glass was half empty, her cellphone rang. She looked at the screen. A tremor of anticipation rippled through her as she took the call.

"Hi, Mark. Your message was a surprise. Did you call to wish me a happy anniversary?" She regretted the words the moment they escaped her lips.

"Huh?"

"You don't remember what day it was yesterday?" She couldn't seem to stop herself.

He hesitated. "September 26th? Oh!"

She heard a lot in that syllable – surprise, guilt, dread. Regret?

"Yeah, that was our anniversary, wasn't it?" he said. "Sorry. I didn't think it still counted after you were divorced." His chuckle sounded hollow. "Anyway, happy belated anniversary."

"You, too."

"So! Good to hear your voice, April. How's it going?"

"Oh – okay." She failed to keep the despair out of her voice, then wished she could hit rewind.

"You don't sound okay. What's wrong?" Evidently Mark still recognized her "Not Okay" voice.

She picked up a throw pillow from the sofa and clutched it to her chest. "It's been a lousy day. I'm in hot water with my department chairman and I have to meet with him on Wednesday."

"All right. So, go get him, tiger!"

April wasn't looking for a cheerleader. She kneaded the pillow. Why couldn't men understand what women wanted?

"You don't know this guy," she protested. "His lover gave a case presentation today that wasn't up to par and he took her apart in front of everyone."

"Hoo boy!" He chuckled again.

She gritted her teeth. "I could use some moral support." She was digging herself into a deeper hole. Why did she have to spell it out for him? But what had she expected?

"Okay," he said. "Good luck. Hang tough."

She clucked her tongue in disdain.

"C'mon, April." Mark's voice was high and impatient now. "When are you going to stand up for yourself?"

"How about right now!" She terminated the call and threw her phone at the far corner of the couch. Too bad Mark couldn't hear it bounce off the cushion.

Stupid, stupid, stupid! Why had she been needy enough to crawl to her ex for the emotional support he'd never provided? April drained the last of her wine in two long swallows. As she got up to go for a refill, her phone rang.

He'd called back. She considered ignoring the call.

"Look, Honey," he said when she picked up, "I'm sorry you're having a bad day."

Honey? There was a word she hadn't heard in months. The tension in her jaws eased. She'd been starving for even a few crumbs of affection. "I shouldn't have hung up on you," she said.

"True," he said. "Exactly the point I was making. You need to face conflict head on, April, not avoid it."

"Thanks for the advice," she muttered. Mark might be right, but she still wasn't getting what she needed from him.

He rushed on. "Anyway, enough of that. The reason I called is I've been thinking about you a lot lately. I wondered if maybe, we could, you know, try spending some time together? See what happens?"

Her whole body tensed. She'd skated onto thin ice. This time, her reaction to danger was fight, instead of flight. "What about your girlfriend?" she demanded. "Holly – was that her name? Is she going to hang out with us, too?"

"That's been over for months."

Mark's tone implied April should have known this. Had she missed a press release, or something?

"It was never serious," he continued. "She was too immature. We had nothing in common besides work."

Was that supposed to make her feel better? That the marriage was ruined over an affair that wasn't even serious? She realized she was grinding her teeth.

Mark pressed on, oblivious. "So, what do you think?" When she remained silent, he continued. "All right, I know I probably treated you like shit toward the end. I was so totally focused on getting promoted. I guess I did neglect you."

"To put it mildly."

"But I've changed, April. I get it now, that I need balance, that there's more to life than a successful career. Like you were always telling me."

His words sounded rehearsed. The reconciliation speech, Act Two.

"I'm not asking you to commit to anything," he assured her.

Somehow, she thought, that actually made it worse.

"Look," he went on, "why don't you take the train in this weekend? I'll meet you at Penn Station. We can go to a museum, have brunch. Or maybe you'd like me to get tickets to a matinee. You always wanted to do stuff like that, right?"

Yes, she thought. And we never did. "Mark, you dumped me for a younger woman." April felt her face growing hot. "And now you want to pick it up like nothing happened? You expect me to come crawling back like some – "

"Well, if you're not even going to give it a chance…"

He sounded like he was pouting. So, now he'd become the injured party?

"Look, April –" Mark sounded so very patient. "At least take some time and think about it, will you? Call me Wednesday and let me know how your meeting went, and we'll talk more then. Okay?"

Like he cared. "Okay, Mark. Whatever." She didn't have the stomach to argue with him.

She hung up and picked up her wineglass. Probably, Mark was right about her conflict avoidance – especially with men. Maybe she'd stopped expecting much from them. A memory of her stepfather arose, unbidden. One of those times she'd gone to hug him, only to feel him stiffen and pull away.

She went to the kitchen for more wine.

As for her biological father, April had no memories of him at all. She knew from her mother that he'd been the keyboard player for a one-hit rock band until he OD'd on drugs. All he'd left April were the genetic roots of her thirst for wine.

She pulled the bottle from the refrigerator. It was still about a third full.

She'd been so hopeful when she married Mark. Too bad marriage didn't come with an owner's manual. As he'd relentlessly pursued the corporate fast track, his hours grew longer, his temper shorter, and their sexual relations became non-existent. When Mark's big promotion finally came through, April really didn't want to move to New York with him.

She uncorked the wine.

Enter the younger girlfriend. It wasn't all Mark's fault. Instead of speaking up and asking for the attention she craved, April had complained about little things, withdrawn into her own work and grown distant and cold.

She lifted the wine bottle, then put it back down.

A wave of disgust at her own self-pity flooded her. How had she allowed herself to become so beaten down? She needed to prove she was worth something. Even to that bully, Morgenstern.

Especially to him.

She thrust the cork back into the wine bottle. Suppose she took the bull by the horns? Instead of waiting and dreading the meeting on Wednesday, what if she showed up at Morgenstern's office first thing tomorrow morning and insisted on having her say? Maybe she could catch him off-guard, level the playing field a little.

She put the wine back in the refrigerator and pulled a clean glass from the cabinet. Another idea occurred to her as she filled the glass with spring water. Why show up empty-handed?

Filled with resolve, April headed to the desk in her bedroom and booted up her laptop. Even if it took her all night, she was going to draft a research proposal to bring to her showdown with Morgenstern tomorrow.

The cats trailed her into the bedroom and hopped onto the bed. They looked at her with encouragement. Or maybe that was just her projection. Your expression tended to be ambiguous when you lacked the eyebrows and muscles to move them on your furry little face.

"All right!" She grinned at them and pumped her fist. "Go team Simon!" She turned back to the keyboard.

Maybe she had a shot at becoming an Amazon after all.

17

PACIFIL SUBJECT: **Carlee Randall**

Carlee Randall stared at the cockroach she'd impaled on a pin. She hadn't planned this macabre ceremony, but after she'd winged the insect with a rolled up magazine, she couldn't resist. Now it writhed on her kitchen floor and would have wailed, if it had a voice.

She had her materials all assembled. Not the stupid rubber bands, ice cubes and chili peppers they'd talked about in group. Something darker. She didn't know why she had to do this, couldn't remember when these compulsions had started.

She certainly had no intention of discussing the matter in the Survivors Group. Not that she didn't like Dr. April. The women in the group were okay, too. But Carlee knew without a doubt that her new rituals were not to be mentioned – to anybody. In fact, she questioned whether talking about personal matters in general was a good idea. Like bringing up her half brother today in group. That had been a mistake. Now she couldn't get him out of her head. The things he did to her.

Lifting the pin holding the squirming insect, Carlee placed it on a piece of aluminum foil. Next, she struck the safety match. She studied the flame for a moment, her expression impassive, and dropped the lighted match onto the roach. Its twitching continued for a few moments, until it blackened and shriveled within the flame.

Carlee smiled.

Tuesday, September 28

18

April's eyes shot open at around 4:00 AM. She'd labored over her research proposal until the words became a blur, then staggered to bed. She dropped into a heavy slumber that lasted only a couple of hours. Once awake, her brain kicked into overdrive, anticipating the confrontation with Morgenstern. By six, she abandoned the idea of getting any more rest.

Over a cup of coffee, she re-read her work, added a few finishing touches, and decided it wasn't half bad. A quick shower augmented the effects of the caffeine. She selected her personal version of a power suit from the closet – fitted black pants, gold silk jacket and black tee. She added a small gold chain and earrings, put a little extra care into her makeup, and nodded at her reflection. She'd nailed the polished professional look.

"Wish me luck," she told Boris and Natasha. If they did, they didn't say so.

All through the train ride into Center City, then the walk from Suburban Station, April debated the wisdom of her mission. Her faculty appointment was at stake. Was it wise to confront the chairman? Perhaps it would be more prudent to wait and show him her research proposal when his state of mind was more receptive.

As she reached her destination, she formulated a strategy. Plan A: Walk into Morgenstern's office and demand – well, request – five minutes of his time. Plan B: Wait thirty minutes, if he wasn't there. Plan C: Leave her research paper on his desk and get the hell out of Dodge.

The security guard eyed April's ID and nodded her through to the lobby of Morgenstern's building. She rode the elevator up to the third floor and walked down the hall to his office. The outer door to the suite was open, but Dana's desk was unoccupied. Morgenstern's door stood ajar, the lights on inside.

"Hello?" April called out. "Dr. Morgenstern?" She knocked tentatively on his door. No response. She rapped again, harder, with the same result. She stuck her head in for a quick peek. No one there.

On to Plan B.

There was a small sofa in Dana's office, apparently for those awaiting audience with the chairman, and April sat down to begin her vigil. She looked at her watch: 8:13 AM. She waited, her level of tension increasing with each passing minute.

Brriinngg!

The phone in Morgenstern's office rang, along with the extension on Dana's desk, then stopped, the call evidently going to voicemail. Silence returned. She looked at her watch again: 8:22 AM. She thought she heard a clock ticking in Morgenstern's office and tried to remember if she'd noticed one when she'd been in there before. She realized she was jiggling her right leg up and down and forced herself to sit still.

The next time she looked, her watch said it was 8:30 AM. No way would she get through another ten minutes of watchful waiting. Shift to Plan C, she decided.

April went over to Dana's desk and glanced at the supplies neatly arrayed there. She found a pad of Post It notes and helped herself to one. Pulling a pen from the caddy, she wrote a short message and affixed it to her research proposal. She took a deep breath and pushed open the door to Morgenstern's office.

She walked over to his desk, and froze at the sight that greeted her there. Morgenstern lay sprawled on the floor – eyes lifeless, face blue, his expression utterly serene.

With a gasp of horror, April rushed to his side. Kneeling, she felt the chairman's neck, finding no pulse. His skin was cold to the touch.

"Oh, dear Lord!"

April whirled at Dana Costelli's shrill voice.

"What's wrong?" the secretary cried.

"I think he's dead." April started to get up from her crouch. "Call 911, right away!" As she took a step toward Dana, the woman backed away, her eyes widening in terror.

"My God!" she shouted at April. "What have you done?"

19

A few blocks away, at Police Headquarters, Sam Perone's partner, Justin, gaped at him.

"Another one?" he asked.

"Yup," Sam confirmed. "Third missing dog reported this week." He sipped his cup of takeout coffee. "Also four cats," he added.

"Where this time?"

"The dog? Over near U of P."

Justin nodded thoughtfully. "West Philly again. Any leads?"

Sam put down his coffee, looking as if he'd lost his taste for it. "Officers found a mutt answering the description about a half mile away from the owner's house."

Justin brightened. "Hey, good news."

"Not exactly." Sam grimaced. "Its throat was cut."

"Aw, shit."

"I've been thinking. I have a contact at The Inquirer who owes me one." Sam referred to the Philadelphia daily newspaper, not than the national tabloid – although, he thought, they'd probably like the story, too. "Maybe if they ran an article about a recent spate of missing animals, we might get more calls, pick up some leads, and – "

His cellphone rang. Sam reached over to his desk, where he'd set it down, picked it up and looked at the display.

"Uh-oh," he muttered. "Better take this."

Justin watched him take the call.

"Yes, Inspector." Sam frowned as he listened. "Now, sir?"

Justin's eyebrows arched with curiosity. Wanting some privacy, Sam swiveled his chair so his back was turned to his partner.

"But, Inspector – " Sam's shoulders slumped as he listened. "Certainly, sir. Yes, I know where it is." He nodded. "On my way." Sam ended the call and spun around to face his partner.

"So what's up?" Justin asked.

"Ah, politics." Sam picked up his half-empty coffee container and tossed it in the waste basket. "Some big deal shrink at Franklin was found dead in his office a few minutes ago." He sighed. "And I'm the lucky guy who gets to go over there and check it out."

20

April couldn't say which made her more uncomfortable – sitting a few feet from an office containing a dead body, or enduring Dana Costelli's baleful stare from across the room. The police officer that'd secured the scene had dispatched them to Dana's office, then gone back inside to watch two paramedics minister to the chairman – or, more likely, attend to his remains. April and Dana were ordered to await the arrival of the detective.

"I can't believe it!" Dana wailed from her desk. "I can't believe he's gone!"

April started to get up from the sofa, instinctively moving to offer comfort.

"You! You stay away from me!" Dana thrust out her hand in a "Stop Right There" signal, and April sank back onto the couch. She herself felt mostly numb with shock.

A stony silence descended for the next fifteen minutes, broken only when the secretary hissed: "You weren't supposed to be here until tomorrow."

April bit back a rejoinder. It was preposterous for Dana to blame her for whatever had happened, but the woman was so clearly shattered by her boss's death that April could see no benefit in arguing with her. She wished the detective would show up, so they could get this over with.

Without warning, the door to Dana's office swung open. A dark-haired man in a grey suit walked in and nodded to the two women.

"Detective Sam Perone, Philadelphia P.D. This the chairman's office?"

"In there." April pointed. "Detective, the officer said you'd want to question us, and – "

He was already walking toward Morgenstern's office, but he stopped and turned back to stare briefly at April. "That's right," he said. "Please wait." He continued on into Morgenstern's office.

Dana shot her a smug look.

April felt a cold twinge of paranoia. Could she somehow get into trouble over this?

"What've we got?" Sam asked the young officer who greeted him inside.

"A dead professor, Detective. Wanna take a look?"

No, Sam thought, but didn't say. He'd rather not be here at all. "Yeah, show me," he replied. He extracted a pair of latex gloves from his coat pocket and pulled them on. He nodded toward Dana's office. "Who're they?"

"The one who found him and his secretary."

"Make sure they stay until I'm done here." Sam surveyed the room. No blood. No signs of a struggle. No weapons. Was it a crime scene? Or did this shrink just drop dead of a heart attack?

Sam approached the paramedic leaning over Morgenstern.

"You the detective?" the man asked. Before Sam could answer, he added, "because if you wanted to interview him, you're too late."

Everyone was a comedian. Sam chose to ignore the gallows humor. "Uh-huh. What do you think happened here?"

"I'm no medical examiner," the paramedic replied. "Hell, I'm no doctor. But between you and me...?" He paused. "I'd bet on respiratory failure. See the color of his face?"

Sam crouched beside the body. No strong odor. No marbling of the flesh, or fluids leaking from any visible orifices. He reached out two fingers and touched the body. Cold. A bit stiff. Sam was no medical examiner, either, but knew enough to guess that Morgenstern hadn't been dead long. A deceased psychiatrist. Unfortunately, not the one he'd like to see dead.

Sam took a breath. Be professional, he reminded himself. Stuff down those kind of reactions while you're on the clock.

The other paramedic leaned in and pointed at Morgenstern's blue-tinged face. "Check out his nose," he said. "The nostril's all red. Maybe he had a cold."

"I see what you mean," the first paramedic agreed. "Think he was snorting coke?"

Sam's gaze panned out from the inflamed nostril to the carpet surrounding the corpse.

"What's that?" He retrieved a small plastic bottle lying a couple of feet away and studied the label. "Nasal spray."

Nothing suspicious there – except for its presence next to the fresh stiff. People didn't keel over from head colds. Sam's intuition whispered foul play – and he'd learned to pay attention when it did that.

"I want this sealed off as a crime scene," he told the police officer. "We're going to need an autopsy and tox screen." He held up the nasal spray. "And this goes to the lab."

Outside in Dana's office, April fidgeted and once again checked her watch – after nine now. She fumbled in her purse for her cellphone, so she could call Praxis and tell Cynthia, what? That Morgenstern was dead and the police were holding her for questioning? She hesitated. Better to simply say she'd been delayed. Before she could dial, the detective emerged from the inside office.

"Which of you found the body?" His eyes moved from Dana to April.

"It was me." April put away her phone. A vision of Morgenstern's corpse filled her mind and she suppressed a shudder. She rose from the sofa and went over to join the other two by Dana's desk. She started to offer a handshake, but stopped. The detective was pulling latex gloves from his hands. She settled for saying: "I'm Dr. April Simon."

He nodded at her and turned to Dana. "And you are…?"

"Dana Costelli, Dr. Morgenstern's secretary."

"I have some questions for the two of you." He pulled a notebook and pen from his breast pocket.

"Detective, what happened to him?" Dana asked.

April gave her credit for taking the initiative in this interview.

"We won't know until an autopsy is completed." The detective turned to April. "Dr. Simon, what do you do around here?"

"I direct the Psychiatric Rehabilitation Program, called Praxis. Right across Vine Street. I really should be getting over there." Her nerves were making her prattle.

The detective's brown eyes fixed on her. "You a psychiatrist?"

"Psychologist."

His eyes narrowed. "There's a difference?"

April was used to explaining the distinction. "Psychiatrists are medical doctors. They can write prescriptions. Psychologists hold academic degrees. We do psychotherapy, testing, research…" She trailed off, babbling again. She wondered whether talking too much came across as a sign of guilt, and vowed to keep her responses brief – just to be on the safe side.

Dana jumped in. "Dr. Morgenstern was a psychiatrist," she beamed.

The detective grunted, obviously unimpressed, and resumed questioning April. "What were you doing here this morning? Did you have an appointment with him?"

"She didn't!" Dana interjected. "Her appointment wasn't until tomorrow." A frosty look from the detective silenced her.

"Exactly what happened when you came in here this morning, Dr. Simon?"

April stammered. "I, ah, came to speak with the chairman for a few minutes." She held up her research proposal. "I wanted to drop off a paper for him to review." She couldn't resist flashing Dana a triumphant look. "Before the meeting we had scheduled for tomorrow."

The secretary pursed her lips.

"When did you get here?" he asked.

"A little before eight-fifteen," April said.

"And?"

April gave a halting account of her arrival, wait and subsequent discovery of Morgenstern's body while the detective jotted notes. Watching him write down her words made her squirm. Suppose she left something out, or got some detail wrong? Was there a penalty for that?

"Anything else?" he asked. "Did you see anyone in the hall when you got here, or afterwards?" He looked up from his notes and again, she felt those dark eyes boring into her. She swallowed, her mouth dry.

"No," she said.

"Oh my God!" Dana cradled her head in her hands and suddenly burst into tears again. "I can't believe Doctor is gone!"

"I'm sure it was a terrible shock."

April was surprised by the detective's soothing tone.

"For both of you," he added, flashing April a look of sympathy.

An attractive man, she thought, admiring his strong, hawk-like features. She looked away, embarrassed to think he might have caught her staring.

"Ms. Costelli," he asked, "do you know if Dr. Morgenstern had any medical problems?"

"Not that I know of, Detective. He was such a strong, healthy man." Dana sniffled. "A tennis player."

The detective nodded. "Was he having any other problems that you noticed?"

"Oh, no! Doctor was a very, very positive man!"

April gaped at the detective. "You're thinking this could have been suicide?" She'd have thought Morgenstern incapable of it.

He shook his head. "I'm not making any assumptions." He cleared his throat. "Ms. Costelli, was Dr. Morgenstern embroiled in any conflicts that you know of? Did he have enemies?"

A jolt of alarm seized April, as several plausible candidates popped unbidden into her mind. Too late, it occurred to her that the detective could probably read her expression. His appraising look confirmed her fear, and she quickly lowered her eyes.

"Detective Perone!" Dana grabbed at Sam's arm. "What do you mean? Who'd want to kill Dr. Morgenstern?"

April thought grimly, who wouldn't? She looked back at the detective and their eyes met.

"Ms. Costelli," he said, stepping back to extricate his arm from her grasp. "If you'll allow me to use your office for a few more minutes, I'd like to talk to Dr. Simon alone."

21

April watched Dana close the office door behind her, her stomach knotting with dread. She was alone with the detective. What did he want from her? Tightness gripped her chest and she felt light-headed.

"You okay?" He thrust the notebook back into his pocket and quickly stepped over to take April's arm. "Why don't you sit down?" His outstretched hand indicated the loveseat. April hesitated. Did he intend them to share it?

"Come on." He steered her to the small sofa. "Would you like me to get you some water?"

"No, thanks." Warily, she perched on the loveseat. "I'm fine."

"You sure?" He eyed her with an expression of concern. "You know, sometimes people experience a delayed reaction to a shock like that." He angled his head toward Morgenstern's office.

"I know how people react to trauma," she fired back, immediately regretting her defensive tone. "I'm all right," she said, giving him a tentative smile. "Thanks."

"Good. Then you won't mind a few more questions?"

Without waiting for her response, the detective pulled out the chair from behind Dana's desk and wheeled it over. He smiled and sat down across from her. He regarded her quietly for a few moments. April couldn't read his inscrutable expression. Despite her resolution to hold her tongue, she broke the silence.

"What did you want to ask me?"

He let her question hang unanswered for several beats. "Who do you think wanted to kill him?" He leaned forward, as if eager to pounce on her response.

"Kill him?" The question startled her. "But you said you weren't – that you had no assumptions about how he died."

"I didn't. Until I saw a look on your face that said you might."

"I might what?" She was confused. Probably that was his intention.

"Might have some idea about why he's dead," he said quietly.

"Are you accusing me?" She felt completely alone and helpless. He was interrogating her!

"Whoa!" He held up a hand and made a slow down gesture. "I meant that when I asked his secretary if he had any enemies, you looked like something occurred to you."

"To me?" April shook her head vehemently, her thoughts racing. She pictured Clarence McKay, Sandra Chang, and Stuart Hartman. There were so many people with reasons to hate Lowell Morgenstern. And they were all her colleagues. Two of them could easily kill her chances for promotion. No way did she want to be pulled into this any further.

"I told you," she said, "I came in and found him like that. I don't know anything about what happened to him."

She watched the detective swivel in the desk chair. She fought a wild urge to shove his chair away and bolt out of the office. He had no right to put her on the spot. She hadn't done anything.

"Tell me about your relationship with Dr. Morgenstern." He posed the question casually, as if they were having a friendly chat.

April bristled at the implications. "What's that supposed to mean?"

"You want me to repeat the question, Dr. Simon?"

Her muscles tensed at the hint of menace in his tone. She'd read journal articles about people confessing to crimes they'd never committed, under the pressure of police questioning. She'd always been skeptical, wondered how that could possibly happen, but now had an inkling. She took a breath to compose herself.

"Dr. Morgenstern hired me to launch a clinical program here, a little over a year ago. I worked with him, not all that closely." She deliberately stopped talking. No point in volunteering how she'd felt about the man.

"Yet there you were in his office, bright and early, no appointment needed," the detective observed. "Makes a person wonder."

Her face burned. What was this, some kind of witch hunt? "Speculate all you want, Detective. I've told you what I know, which is nothing."

A sharp rap on the office door.

"What?" her interrogator called out.

A man carrying what looked like a medical bag entered. "You called for a crime scene technician, Detective?"

"Hi, Marty. Yeah, thanks." He pointed at Morgenstern's office. "In there."

The technician headed inside.

April looked at her watch. "May I get back to directing my program now, Detective Perone? Or do I need to call a lawyer?"

"Whether you call an attorney is up to you, Dr. Simon." He smiled, disarmingly. "We're done here for now," he added. "Where can I reach you in case I have further questions?"

Tight-lipped, she reached into her purse and pulled out her business card. She stood and held it out to him.

He rose and took the card. She turned to go.

"Dr. Simon?"

His voice was gentle, almost tender, and stopped April in her tracks. The man was utterly unpredictable, attacking one moment, solicitous, the next. Deliberately keeping her off balance? She stood with her back to him, unwilling to turn. She itched to escape that room.

"Take it easy," he told her. "You've had a nasty shock."

April hurried down the hall to the elevator, desperate to get away before Detective Perone changed his mind and came after her – like in those classic Columbo episodes she used to watch on re-runs. The rumpled, innocuous detective would play cat-and-mouse with his suspect. When he was about to leave, he'd turn and say, "By the way…" and the unwitting suspect ended up skewered by the rapier-like question or observation Columbo thrust at him.

Or her.

When she reached the elevator, April glanced back toward Morgenstern's office to make sure Sam Perone wasn't stalking her with a rapier of his own. The coast was clear. As she pressed the elevator button, she noticed her hand was shaking. She exhaled once she was inside the elevator and no hand or foot shot out to block the doors from closing. She'd eluded her own Columbo, at least for the time being.

Not that Sam Perone looked anything like the Peter Falk character, April reflected as she rode down to the lobby. He wasn't rumpled, dumpy or frumpy. Actually, he was pretty hot. Probably knew it too, the way he used those penetrating dark eyes. Her mouth pinched with annoyance – whether at the detective or herself she couldn't say.

She stepped out of the elevator into the lobby and paused to get her bearings. She needed to shake off the disastrous events of the morning and get back to Praxis. She'd explain to everyone there that…

She froze. She had to decide what to tell people, or not tell them. Did the detective give her any instructions about that? She left the building and walked slowly down 15th Street to the intersection at Vine.

This wasn't going to stay a secret. Dana Costelli had probably begun spreading the news as soon as she'd left the office. Gossip at Franklin traveled like an airborne pandemic. April wouldn't be surprised if people at Praxis greeted her with word of Morgenstern's death the moment she walked in there.

She reached the other side of Vine Street and stopped in her tracks – Sandra Chang. The resident would be devastated to learn of Morgenstern's death. She shouldn't hear about it through the rumor mill.

April decided to find Sandra and break the bad news herself. She quickened her pace, hoping to reach her before the grapevine did.

22

Sam Perone set out to deliver the bad news to Morgenstern's wife. He drove to Lower Merion, pulling up in front of the Morgensterns' colonial. He walked past a lush front lawn, glad he wasn't the one who had to mow it, and up to the front deck. A tall door held a brass knocker with a little gargoyle face sticking out its tongue at him. He opted for the doorbell instead, although he had second thoughts when it tolled the opening notes to Beethoven's Fifth Symphony. Why was it necessary for so many inanimate devices to express themselves these days?

Footsteps approached and in a moment the door, still chained, opened a few inches. A face peered through at him, composed and skillfully made up to create a natural look that probably took the better part of an hour to produce. A cool voice inquired, "Yes?"

Sam produced his badge. "Detective Perone, Philadelphia PD. Are you Mrs. Morgenstern?"

She arched a neatly plucked brow. "I am. What's happened?"

"May I come in? There's something very serious I need to discuss with you."

The door closed slightly as she unlatched the security chain, then reopened.

"Come in, Detective." Her silky lavender tunic, with iridescent beading around the neckline, shimmered as she moved. Even her hair shimmered. Sam thought about the expression "a woman of a certain age," fully appreciating its meaning for the first time.

No doubt, money helped.

She led him into a living room the size of a football field. Sunlight shone through high, arched windows. Sam eyed the pricey fabric arrangements, the plush white rug and gleaming hardwood floors. Throw pillows decorated the furniture, also white, adding little splashes of color and texture. Not a room that looked as if it had ever welcomed muddy sneakers or sticky fingers. If he had the chance to sit here for a while, he might achieve spiritual enlightenment.

But Sam didn't expect to stay that long.

Gesturing Sam toward the sectional, Miranda Morgenstern sat in a chrome and leather chair.

"So, Detective," she asked, "what is it you've come to discuss with me?"

Sam braced himself. He hated doing this, knowing only too well how it felt to be on the receiving end of the announcement he'd come to make.

"Mrs. Morgenstern, I'm afraid I have very bad news." He paused. "Your husband was found dead in his office this morning."

She gasped. "Lowell?"

"I'm afraid so."

"But, how? What happened?" Her eyes flooded with tears. She blotted them gingerly with her fingertips, as if protecting her mascara.

Sam pulled a handkerchief from his breast pocket and handed it to her. "We don't really know yet. The medical examiner will conduct an autopsy."

"Why would they do that?" Miranda frowned, as if the notion of something as messy as an autopsy had no place in her pristine life or living room. "Was there something suspicious? Signs of violence?"

She dabbed at her eyes with the handkerchief.

"No, it's required by law," Sam explained, "in cases where no physician is present at the time of death."

"Oh."

A tiny twitch rippled across her mouth. Did it have a meaning?

"Where…where did he….?" Miranda trailed off.

"He was found in his office early this morning," Sam told her.

"Who found him?" Her tears had subsided.

"One of the faculty."

"Which one?"

Sam hesitated. He didn't have to reveal that information, but decided it might be worth seeing her reaction. "Dr. April Simon."

Miranda squinted at him, her forehead betraying no hint of a furrow. "What does she look like?"

"Early thirties, slender, shoulder-length hair." Sort of a coppery color, he thought, picturing her.

"Don't think I know her." Another micro-expression flitted across Miranda's face.

It made Sam suspicious and he played a hunch. "What sort of relationship did you and your husband have?" He expected her to bristle at the question.

She didn't. "We've been married for eighteen years." Miranda's expression remained impassive.

"How did you get along?"

She shrugged. "Like we were married for eighteen years." She gave Sam an appraising gaze. "Look, Detective, I'll save you some time. I don't know who this Dr. Simon is, but I do know, did know, my husband. He was carrying on with someone."

"How do you – "

"Experience, Detective," she said with a bitter smile. "Plenty of experience. If your Dr. Simon is young and attractive, I'd suggest you look into what sort of relationship she had with Lowell."

She was young and attractive, at that. Sam's mind conjured the image of a pair of almond-shaped green eyes, a generous mouth with a delicate Cupid's bow on the upper lip.

"Detective?"

Sam mentally shook himself to banish the vision, feeling as if he'd been caught leafing through Penthouse instead of doing his homework. What the hell was the matter with him? And why was the widow so eager to point a finger at someone?

Maybe they were both too interested in April Simon.

Again Miranda interrupted his thoughts. "Did Lowell say anything before….?"

Sam shook his head. "He was gone when they found him. The autopsy will tell us more about the time of death."

"When will I be able to claim my husband's body?" She sounded as if she were pushing a mechanic to have her car ready.

"As soon as the autopsy is completed. They'll call you." She nodded and Sam continued. "Did your husband suffer from any medical conditions that could have contributed to his death?"

"None. Lowell was healthy as a horse. Even down to his cholesterol level. Except for recurring sinusitis and occasional tennis elbow, he was fine."

"Okay, then. I don't want to take up any more of your time." Sam turned as if to go, then looked back at her. "Sinusitis, you said?"

"That's right."

"Did he use any medications to treat it?"

"Antibiotics when it flared up, otherwise, no. Just saline nasal spray. He used that all the time."

Sam felt a prickle of interest. "Did he carry his nasal spray with him?"

She raised her eyebrows, her forehead still smooth as glass. "I couldn't say. He kept a container on his night table. When we went out, he'd often have it in his pocket. I don't know what he did at work. Maybe you should ask the people there, if it's important. I'm sure his secretary, Dana, would know."

"I'll do that," Sam said. "The container on his night table – if it's there now, I'd like to take it."

She moved to get up. "I'll get it."

He held up a hand. "A few more questions. I'm sorry to have to ask, but did your husband have any enemies that you knew of?"

The muscles worked in her jaw, as if she were chewing on the question. When she spoke, her words were slow and deliberate. "Detective, my husband had a very – forceful – personality. Always said what he thought. He could be blunt. Didn't suffer fools, as they say."

"So, he might have ruffled some feathers on the job?"

"I wouldn't be surprised," she replied.

"Anyone in particular?"

"No." Her gaze skittered away from his. "Shall I get you that nasal spray?"

"Yes. Thank you."

Miranda Morgenstern exited the room, tunic shimmering. She'd left him with two distinct impressions. The widow was hiding something. More certain, April Simon was a definite person of interest –someone he intended to pursue.

23

Although she was long overdue at Praxis after her encounter with the detective, April hurried straight up to the outpatient clinic. She needed to find Sandra Chang and come up with some gentle way to break the news of Morgenstern's death.

April checked with the clinic's receptionist, who informed her that Sandra was in her office, wrapping up her last patient med check. Grateful for the fortuitous timing, April waited outside the resident's office. A couple of minutes later, the door opened and a young man exited, prescription in hand.

April poked her head through the open door. "Sandra?"

"April! I'm glad you're here." Sandra's face was pinched with worry. "I need to talk to you. Something's happened. Something very serious." Her voice broke.

Could the news have traveled so fast? Sighing, April walked in and sank into a chair across the desk from Sandra. "Then, you know," she murmured.

"Of course." Sandra cocked her head and stared at April with a look of puzzlement. "But how would you?"

"I just came from Lowell's office," April explained. She braced herself for the inevitable tears and questions.

Sandra looked stunned. "And he told you? That I'm pregnant?"

April felt a wave of shock, followed by dismay. The conversation with Sandra was going to be even harder than she'd expected.

Ψ

It was well past 10:00 AM, before April could extricate herself from her painful session with Sandra. She'd convinced the poor woman to take a sick day and go home. Sandra was far too distraught to be useful to patients. April herself felt drained, yet dry-eyed. Where were her tears? If not for Morgenstern, at least for Sandra?

She had no time to mourn once she got to Praxis. April threw herself into the flow of activities there, trying to maintain a normal program routine. It wasn't as if her patients knew Morgenstern – except for his four research subjects.

The staff was another matter. By noon, the whole department of behavioral health sciences buzzed with the news of the chairman's death. Shock was universal. The man had been a force of nature, his demise so sudden and unexpected. Rumor and speculation spread like brushfire.

At her lunch break, April sought refuge in James's messy office. She'd declined his offer to pick up a sandwich for her from the Chuckwagon, but gratefully sipped the hot tea he'd insisted on bringing her. She also availed herself of his sympathetic ear.

"It was so unreal," she concluded, as she described the morning's events. "Like, I was standing outside myself, watching myself stare at him there on the floor." Although Sandra's confession weighed on her mind, April decided to confine her account to Morgenstern's death. The dead might forfeit their claims to privacy, but the living didn't.

"So, now you know what derealization feels like," James said. "Like the textbooks say, it's as if events aren't really happening to you. A primitive defense, but pretty handy if you're traumatized."

"I guess so," April mused. Had she been traumatized? She hardly knew what she was feeling.

James regarded her with a look of concern. "Red, why don't you take the afternoon off, go home and take care of yourself?"

April shook her head and swallowed a sip of her tea. "I'd rather stay. I may be numb right now, but once I get home, the emotional Novocain is bound to wear off, and I'll crash. I'd just as soon hold off on that."

"In that case..." James hesitated.

She looked up from her tea. "What?"

"How do you want to handle the Pacifil Four? We'll need to break it to them that their shrink is dead."

"Oh, God! You're right." She leaned back in her chair, thinking. "How about if you and I meet with them as a group to discuss it?"

James nodded slowly. "Maybe that way they could support each other." He frowned. "But who's going to prescribe for them now? For that matter, is the study even going to be continued?"

April massaged her temples, trying to ease the tension that had been steadily building there. This small act of comfort almost brought tears to her eyes. Maybe her emotional Novocain was wearing off sooner than she'd anticipated. She pushed aside her distress and focused back on the problem.

"The pilot study only has another two months to go," she said. "Maybe we won't have to abandon it. The project is good for Franklin and the Pacifil seems to be working with the patients." Except for Felipe, she mentally added.

"Uh-huh."

"I'll bet Clarence could take over the pilot," she said. "He could do the prescribing and finish out the study. We're doing most of the symptom ratings here at Praxis, anyway."

"Makes sense." James nodded. "Think he would?"

"I'll talk to him. He'll get a publication out of it. And he does have a responsibility to the patients."

"Sounds good, Red. The sooner you can pitch it to him, the better. It really would help if we had a plan in place when we talk with those Pacifil patients."

24

"The nasal spray angle – that's interesting," Justin said, after Sam briefed his partner on the situation at Franklin. "But you know those guys at the lab. You won't hear from them for a couple weeks at best."

"Yeah. Ahhh, what the hell," Sam said. "It's not like this is such a red hot case. Better to put our energy into –"

"What, dogs?"

The ringing of his desk phone spared Sam from answering, and he took the call. Justin watched his partner suddenly sit up at attention.

"Yes, sir," Sam said. "I understand. I'll –" He listened, then nodded. "I'll make it my top priority, sir." He hung up, scowling.

"What was all that?" Justin asked.

"That," Sam replied, "was our esteemed Inspector."

"Yeah?"

"Who said he just got off the phone with the Chief of Police."

"Uh-huh?"

"Who just spoke with the Mayor."

"Nice to know where you are in the pecking order, right? So – ?"

"It's about the Morgenstern case. Seems the Mayor's Chief of Staff is on the board of trustees at Franklin. They're all worried about bad PR over his death and the heat is on us to close the case." He sighed. "Guess the shrink goes back on the front burner."

"So, the best case scenario is the guy died of natural causes, right?" Justin asked. "And your nasal spray is just – "

"Nasal spray." Sam grimaced. "Somehow I've got a feeling it's not going to be that simple."

Ψ

A few miles away, at the office of the Philadelphia Medical Examiner, one of the veteran pathologists pulled off his latex gloves and stepped back from the autopsy table.

"That's it," he announced.

"What's the cause of death?" his pathology resident asked.

"Can't say yet. He asphyxiated, but I found no obstruction, no evidence of heart attack." The ME's tone betrayed his frustration. "No evidence of anything. We'll have to wait for the results of the tox screen."

"But that could take weeks, right?" The resident was already getting the hang of the bureaucracy.

The pathologist sighed, something he often had occasion to do. "I guess we can try pulling some strings to get it expedited. The guy was pretty important."

The wall phone rang.

"Yes?" the pathologist said, as he picked up the receiver. He listened for a few moments. "Really?" His voice rose with excitement. "Incredible! Yes, it will. Thank you." Hanging up, he turned to his resident and grinned. "We caught a break."

"On him?" The resident nodded at Lowell Morgenstern's lifeless body.

"Uh-huh. The crime lab analyzed a container of nasal spray found next to the body."

"So soon?" the resident asked.

"Yeah, warp speed. Looks like somebody already pulled those strings."

"And?"

"Of all things, the spray was laced with Botox," the Medical Examiner said "Now, there's a cause of asphyxiation!"

"Botox!" the resident echoed. "Jeez! So now….?"

The ME finished his sentence. "We test the body for Botox."

25

Clarence McKay frowned. "Can't one of the residents do it?" he protested, when April concluded her pitch for him to take over the Pacifil group. "The president just asked me to step in as acting chairman. I don't have time to take on a research study."

"Don't think of it as a study," April coaxed. "All you'd have to do is see four patients once a month, write their scrips and fill out a brief symptom checklist at the end of their visits. It's only for two months." She resorted to flattery. "Please, Clarence. We need your clinical expertise. Besides," she added, saving her most compelling argument for last, "you'll get a publication out of it."

He continued to frown for a few moments, then sighed. "All right. I'll do it for now. But if I find I can't keep it up, I will transfer it to one of the residents and you will accept it. Yes?"

"Absolutely."

"Is that it?" He shook the mouse on his desk to awaken his computer screen.

"Well," April began.

Reluctantly, Clarence let go of the mouse.

"It's about Felipe Diaz," April continued. "We referred him to Freedom House for rehab before we take him back at Praxis. For the sake of the study, can he still come to you for his Pacifil? We can get someone from Freedom House to bring him for the med visits."

"Whatever," McKay sighed. "It would appear Lowell's death settled that problem for you. Now are we done?"

She hesitated. "There is one more thing. You remember Lowell promised me a faculty appointment when I submit a research plan for Praxis?"

"It rings a bell." He fiddled with the mouse again.

"Maybe this isn't the right time, Clarence, but I've drafted the proposal. As the acting chairman, I thought at some point, you might – "

"Not up for discussion now," he said flatly. "Meeting over." He turned to his computer monitor.

He sounded like a chairman already. April reluctantly rose to leave. She'd wait, if she had to, but she had no intention of dropping the matter of her promotion. In the meantime, she decided, she'd ask Larissa to look over her proposal and give her feedback.

She took the stairs down to Praxis, rather than wait for the elevator, and found James about to go in and start his afternoon therapy group. Flagging him down, she flashed him a thumbs up sign.

"Clarence said he'd do it," she told him. "Let's meet with the Pacifil folks after your group."

Ψ

An hour later, the Pacifil Four – minus Felipe – sat in a group room with April and James. Carlee Randall, as usual, divided her attention between the floor and her dark brown hair, which she twisted around a finger. Tyrell Johnson wore a goatee, droopy jeans and his signature scowl. Brittany Jacobs maintained her biker chick insouciance. Beneath the spiky blond hair, multiple piercings and relentless gum chewing, was a fragile girl who'd been undone by drugs and partying in her first attempt at college and was now gearing up for a second try.

With a glance at James, April cleared her throat and began. "We called you in to meet with us because we have some very sad news."

Brittany popped her gum.

"I'm sorry to tell you that Dr. Morgenstern died this morning," April said solemnly.

"You shittin' me?" Tyrell exploded.

Carlee continued to watch the floor and play with her hair.

"No, Tyrell, I'm afraid it's true," April said. "It was very sudden. We don't know the cause yet."

"I can't believe it!" Brittany exclaimed. "I just saw him the other day."

"I know it's a terrible shock," James said.

"But what about us?" Tyrell demanded.

"You'll continue to receive your medication," April assured him. "Dr. McKay will take over as your psychiatrist. He's very good, and – "

"No! No! This ain't right!" Tyrell thundered.

"We're supposed to see Dr. Morgenstern!" Brittany protested. "This is a study, right?"

Carlee began to cry.

Shit, April thought. Who knew Morgenstern was so popular?

It went downhill from there.

Ψ

When it was over, April and James retreated to her office.

"Jesus!" James blew out a breath. "What a scene!"

"Unbelievable," April agreed. "Every borderline trait in the book."

"Intense, angry, unstable." James began ticking off typical traits of the disorder. "Putting Morgenstern on some kind of pedestal," he added.

"From their perspective, he abandoned them," April said. "The number one fear of every borderline patient." She shuddered. "God, I hope this doesn't trigger any suicide attempts or self-injury."

"We'll keep a close watch on those three," James said. "But there's still Felipe."

"I know. At least we've got a plan in place." April sighed. "Guess I'll call and ask him to come in and meet with me. It wouldn't feel right to tell him over the phone."

"Brave woman," James said. He scratched his head. "I still think their reactions were really over the top, even for borderlines."

"Maybe they triggered each other," April speculated. "Anyway, as you said, we'll keep an eye on them."

26

"Botox?" Sam repeated to the crime lab technician who'd phoned him. "You're kidding!"

"No joke. Definitely a lethal dose. Probably killed him within minutes."

"Huh. Our fair city leads the country in gunshot killings and this poor bastard gets it with Botox. I suppose it's unlikely he put the stuff in there himself. Or bought the spray that way."

"Not likely at all. It took time and effort to rig that container. See, Botox comes as a powder. You have to reconstitute it to get it into liquid form. Then it only has a shelf life of 24 hours. Plus, it has to be refrigerated. So it wouldn't make sense for some psycho to try to contaminate over-the-counter nasal spray with Botox and expect it to kill anyone."

"Say, I'm impressed," Sam said. "You going to med school at night, or something?"

"Nah, I looked it up on the Internet. Anyway, the suicide angle doesn't make sense, either. Too complicated. The guy would have to be some kind of obsessive-compulsive nut. Besides, he was a medical doctor, right? If he wanted to kill himself, he had access to easier ways."

"And Botox is pricey, right?" Sam asked.

"About $600 a syringe."

Sam whistled. "Sounds like somebody spared no effort or expense to kill Dr. Morgenstern."

"Pretty ingenious method, too," the technician said. "If you knew the guy used this nasal spray and you could plant the rigged container, it would work like a time bomb.

You could have your alibi all lined up. You wouldn't have to be anywhere near him when he took the dose."

Sam thought for a moment, absently doodling on a memo pad. He'd drawn a crude sketch of a syringe. "Interesting," he said. "So someone could have planted the spray container in his office, say, last night, or early this morning. Or maybe given it to him before he left the house."

"Well, remember, the stuff has to be kept cool. So last night might be a stretch. But this time of year? Yeah, this morning makes sense."

"Would it take a physician, or someone with medical training, to do it?" Sam asked.

"Not necessarily. The person would have to know how to use a syringe, but it's not like they'd have to hit a vein. But the killer was smart. See, the Botox powder has to be reconstituted with sodium chloride – "

"You mean, salt?"

"Well, yeah, saline solution. Which is exactly what the nasal spray is. So if you wanted to make sure the victim got a good, strong dose, what you'd do is use the syringe to extract the nasal spray from the container – "

"Which wouldn't leave any mark on the container, right?"

"Not if you stuck the syringe right into the opening. Then you'd inject the nasal spray into the Botox vial, mix it with the powder and re-inject the mixture into the nasal spray bottle. And *voila!* A lethal delivery system."

"Interesting." Sam frowned. "Any prints on the nasal spray?" He doodled a handprint that looked more like a paw.

"Only the victim's."

"Figures. Okay, thanks for the quick turnaround on this one. Not to mention the education.

If we can keep this quiet, maybe the killer will get overconfident and sloppy."

"Yeah. Good luck."

27

Back at Franklin, in the Anatomical Pathology Residents Room, a pathology resident sat hunched over a microscope, studying a slide. His friend, a dermatology resident, padded over, crepe-soled shoes silent on the floor.

"Hey!"

"Aargh!" Startled out of his intense concentration, the path resident banged his head against the microscope when he turned at the sudden sound.

"Whoa! Sorry dude. You getting jumpy working around all those stiffs?"

"No. They don't sneak up on people." He massaged his head. "Anyway, I was looking at your patient, Mrs. Williams's, specimen. No melanoma, just a birthmark. Nothing to worry about."

"Hey, great."

The path resident chuckled. "Man, if you like that news, wait'll you hear what else I found out."

His friend motioned a "gimme" hand gesture.

"You see," he continued, "I have a buddy who's over at the Medical Examiner's office for the month." He paused, for effect.

The dermatology resident obliged him. "Yeah, and – ?"

"He assisted the pathologist who did the post on Morgenstern."

This time his friend waited him out.

"So, I just got off the phone with him," the path resident went on, "and he told me the ME found that Morgenstern asphyxiated, but couldn't come up with a cause."

"That's the big news?" his friend asked.

He grinned. "Nope. The scoop is that Morgenstern died of Botox poisoning."

Thus, the rumor mill was set into motion.

Ψ

The dermatology resident caught his department chairman first thing after lunch. Dr. Chad Klein was swapping his black leather jacket for a white lab coat when the resident rapped on his office door.

"Dr. Klein? I just came from pathology and thought you'd want to know. Mrs. Williams is negative for melanoma. It turned out to be a birthmark."

"Good," the head of dermatology replied. "Thanks for letting me know."

"Say, umm, Dr. Klein, I'm sorry about your loss. Lowell Morgenstern was a friend of yours, wasn't he?"

Klein shook his head ruefully. "I can't believe he's dead. Healthy guy like Lowell."

"You know, I was talking to someone with a contact at the Medical Examiner's," the resident said, "and he told me Dr. Morgenstern might actually have been killed."

"What?" Klein gaped at him.

"And even more strange is how they think he was killed," he added.

"Well!" Klein snapped. "Spit it out!"

"He died of a lethal dose of Botox. Isn't that bizarre?"

All the color seemed to drain from his chairman's face.

The resident reached for his arm. "Dr. Klein?" he asked. "Hey, are you okay? Maybe you ought to sit down."

28

When her workday finally ended, April headed for Suburban Station, her thoughts churning over the double shock of Morgenstern's death and Sandra Chang's pregnancy.

"Hey, heads up!" Chris Willis put out an arm to stop her, as they nearly collided.

"Sorry, Chris," she said sheepishly. "I was distracted."

He clutched her shoulder. "I heard you were the one who found Morgenstern this morning."

She sighed. "Yeah. I was fine all day, but I think it's catching up with me."

"I can imagine."

"Anyway, I'm gonna head home and take it easy tonight." She turned to go, and he reached for her elbow.

"What do they think happened to him?"

She shrugged. "No one seems to know yet. I guess there'll be an autopsy."

"Huh." He lowered his head to peer at her face. "Look, are you okay to make it home? You seem pretty shaky. My car is right over in the lot if you'd like a lift."

She smiled. "Thanks, Chris, but I'll be fine. It's such a beautiful evening, maybe the walk to the station will help clear my head. And I live right next to the train station in Jenkintown."

"Okay, if you're sure. I'll give you a rain check for next time."

"Next time I find a body?"

"Next time you want a lift."

"Deal. Thanks, Chris."

She walked up Broad Street, mentally kicking herself for refusing Chris's offer. She'd sensed some chemistry between them, but told herself it was probably wishful thinking on her part. He was single, attractive and smart. Plus he was a doctor, which all nice Jewish girls were trained to grab for like the brass ring on a merry-go-round.

Why hadn't she gone with him? She chided herself for not being more spontaneous. She always seemed to back away from opportunities.

A sudden tap on her shoulder made her turn, hoping for a second chance. "Well, now that you mention it – "

But it was Felipe Diaz, not Chris Willis, who stared back at her, his pupils pinpoints in the fading afternoon light.

"We gotta talk. I want to come back to the program." He was twitchy, as if unable to stand still.

"Felipe!" She felt uneasy. "Were you waiting for me?"

"We gotta talk," he repeated.

"We do," she said. "I'm sorry to have to tell you this, but Dr. Morgenstern died today."

"What? No way! You're lying!"

"No! Listen, Felipe, we've worked out a plan so you can continue getting your meds."

"You're trying to get rid of me, but it won't work. I'm gonna call Dr. Morgenstern. He won't let you do this."

"Wait, let me explain!"

He stepped close enough to be right in her face. "You won't get away with this!" he hissed. He pushed her roughly, then turned and walked away.

Ψ

All the way from the Jenkintown train station, April craved a glass of wine. Maybe a few. The craving only intensified when she walked into her apartment. After a day that featured a dead body, a room full of borderlines and a run-in with an angry druggie, she felt entitled. Her conscience argued otherwise. If she fell into the habit of drinking to relieve stress, she'd be in trouble, stress being a prominent feature of her life. But tonight was different, she rationalized. It wasn't as if she ran into corpses every day.

She shuddered, picturing Morgenstern's blank, blue face, the way it contrasted with the maroon rug below his body.

Maybe one glass.

How long had she been doing this – drinking almost every night? Since the divorce? Since the separation? Along with the cats, wine had become her constant companion at the end of the day. She poured a glass of Pinot Grigio, thinking about how much she hated being alone.

Of course, that was the real issue. Being alone brought out the worst in April. Without a relationship, she drifted. She didn't reach out to friends enough, or take the best care of herself. It wasn't something she was proud of.

She took her wine into the living room and debated calling Mark. After all, she'd agreed to tell him how the meeting went. (Piece of cake! He didn't give me any grief at all!) But he'd want to know if she'd come to New York this weekend, and she hadn't decided. Absently, she picked up the remote and flipped to the Weather Channel, muting the sound while she waited for the local forecast.

She took another sip of wine. The extended forecast crawled across the TV screen. Rain for the weekend. Not so good for travel, or wandering around New York. But why should she be the one to travel, anyway? April reached for her cellphone, jostling the cats, who yawned and stretched. Boris meowed in protest while she made the call.

"Hey," Mark said, picking up. "I was about to call you. How'd your meeting go?"

April filled him in. He offered a cursory expression of sympathy, then quickly switched gears.

"So, what about this weekend?"

"Actually…" She paused. "I finished a draft of a research paper and I'd like to work on some revisions this weekend." Even though no one is willing to read it, she reminded herself. "How about you coming down here?"

Now the pause was on the other end. "You mean, come all the way down to Philly so I can hang around while you write?" he said. "I thought the whole point was for us to have time together."

"We would!" she protested. "I'll only need to work for a couple of hours. Or you could come down on Sunday."

"So bring your laptop!"

"No," she said. "There are some books and other references here I might need. I'm not hauling a bunch of stuff on the train."

"Look, April, trekking down to Pennsylvania isn't convenient for me right now."

"Oh? Well, trekking up to New York isn't very convenient for me."

"You're putting me off to work on a stupid paper?"

"It's not stupid. It's important to my career."

"Whatever. It still shouldn't come before us."

Us? April wondered. They only seemed to become an "us" when it suited him. "Sorry, Mark," she said, "but this is a priority for me. I can't come to New York this weekend. If it's not convenient for you to come down here, getting together will have to wait."

"Fine," he snapped. "Have it your way." He hung up.

She drained her glass of wine and went to the refrigerator for more.

29

Curled up amid a stack of pillows on what used to be her side of the king-sized bed, Miranda Morgenstern wrapped up a phone conversation of her own.

"No, they don't seem to know the cause of death yet. There's a detective on the case – some Italian-sounding name – who said they'd be doing an autopsy. I'm all right, really. No, don't come tonight. Maybe when things settle down we can get away for a bit, okay? All right. Call you tomorrow, Stuart."

She hung up with a sigh. Shouldn't she feel more excitement at the prospect of seeing her lover without sneaking around? But the truth was, Stuart Hartman wasn't all that exciting. He was attentive and dependable – a beta male. But no Lowell Morgenstern.

A tear trickled down Miranda's cheek. What a shame he'd had to die.

Ψ

Felipe Diaz shivered and turned up the collar of the denim shirt he wore over his tee shirt. He wasn't dressed warmly enough for this September night. He'd been walking the streets of Center City for hours and he was hungry, as well as cold.

Where could he go?

Mamita wasn't about to take him in. And his friends – his so-called *amigos* – wouldn't welcome a visit if he showed up empty handed.

He'd smoked the last batch of meth after all. What the fuck. Now he had nothing left to offer.

That *puta,* Dr. April. If she hadn't kicked him out, he'd at least be able to go to Praxis in the morning and put some moves on the people there. A lot of them were real saps. He'd talked them into lending him money before. Okay, maybe "lend" was a generous way to put it.

He reached into his pants pocket and removed two singles and a handful of change. About enough to cover a Value Meal at Mickey D's. If only he hadn't lost his cellphone, maybe he could call someone.

Looking up from his meager stash of funds, Felipe saw a rare sight – a pay phone on the corner. It might be worth the investment of his spare change.

He couldn't remember her exact address, but at least he knew the street her apartment was on. Enough to get her number from Information. He fed his coins into the phone and the operator put through his call.

She answered after two rings.

"Carlee? It's me, Felipe. Hey, I'm out here on the street and it's fuckin' cold. Please – can I come over?" He listened, a smile spreading across his angular face. "Great! I'll be there in fifteen. Lady, you da best!"

He hung up the phone, saluted the night sky with a fist, and headed down the street. Carlee Randall had bailed him out tonight.

But April Simon was going to pay.

Wednesday, September 29

30

On his way to meet with Clarence McKay, Stuart Hartman was smiling for the first time in days. There was a spring in his step. Morgenstern's death could open up some fine opportunities for him. For one thing, his well-preserved widow would no doubt come into a tidy inheritance, which certainly enhanced her attractiveness in Stuart's eyes. Miranda could be demanding – even bitchy, to put it bluntly – but her late husband's assets would no doubt improve her mood.

Then there was the question of that ridiculous Ph.D. program that Morgenstern was so gung-ho on launching. The new program would amount to a functional demotion for Stuart. But it might not be too late to stop the project, now that Morgenstern was out of the picture. The meeting Stuart was about to have with the acting chairman was a great opportunity to make his pitch.

Yes, things were definitely looking up.

Ψ

Meanwhile, the Franklin rumor mill ground its way forward.

When Clarence McKay answered his phone, the incoming call showed the ID of the chairman of the FU pathology department.

"Hello, Jim," McKay said.

"Clarence! I'm probably catching you at a busy time. Heard you're filling in for Morgenstern as acting chair."

"It's pretty hectic, but I've got a few minutes. What can I do for you?"

The path chairman hesitated. "Uh, Clarence, it's a hell of a thing. I debated with myself about whether to even tell you this."

Clarence sat up straighter. The man now had his full attention.

"But if the positions were reversed," he continued, "I'd sure want to know."

"To know what, Jim?" Clarence felt a sense of foreboding.

"It's about Lowell. Look, you can't tell anyone about this, but – he was murdered."

"What?"

"One of my residents heard it from a friend at the Medical Examiner's office. It turned out Lowell's goddamned nasal spray was laced with Botox."

"Botox!" Clarence repeated.

"Yeah. Apparently, he inhaled it and suffered a fatal paralysis."

"That's unbelievable! Jim, are you sure about this?"

"Afraid so. Look, Clarence, there's bound to be an investigation. I just thought that, you know, as one department chair to another, I ought to give you a heads up."

"I appreciate it, Jim."

"But you'll keep this between us, right?"

"Of course." Clarence hung up and let his head sink into his hands. He massaged his temples as if this might eliminate the ache he felt. He'd been relieved to know that Morgenstern's death would take him off the hook. No one else could possibly know about his fudged research data. No one but Lowell knew about the way he'd crunched those numbers.

Clarence had no doubt that Morgenstern would have made good on his threat to report him to the NIMH, throwing him to the proverbial wolves.

But Clarence also felt wracked with guilt. He shouldn't have let the pressure get to him, shouldn't have made such a terrible mistake. Shoulda, woulda, coulda, he reflected grimly. Deep in his troubled thoughts, he was startled by the rap on his partially open office door.

31

Elsewhere on the Franklin campus, Sam Perone opted to start his investigation with the dermatology department. Follow the Botox, he figured. He badged his way in to see the chairman. Shaking hands with Dr. Chad Klein, Sam reflected that the man just needed a tee shirt and earring to pass as Mr. Clean. Or Dr. Clean. Brawny, with a dark tan that included his shaved head, Klein looked better suited to the tennis court than the hospital.

"How can I help you Detective – " he peered at Sam's card. "Perone?"

"I'm investigating a case and you could be very helpful by clearing up some things for me about Botox."

"Botox?" Klein chuckled uncomfortably. He made a show of scrutinizing Sam's face. "You do have a slight furrow there in the forehead. Want me to touch it up? It'll make you look more inscrutable to suspects." He chuckled again.

Sam didn't. "No, thanks. Where do you store your Botox?"

"My Botox?" Klein's tone implied the question was absurd.

"Any Botox, Doctor. Yours, for instance."

"Uh – how much do you know about Botox, Detective?"

"I've learned a few things."

"Then you're probably aware that it comes in a powder form and has to be reconstituted with liquid. Once you do that, you've got to refrigerate it. So, to answer your question, we keep the vials of powder in a locked medication cabinet, and the reconstituted vials in a refrigerator."

"And this refrigerator, is it kept locked?"

"Our refrigerator?" Klein repeated. "No. We don't keep narcotics or dangerous drugs in there. And the fridge is in the treatment room, so my staff and I are in and out of there all day. It's not like it's left unattended."

"And the locked medication cabinet – where do you keep the key?" Sam waited for another echo response from Dr. Clean, but received a non-answer instead.

"I have a copy, of course."

"And?" Sam persisted.

"We – uh – keep a spare in a drawer in the supply room. You see, several of my staff need access to the cabinet, and I don't want a lot of keys floating around, so – "

"So, basically, anyone could get into that cabinet," Sam concluded.

"Detective, I hardly think – "

"I'd say your procedures sound pretty lax, Doc. Tell me, has any of your Botox gone missing recently?"

The dermatologist's bronzed forehead furrowed. Sam had to wonder about a dermatologist who apparently spent so much time in the sun. And didn't even avail himself of his own services.

"I couldn't really say." Klein looked away from Sam's gaze.

"You don't keep track of your supplies?"

"Of course we do. When we're running low, we have to order more."

"Who's in charge of doing that?" Sam asked.

"My assistant, Gretchen."

"All right. Please have her tally your Botox supply and see whether any of it is unaccounted for."

"I don't see why – " Klein froze at Sam's flinty expression. "Okay," he relented. "I'll call you with the results."

"Thanks, Doctor. By the way, did you know this Dr. Morgenstern who died the other day?"

Klein went wide-eyed for a moment, then recovered his composure. "Yes, I did. Lowell was a close friend." He shook his head. "A terrible loss."

Sam nodded. "My sympathies, Doc." He turned to go, then looked back. "I'll be expecting your call."

"I'll get right on it, Detective."

As he left, Sam reflected that the dermatologist hadn't even asked him whether Morgenstern's death had anything to do with all those questions he'd asked about Botox. That struck him as odd, especially considering Morgenstern had been Klein's friend.

As soon as Sam was out the door, Klein scrambled for the phone.

Ψ

"Not another one!"

Miranda Morgenstern rolled her eyes in response to the phone's incessant ringing. After all the calls she'd made and received since yesterday, she considered letting this one go to voice-mail. But when a glance at the caller ID showed a Franklin University number, she decided to take it. It could be something about Lowell's pension.

It wasn't.

"Miranda?" said a familiar voice, "Chad Klein. Hun, I'm so sorry about Lowell. Jeez, I'll miss the guy. How you holding up?"

Miranda assumed her grieving widow voice. "Oh, you know. As well as can be expected, I guess. Good of you to call, Chad."

"Yeah, well – actually, Miranda, I've got a little problem here."

"Oh?" Her tone frosted over. She was bereaved and he had a problem?

"See, there's this detective who came around asking me a lot of questions about Botox."

Miranda received this information in stony silence. She wondered, could it be the same detective who'd come to the house yesterday? What was going on?

Chad Klein continued. "He wants me to check my inventory. You see the problem?"

What the hell was the man babbling about? "No, Chad, frankly I don't. In fact, I don't see why you're bothering me about this at –"

"I know, I know it's a terrible time," he said. "It's just – I was wondering, Miranda, do you still have the two vials I gave Lowell earlier this week?"

"What?"

From the outrage in her tone, he might as well have asked her bra size. Klein cringed, but had no choice but to forge ahead.

"Look, Miranda, I've given Lowell – oh, about $5,000 worth of Botox for you over the last couple of years. You know? And I was happy to do it," he added quickly. "But now, if this comes out, it could look really bad. I'll have to account for the shortfall, maybe even pay for it. So, I wanted to let you know that I might need to…uh …"

"You're calling me to ask for money at a time like this?"

"No, not right away! But if you still have the last two vials, maybe I could come by and pick them up, so, at least – "

"I do not! And if I did, I wouldn't give them to you. You've got some nerve, Dr. Klein!" She slammed down the receiver.

32

"Clarence?" Stuart Hartman stood in the doorway to McKay's office. "You ready to meet?"

"Huh?" McKay looked up, startled.

"Our ten o'clock appointment, remember?"

"Oh!" Clarence looked down at his watch. "Oh," he repeated, his face blank with distraction.

Stuart hesitated. "If this is a bad time…"

Clarence gave a small shake of his head. "No, it's fine, Stuart. It's just – "

Hartman took a step into the office. "Something wrong? You seem preoccupied."

Clarence frowned. "Close the door." He motioned for Stuart to take a seat.

Stuart sat in the chair opposite McKay, waiting, while Clarence drummed his fingers on the desk, apparently wrestling with his thoughts. Finally, he looked up.

"Stuart, I'm going to tell you something and I want your word you'll keep it in the strictest confidence."

Stuart felt curious, but wary. A vague premonition warned him that his personal agenda for this meeting was about to be derailed. "Of course, Clarence," he said. "You can count on my full support."

Clarence sighed. "It's about Lowell."

Five minutes later, Stuart raced out of the building. As soon as he reached the street, he pulled out his cellphone, glanced around and made a call.

"Miranda?" he said. "It's me. I just heard the most unbelievable – "

"Hah! You?" Venom suffused her voice. "You want to talk unbelievable?" she said. "That goddamned Chad Klein had the nerve to demand I return his stupid Botox! Can you imagine, at a time like this? The man is an absolute –"

"Fuck Chad Klein!" Stuart shouted, cutting off her harangue. He looked around nervously, hoping no one had overheard his outburst. He was alone. "Jesus, Miranda!" he hissed. "I just heard that Lowell was poisoned with Botox."

"Poisoned? From Botox?" Her tone was scornful. "How is that even possible? You can't OD from Botox injections. Besides, Lowell wasn't even getting Botox injections."

"Miranda, will you listen to me?"

The urgency in his voice silenced her.

"This wasn't an accident," Stuart continued. "Someone spiked Lowell's nasal spray. He was murdered." He paused. "But why was Klein calling you about Botox?"

"Oh my God, Stuart!" Miranda wailed. "Chad said the police were there, asking about his Botox supply. He was having a conniption over all the Botox he gave Lowell for me. He wanted me to return the two vials he gave Lowell this week."

"Miranda, did you?"

"What? Return them? No. I – I told him I didn't have them anymore. But, Stuart, I do have them. Don't you see? The police are already investigating. They're going to find out I've gotten all this Botox from Klein, and they'll think…" She fell silent and they both followed the same alarming train of thought. "Oh my God, Stuart, what should I do?" she demanded.

"Listen, Miranda, I have an idea" Stuart said. "I want you to give me the Botox."

"But, why?"

"Don't worry. It'll be all right. You trust me, don't you?"

"But – "

"Let me take the stuff from you today, this morning. You're right. It's better you don't have it. Should I come to the house, or meet you somewhere?"

"Oh God, Stuart, I don't know. All right, come here. If people are there, we'll act like you're paying a condolence call."

"Fine," he said. "I'll be right over." Stuart ended the call and pocketed his phone. A small smile curled his lips at the thought of playing the hero.

Hanging up at her end, Miranda blew out a sigh of relief. She glanced down at her nails, wondering if she'd have time to go for a manicure before Stuart showed up.

33

PACIFIL SUBJECT: Tyrell Johnson

The brown mongrel dog was there again, sniffing around the trash cans in the back alley of West 52nd Street, as Tyrell had hoped. He had a mission to carry out this morning, on his way to Praxis. Tyrell knew exactly what he had to do, even if he didn't know why. He'd felt rotten since they'd told him about Dr. Morgenstern's death – so anxious, like his skin was crawling, or something. Tyrell couldn't explain this overwhelming feeling of wrongness. It wasn't as if he'd even liked the psychiatrist all that much.

But now, here was the stray dog, skinny and scruffy, as if he'd been waiting for Tyrell's arrival.

"Hiya, boy. Good boy."

The dog looked up and cocked his head. He held his tail low, but wagged it tentatively.

"Atta boy." Tyrell reached into his back pocket. The dog treats were right there, next to the knife. "You hungry, fella?"

Tyrell approached the unsuspecting animal slowly, displaying a couple of the treats in his outstretched hand. "Good boy," he said as the dog sniffed his hand. The hungry animal licked at the biscuit. "That's right," Tyrell said. The mutt gobbled the treat from his hand and crunched on it greedily.

Tyrell glanced around the alley. He was alone with the dog.

"Want some more, boy?"

The dog wagged his tail and Tyrell reached back into his pocket. He retrieved another treat and tossed it a few feet further into the alley. "Go get it, boy!" he urged.

As he followed the dog, Tyrell pulled the large knife from his pocket.

34

Faculty, staff and students had gathered in the Franklin auditorium to pay their respects to Lowell Morgenstern. Several colleagues delivered tributes, and Clarence McKay concluded the memorial service by requesting a minute of silent reflection in the late chairman's memory.

April found summoning charitable thoughts about him to be a challenge. She did appreciate that Morgenstern had given her a job, and tried to focus on gratitude for that. But her mind wandered into speculation about what others in the auditorium might be thinking. Only Sandra Chang's sniffling gave her any inkling.

After an interminable minute, Clarence quietly dismissed the assembly. April stood and joined the flow of people moving toward the exit.

"Hey!" Larissa Lewis caught up with her as they merged into the central row of the auditorium.

"Hi,"

Larissa took April's elbow, leaning in to assume her familiar "have you heard the latest?" posture.

"What is it?"

Larissa murmured the news into her ear.

"What?" People turned to stare. "You're kidding," April said, lowering her voice. "Botox? That's bizarre! You and I were just talking about that yesterday."

Larissa held a finger to her lips. "Strictly confidential," she whispered. With a quick wave, she maneuvered her way through the crowd with the deft speed of the native New Yorker she was.

Pondering Larissa's startling news, April inched forward with the throng until she passed through the door into the lobby. She glanced around for Larissa. A tap on her shoulder caused her to turn. Detective Sam Perone stood beside her.

"Dr. Simon." He extended his hand. "Nice to see you again so soon after our chat yesterday."

She rolled her eyes. "What a lovely surprise." She suspected their meeting was no coincidence. She shook his hand. His grip was warm and firm. Did she imagine it, or did he hold onto her hand a little longer than manners required? She met his gaze and his brown eyes caught her off guard. She'd forgotten how attractive he was. She looked away.

"How are you?" he asked. "Any after-effects from your experience yesterday?"

She assumed he meant the experience of discovering her chairman's body, unless it was a trick question. "I'm fine, thanks." She reminded herself to keep her responses brief, not to volunteer information.

He peered at her face. "Then why do you look like you've just seen a ghost?"

"I haven't! I mean, I don't." But the implications of Larissa's bombshell suddenly detonated in April's head. "My God!" she whispered.

"What is it?" The detective was reading her again.

"Is it true Dr. Morgenstern was murdered?" she blurted out. "That someone put Botox into his nasal spray?"

"Actually –" He coughed, but took a deep breath and controlled it "I could use a cup of coffee. How about joining me at the Starbucks?"

"I don't –" Should she make a run for it?

He smiled. "Come on. You look like you could use a cup, too."

The atmosphere at Starbucks was a mix of study hall and day care center. Several Millenials, with the unshaven look of grad students, pecked at their open laptops, while a frazzled, obviously pregnant woman tried to quiet two screaming toddlers in the corner. April and Sam stood by and sipped their coffees until a man in a business suit finally grabbed his briefcase and rose from his seat. They made a beeline for his table.

"So, tell me," the detective said when they were settled, "where'd you hear this story about the Botox?"

April fingered her coffee container, studying the foam on her cappuccino. He'd asked the question in a casual tone, but she feared she was in for another interrogation. She shouldn't have asked him about the Botox. But she wanted to know if Larissa's story was true.

"One of my colleagues told me about it," she said.

"But how would he know?" The detective frowned. "That information is part of a confidential investigation."

"She."

"Huh?"

"My colleague. It's a she." She sipped her coffee. "News travels very fast around here, Detective Perone. And my friend always has her ear to the ground."

"I see." He looked down at the table and shook his head, a half grin twisting the corner of his mouth.

"Welcome to academia." April raised her coffee cup. The detective had no idea what kind of juiced-up grapevine he faced at Franklin. He brushed the rim of his cup against hers. While he drank she studied him. Today he wore a tweedy brown jacket that looked less official than yesterday's suit.

His strong cheekbones and aquiline nose gave him a hawk-like appearance, softened by the fullness of his lips pressed against the coffee cup. She dropped her guard and mused aloud.

"But it is ironic."

"What is?" He lowered the cup and looked at her.

"The other day Larissa, my colleague, was talking about a faculty party where Dr. Morgenstern bragged about getting free Botox for his wife."

"Quite a coincidence," the detective remarked. "What's Larissa's last name?"

April pinched her lips together. "Lewis," she mumbled.

"Did she tell you where Morgenstern was getting this Botox?"

April stalled, taking another sip of coffee. He was better at this than she was. She glanced up and met his eyes.

"You never did answer my question, Detective." She sat up straighter in her chair. "Was he poisoned with Botox?"

He grinned. "Who's asking the questions here?"

So he'd decided to play the good cop today. He did have a nice smile.

"Looks like we both are." She sat back, brushing her hair away from her face. The stray strands were the color of the cinnamon dusting the foam on her cappuccino.

His eyes lingered on her face. "Dr. Simon," he began. "April…" He drew out the syllables of her name, as if sampling their taste.

The effect was hypnotic.

"Nice name." He smiled again and the corners of his dark eyes crinkled. "Different. Was that the month you were born in?"

"Uh-huh. A couple weeks earlier, and I'd have been stuck with March."

He chuckled. "I see what you mean. April suits you better." He leaned in. "I wish I could answer your questions. You found your chairman dead yesterday. You want to know what's going on." He smiled ruefully. "But I really can't discuss it. I'm sure you can understand."

Instead of trying to intimidate her, he was acting reasonable. Seductive, even. The man had a lot of tactics at his disposal. "But you want me to repeat things that others told me," April objected.

"That's right. Look, suppose your chairman was murdered. Why wouldn't you want to cooperate with an investigation?"

She couldn't think of any logical answer. Or one that wouldn't make her sound like she had something to hide. And she didn't, so why play cat and mouse?

"Larissa said he got it from his buddy, Chad Klein," she said, "the head of the dermatology department here."

"Why do you suppose Dr. Klein would do that?"

April shrugged. "Apparently he owed Lowell a favor."

"And Morgenstern bragged about this at a party?"

"According to Larissa, Lowell claimed he helped himself to Botox out of their fridge, like it was his personal candy store."

"Huh. So who was at this party?"

"I don't know. Faculty from our department and their spouses, I guess."

"Weren't you and your husband there?" He eyed her left hand, where she no longer wore a ring.

"No, Detective Perone." She pulled her hand into her lap.

"Call me Sam."

"Is that allowed?" she shot back. "When you're on duty?"

He gave her that smile again. "It's part of our community relations program."

And it's working, she thought.

"So how come you weren't at this party?"

"It, uh, wasn't a very festive time for me."

He waited.

"I was going through a divorce."

"Sorry," he said. "Didn't mean to pry."

Like hell. April lowered her eyes, taking refuge in another sip of cappuccino. She peered at the detective from beneath her eyelashes. His brown hair was soft, shiny, and a little on the shaggy side. She glanced at his hand. He didn't wear a ring, either.

"Can I ask you something else?" he said.

Like she could stop him? "What?"

"Same question as yesterday. Who wanted to kill Morgenstern?"

"Same answer as yesterday. I don't know."

He leaned in to close the space between them. "Come on, April. Who had issues with him around here?" He raised his eyebrows, his expression all innocence. "Why won't you help me out?"

He kept sounding so reasonable. Damn, he was good at this! She sighed. "Look, Sam, this is academia. Home of the giant egos. Morgenstern's was probably the biggest. There are bound to be conflicts. But that doesn't make my colleagues a bunch of murderers."

"I'm only looking for one."

She flashed a triumphant smile. "So it was murder!"

He held her gaze, his expression impassive. "Tit for tat. At least help me figure out who else to talk to."

Names sprang to mind, but she held back. She had a promotion at stake. It wouldn't do to start ratting out her colleagues. Even if some of them occasionally acted like assholes, she thought, remembering Stuart's scene at the Chuckwagon.

"I'm sorry," she murmured. "There's really nothing I can tell you." She reached down to pick up her bag. When she sat up, the detective held out his business card.

"Please," he said. "Call me if you think of anything I should know."

As she took the card, their fingertips brushed. "I will," she promised.

35

Person of interest, indeed.

As he watched April exit the Starbucks, Sam found her back view as attractive as the front – that coppery hair and slender frame. Curves, too. She was intriguing in other ways, as well. He'd tried to charm her into giving him some leads, and she'd bested him. Instead of coming away with a list of suspects, he'd ended up confirming the rumor that her chairman was murdered. His slip-up surprised him. Even more surprising was the fact that he didn't really mind.

He'd established some rapport, he told himself. April Simon would come around. For all her guardedness, she didn't strike him as the least bit sneaky. There was something genuine, trustworthy, about her. At least, he wanted to think so. He could use an inside source in this crazy institution, where confidential information circulated at warp speed. How the hell had that Botox story leaked?

The ring of his cellphone interrupted Sam's musings.

"Detective Perone? It's Dr. Klein, from dermatology."

"Yeah, Doc. You check your inventory?"

"We did. Actually there is some missing."

"How much is 'some'?"

"That's, ah, complicated."

"I see," said Sam. "Fortunately, I'm right here on campus, Doc. I'm on my way up to your office."

Ψ

"So, Dr. Klein," Sam asked the dermatology chief, "what's so complicated about your Botox inventory?"

"As I said, there is some missing and – uh, Detective? Can I be frank with you?"

Sam's eyes narrowed. This was a question that usually meant a lie was about to follow. "I think you'd better start telling the truth right now," he said.

"I mean – off the record."

"Is this about you giving away Botox to your buddy, Morgenstern?"

Klein's jaw sagged. "How –? You know about that?"

"Apparently lots of people around here know about it. Seems your pal got loaded and bragged about his candy store at some faculty party." At least April Simon had given him that much. Sam grinned. "Off the record, of course."

"Shit," Klein muttered.

"So why the freebies, Doc?"

"Let's say I owed him a favor."

"What kind of favor would that be?"

"Is that really important, Detective?"

"You never really know what will turn out to be important, Doc" Sam replied.

Klein sighed. "Look, this really does have to be confidential." When Sam made no response, he continued. "Lowell used to, well, cover for me."

Sam looked puzzled. "Cover? You mean, in dermatology?"

"Uh, no. With my wife," Klein explained. "Once or twice, I told her I was playing tennis with him when I wasn't."

"Uh-huh." Between gossiping and screwing around, Sam wondered how these academics got any research done, or kept their patient appointments straight.

"Lowell was a good friend," Klein said. "We helped each other out, that's all. I just wanted to be discrete about it."

"Doc, Morgenstern told people he sometimes helped himself to the Botox from your fridge. Is that true?"

"That's an exaggeration, Detective. First of all, as I told you, Botox is perishable in liquid form, so Lowell would hardly be taking it out of the fridge and running around with it."

"But you said 'exaggeration', not lie, so – "

"If you'd let me finish, what I was saying is there was one occasion when I did tell Lowell he could stop by and take a couple of vials from the refrigerator. Miranda's appointment with her plastic surgeon was moved up at the last minute. Since I wasn't going to be around that afternoon, I told him to take the vials and keep them on ice until she came to pick them up."

"So Morgenstern was lying at that party?"

Klein's tanned face flushed. "Not lying, Detective. Just, I don't know, crowing a little. Lowell could be like that sometimes. You should have seen him when he swept a tennis set."

"Did he know where you kept the spare key to the locked medication cabinet?"

"Absolutely not."

"All right." Sam shifted gears. "Tell me, when was the last time Morgenstern received his Botox stash?"

Klein chuckled uneasily. "I wish you wouldn't talk about it as if it were some kind of illicit drug, Detective. But the answer to your question is two days ago. I gave him two vials on Monday."

"Liquid or powder form?"

"Powder. The usual arrangement."

"And how many vials would you say he's had from you, all told?"

"Umm, I guess about – "

"You guess?" Sam demanded. "I thought you took an inventory."

"Twelve, Detective. That was over the past two years."

"Okay. So that's the discrepancy you found in your inventory?"

"Well…" Klein hesitated.

"What?"

"Apart from the Botox we gave to Lowell, there are two vials unaccounted for."

36

At her desk, April had seized some rare down time to try to put a dent in her mountain of paperwork – memos, program statistics, patient treatment plan reviews. All manner of documentation that accumulated while she gave her attention to the needs of actual human beings. Her phone rang, signaling that yet another one wanted her attention. She glanced at the caller ID and winced.

"Hey, Larissa!" she said with false cheer, sensing trouble.

"It was you, wasn't it?" Larissa sounded angrier than a jostled nest of hornets. "You sic'd that cop on me!"

April gulped. "I – "

"Admit it! He said 'a colleague of mine,' but you're the only one I talked with about Lowell getting the free Botox. Why'd you tell the police about that?"

"Larissa, I'm sorry. He was questioning me, and it sort of slipped out. But," she added, before her friend could yell at her again, "there was nothing the least bit incriminating about what I said. And he is trying to investigate a murder. Lowell was your friend. Don't you want to help find his killer?"

"Did he admit that to you? That Lowell was murdered?" Larissa instantly shifted to gossip mode.

"Not in so many words," April said, worried that she'd once again revealed something she shouldn't have. "So what did he ask you?" she said, trying to change the subject.

"Nothing much," Larissa replied. "He mainly wanted to know who else was at that party when Lowell bragged about the Botox."

"Who was there, anyway?" April was curious.

"The usual suspects," Larissa chuckled.

"Very funny."

"Lowell and his wife, Miranda. Clarence McKay and his wife." Larissa ticked off the list. "Chris Willis, no partner. Stuart Hartman, without his wife." She paused. "Let's see. I think also –"

Sudden shouts and screams erupted from the group room down the hall.

"What was that?" Larissa asked.

"Trouble," April answered. "Gotta go."

She hung up the phone and raced down the corridor. Staff and patients were already pouring out from the adjacent rooms when April reached the closed door. Loud, frightened voices and sounds of chairs scraping against the floor came from inside.

Waving over one of her staff, April murmured: "Take the rest of the patients back to the community room, while I – "

The door flew open with a sudden crash. A patient, Denise, darted out of the room.

An angry male voice boomed from inside. "Shut that fuckin' door!"

Tyrell. Her heart pounding, April recognized the voice of one of the four Pacifil subjects.

"Nobody else leaves!" Tyrell thundered.

Someone in the room reached out and yanked the door closed.

Denise turned to April, her face contorted with panic. "He's got a knife!" she cried. "He's gone crazy!"

"Denise!" April gripped the woman's shoulders, trying to steady her. "Is anybody hurt in there?"

Denise shook her head.

"The therapist!" April demanded. "Who's running that group?"

"James," she said.

Inside the group room, perspiration stood out on James's forehead. He kept his gaze locked on Tyrell, who stood in the center of the room. Swinging a large knife from side to side, wearing a tee shirt streaked with dried blood, Tyrell held the other group members at bay. He reeked of fear and desperation. Eight sets of eyes were glued to him – and especially to that knife. Along with James, two group members, Mickey and Don, were on their feet. The rest cowered in their chairs.

"Nobody leaves this room 'til I get some answers!" Tyrell shouted.

James carefully pitched his voice so it was a notch softer than Tyrell's. "We'll answer all your questions, Tyrell. But why don't we let these other people leave, so – "

"Liar!" Tyrell cut him off. "Prick! You tryin' to trick me! You think I'm some kinda fool?"

Across the room, Mickey and Don exchanged glances.

"I'll call the police!" April started back down the corridor to her office.

"April! Wait!" Chris Willis raced down the hallway toward her. "What's going on? Cynthia told me you needed help."

"There's a patient with a knife in there," she said frantically. "I'm calling 911."

"No, wait." Chris put out a hand to stop her. "Let me see what I can do."

"It's too dangerous!" she protested. There wasn't time, and this was beyond the province of psychiatry.

"Give me ten minutes. April, trust me," he insisted. "This is what I do."

He looked so confident. April swallowed her objections, but not her doubts. She still wondered if they were doing the right thing.

"How many other patients are in there?" Chris asked.

"About seven or eight, besides Tyrell," April replied.

"All right," he said. "I'm going to try to talk him into opening this door."

Inside, James tried to soothe Tyrell. "You're angry and scared," he said. "Whatever it is that's happened, we're still your friends. Tyrell, I know you don't want to hurt these folks. Please. Put down the knife."

Tyrell hesitated. His lip trembled.

At that moment, Mickey and Don rushed at him.

"No!" James shouted.

Pivoting, Tyrell turned his knife on the approaching men. Don skidded to a halt and Mickey crashed into him, sending them both toppling to the floor at Tyrell's feet. As Tyrell stumbled backwards, he saw James grab for him.

"Get away, man!" Tyrell swung the blade at James, who reeled away. With a stricken cry, Tyrell suddenly pulled back the knife and slashed his own arm. A gash opened there, like a bloody grin.

"Tyrell, no!" James yelled. "Stop!"

Tyrell's eyes darted wildly around the room. Blood dripped from his wounded arm and he whimpered in pain. He raised the blade, pressing it against his own throat.

"Stay away from me," he warned James.

James stopped in his tracks. Two of the women in the group seized their chance and ran for the door.

Chris Willis leaped back as the door flew open. The two women barreled into him as they rushed out of the group room.

"Is everyone all right in there?" April asked them.

"He cut himself!" one of them shouted. "He was bleeding bad."

"Who? Who's bleeding?" she demanded.

"Tyrell."

April turned to Chris. "We have to call the cops," she insisted.

"No." His mouth set in a grim line, Chris stepped into the room, leaving the door ajar behind him.

April stood outside the door, quietly motioning the others away. If this went bad, she'd call the cops whether Chris liked it or not.

37

Chris Willis inched cautiously into the group room.

"Tyrell? I'm Dr. Willis." Chris held up his hands so Tyrell could see they were empty.

The young man stared back at him, eyes wide with pain and fear.

Chris stayed just inside the door, advancing no further for the moment. "That's some knife you've got there," he observed.

Tyrell glanced quickly over at James, who stood about five feet away, also holding his position. His gaze returned to Chris and he stared at him as if riveted.

"You okay, man?" Chris pointed at Tyrell's arm. "That's a nasty looking cut." He took another step forward into the room.

"Stop!" Tyrell cautioned him.

Chris nodded. "Whatever you say. You're in charge."

Tyrell exhaled. A look of weariness etched his face.

"You think we could let these other folks out of here?" Chris asked. "We probably won't need them anymore. What do you say?"

Tyrell lowered his eyes and nodded almost imperceptibly.

"Thank you, Tyrell." Chris looked at James. "Take them out," he said softly.

Tyrell stood silently, swaying slightly on his feet, as James motioned the other group members out of the room. At a nod from Chris, James followed behind them. One or two members turned their heads to gape at Tyrell as they passed him. The others avoided looking at him.

"Thank God!" April murmured, as the patients emerged, wide-eyed, from the group room. She clasped James in a quick embrace as he came out the door.

"Everyone's okay. Chris has it under control," he told her. Before she could answer, he added: "Why don't you take them back to the community room? Check them over, debrief them and send them home. I'll stay here, in case he needs any help."

April wanted to argue, but realized he was right. The rest of the patients needed tending to, and James was probably better equipped to assist Chris, if it came to that.

Reluctantly, she nodded. "But don't be a cowboy," she said. "Call 911 if they're not out of there in two minutes."

Alone in the group room with Tyrell, Chris regarded him with a look of appraisal. The young man was obviously on the brink of collapse.

"How about lowering the knife while we talk?" he asked.

Tyrell continued to stare at Chris. "Do I know you?"

"I don't think so," Chris said.

"You a shrink?"

"Uh-huh."

"They told me my shrink was dead," Tyrell said, a tremor in his voice. A sob broke from his throat. "Everything's all messed up."

"You mean Dr. Morgenstern?" Chris asked. Slowly, he moved over to one of the vacant chairs and sat, gesturing Tyrell toward another. "He was your shrink?"

Tyrell nodded. He sank into the chair and lowered his arm, letting the knife blade graze the floor. Tears and snot ran down his face.

"He was treating me with some special new medicine," he mewled. "What's gonna happen to me now?"

"Guess this all happened pretty suddenly, huh?" Chris asked.

Tyrell nodded, wiping his nose with the back of his hand. He gaped at the blood oozing down his arm, as he pulled his hand away.

"Oh, sweet Jesus!" he wailed. "I did something bad! Really bad."

"Want to talk about it?"

Still holding the knife, Tyrell clutched awkwardly at his bleeding arm. "Dr. Morgenstern," he gulped, "he said I was only supposed to talk to him. Ain't supposed to change doctors."

Chris frowned in puzzlement. "What do you mean?"

Tyrell only sniffled.

"Anyway," Chris continued, "you don't have to worry about that. My job is to help people through emergencies. So you can talk to me without making a commitment, you know?"

Tyrell stared at him. "How would you help me?"

"Get your arm taken care of, for openers. Looks to me like you might need a couple of stitches. Give you something to help you feel calmer, if you like."

Chris's voice was soothing, and Tyrell's eyelids seem to be drooping.

"After that," Chris added, "we can sort out what to do about all this. What do you think?"

"Would I have to go into the hospital?" Tyrell asked.

"Do you want to?"

"I dunno," he said. "Maybe."

"Uh-huh. Tyrell?"

"Yeah?"

"How about you drop the knife on the floor now?"

"You won't let them hurt me?"

"No one will hurt you. That's a promise. Now please put down the knife so we can get your arm taken care of, okay?"

With another sob, Tyrell tossed the knife to the floor in front of him. "I killed that fuckin' dog!" he cried. "I'm sorry! I'm sorry!"

38

The blade still had dried blood on it. April looked away in revulsion, as Chris Willis examined the weapon he'd taken from Tyrell. They sat in her office, debriefing.

"Pretty hefty," he commented, weighing the weapon with his hand.. "Looks like a hunting knife."

"Thank God no one besides Tyrell was hurt." She shuddered. "Except that poor dog."

"Tyrell will be okay," Chris reassured her. He'd been escorted safely across Vine Street to have his arm stitched in the medical ER. By now, he was being admitted to the inpatient psychiatric unit. The other Praxis patients had been soothed and dismissed for the day.

"Does he have a history of cruelty to animals?" Chris asked.

"Not that I know of," April said. "He's never been violent. I don't understand what brought this on." She felt a vague sense of foreboding, wondering what effects Morgenstern's death might have on his other research subjects, but tried to put aside her fears.

"Anyway, you really made that look easy," she said to Chris. "I was sure we needed the police."

He shrugged. "Tyrell painted himself into a corner and needed a way out. I was just in the right place at the right time."

He was being too modest, April thought.

"Besides," Chris added, "the cops usually make matters worse in these situations."

That comment didn't sit as well with April, but before she could think of a response, James walked in, extending his hand to Chris.

"Hey, man! I owe you one."

"No problem." Chris shook James's hand. "Glad it worked out."

James leaned against the door frame, using it to scratch his back, a familiar ritual April found faintly amusing. "I wonder why Tyrell thought he knew you," he mused.

"I don't know. He probably saw me around the campus." Chris held up the knife. "I'll take this back with me and have security put it somewhere safe."

"Please," April said. She never wanted to see the thing again. "And thanks for everything you did today."

When Chris left, James plopped into the empty chair and let out a deep sigh.

"You okay?" she asked.

"Yeah, I'm all right." His smile was wan.

"God, that was awful," she said.

James's expression appeared troubled. "I keep thinking I should have seen that coming, but Tyrell caught me completely off guard."

April reached over to squeeze his hand. "Even you can't walk on water all the time, pal. But I still don't get why Morgenstern's death would make Tyrell go berserk like that." She frowned. "Maybe it triggered memories of an earlier trauma."

"Could be." James agreed. "What still amazes me is how he instantly responded to Chris. Hell of a transference reaction. Lucky for us, I guess."

Ψ

April was still mulling over the incident with Tyrell on her way home. None of it made sense to her. For one thing, she didn't really buy James's theory that Tyrell had some kind of instant positive transference reaction to Chris. Why would a tall, thin, white psychiatrist remind a twenty-something black guy from West Philly of some key figure in his life? And why would Tyrell kill a dog? Granted, he sometimes affected gangsta airs, but Tyrell had never shown any signs of cruelty or sadism.

She trudged up the hill from the Jenkintown train station, tired, but wired, her thoughts still churning. In her head, she replayed Chris's intervention with Tyrell. He'd handled the situation so coolly. No question, it added to Chris's charisma. But she thought he might have been too cool and confident – almost to the point of arrogance. There was something else that April couldn't quite put her finger on. He reminded her of someone, but who? Maybe she was having a transference reaction of her own. Anyway, she thought as she reached the entrance to her building, it was too much to sort out tonight.

Ed, the elderly doorman, opened the door to the lobby for her with a flourish, the edges of his moustache curling up as he smiled.

"Evening, Doctress!'

"Hello, Ed." April cringed at the grating honorific. She itched to correct him, but didn't want to hurt his feelings.

She rode the elevator up to her floor and walked down the hall to her apartment, pulling her key from her purse. The hallway was empty, which was fine. She didn't have the energy to chit chat with any neighbors.

As April approached her apartment, something caught her eye. What was that stuff on her door? At first, she thought it was a flyer or a menu someone had taped there. But as she came closer, she saw it wasn't. She froze in front of her door. A message was scrawled on it in bright red. Blood?

Her heart raced with panic. Her stomach lurched. It was a crude, childish drawing of a cat's face. Beneath it, crooked letters spelled out:

KILL UR CAT

"No!" she cried out.

39

An image of Tyrell's bloody hunting knife filled April's mind as she reached out a trembling hand to grope at her apartment door. Her fingers made contact with the red writing.

Not sticky. Maybe not blood, she prayed She brought her hand to her face and sniffed her fingers, recognizing the faint smell of magic marker ink. April let out a sigh of relief and realized she'd been holding her breath. Her hands still shaking, she turned the doorknob.

Locked! Thank God.

She fumbled her key into the lock. Please, please let them be okay. A small whimper of dread escaped her lips as she pushed open the door.

Natasha was right there.

"Oh, sweetie!" She crouched and clutched the ginger-colored cat, who wriggled out of the embrace. April looked around. But where was Boris?

"Boris?" she called. Standing and closing the door behind her, she scanned the apartment. Nothing appeared to be disturbed. Yet there was no sign of the other cat.

"Boris?" April raced through the rooms, calling for him. There was no answering meow. Natasha padded behind her as April opened closets and looked under the bed, behind the couch, in the bathtub.

Not there.

Tears blurred her eyes as she ran into the hallway. She raced toward the elevators, then up and down the other wings of her floor, calling for her cat.

She opened the door to the trash room, filled with terror at the thought of the incinerator inside. No cat cowered among the newspapers and boxes stacked for recycling.

Back in the hallway, she contemplated the elevator doors. Could he have slipped in there? Been taken to another floor?

Or taken someplace worse?

April combed every inch of every hallway on all six floors of her building, trash rooms included – finding no trace of Boris. Panting, her heart pounding, she sprinted through the basement garage, peering under each car and calling him. Exiting through the garage, she ran outside and circled the grounds of Briar Hill for another half hour.

The dusky shadows faded into darkness. With a sinking heart, April realized it was becoming too dark for searching to be of any further use. She couldn't tell which scenario she found more dreadful – the idea that Boris had been killed or taken, or that her beloved declawed indoor cat was out there alone and frightened in the dark. Sweaty and exhausted, but still charged with adrenaline, she trotted back to her building.

Ed, the doorman, gaped at April's tear-streaked face, wild hair and dirt-smudged clothing as he opened the lobby door.
"What's the matter? Are you all right?"

"My cat!" she gasped. "I think someone took him. There's writing all over my apartment door – in red – threatening to kill my cat. And I can't find him anywhere!"

Ed stared at her. "Writing on your door?"

She stepped up close to the doorman and peered into his face. "Ed. Ed! Did you see any strange men come into the building today?"

"Strange men?"

Could he do nothing but echo her words? "Maybe someone who claimed he was delivering something?"

He slowly shook his head, as if pondering the mysteries of the universe. "No deliveries today. Besides, when someone delivers a package, I always keep it down here. I don't let people go up to the apartments, Doctress." He gave her a wounded look. "You know that."

She stifled the urge to scream at the man. "But couldn't there have been a visitor?"

Felipe! April suddenly remembered the patient she'd suspended. He had threatened her, hadn't he?

"Ed, could there have been a young, slender Latino man here today? With an Afro hairstyle?"

He shook his head again, vehemently this time. "No one like that."

April simply wanted to get out of there now. Ed was no help, and she probably sounded like a racist.

"Is there anything else I can do for you?" His mild tone made it sound like she'd been asking about something as trivial as the correct time.

"Just, please, Ed! If you do see my cat, he's a grey tabby, about eight or ten pounds. Please call me right away. Okay?"

She went back upstairs, taking the elevator. There was nothing to hurry for, now.

The sight of her apartment door made April sick to her stomach. She wanted to scrub off that lurid message before all her neighbors saw it. It felt as if the whole mess of her life was on display.

But then again, the writing could be evidence.

She let herself back into her apartment. Natasha greeted her, and April fought down the urge to start the search for Boris all over again.

She could always do that later. Instead, she fished through her purse until she found the card the detective had given her. She pulled it out, along with her cellphone.

If there was evidence here, she needed a cop.

"Detective Perone? Sam?" she blurted out when he answered. "This is April Simon, from Franklin. I don't know if it has anything to do with Dr. Morgenstern's death, but something has happened." Her voice broke. "And I need your help!"

40

"What did you find out?" April asked when Sam returned from interviewing the other residents on her floor.

"Nothing." He stepped into her apartment. "Most of your neighbors were at work during the day, and the ones who were around didn't notice anyone near your door, or see any unfamiliar people in the halls. Probably he was in and out pretty quickly. Your doorman isn't exactly Homeland Security," he added.

April hurried to close the door behind him. She couldn't stand to look at that ugly red scrawl.

"Hey!" His tone strove for upbeat. "Consider the bright side. There's no sign of forced entry and you told me nothing inside your apartment was disturbed. I don't see any evidence that someone got in here."

"Except my cat's gone."

At that moment Natasha mewed, as if seconding her complaint. Sam stared briefly at the cat before turning back to April.

"Look." He patted the door. "You saw those red smudges on the outside, where the intruder smeared the marker. But no trace on the inside."

"What about fingerprints?"

He shook his head. "If there were any prints left on the doorknob, you compromised them when you opened the door."

April bit her lip.

"So…" Sam folded his arms and rested a shoulder against the door. "Now for the sixty-four thousand dollar question. Who do you think did that to your door?"

April inhaled sharply.

"What?" he asked.

"There's a patient in my program," she murmured. "I suspended him and he sort of …threatened me."

"Sort of?" Sam frowned. "What did he say?"

April hedged. "Nothing specific."

Sam pulled out his notebook. "What's his name?"

As he turned to a fresh page, April's eyes widened. "Oh, no! I can't tell you that."

The pen in Sam's hand froze above the blank page. "Why the hell not?" He rolled his eyes. "No, don't tell me – patient confidentiality, right?" She nodded, her face pinched in misery. Her cat was out there somewhere, but her professional responsibility was all too clear. "Anyway, there's no proof he was here."

"But if you gave me his name, I could at least check him for priors," Sam argued. "You're tying my hands."

She heard the frustration in his voice. "I'm sorry."

"You know," he tapped the notebook against his leg in a staccato tempo, "I'm getting a sense of *déjà vu.* Once again, here you are holding out on me."

He leaned closer and a hint of spice aftershave teased at her nostrils.

"Has it occurred to you, Dr. Simon, that this business –" Sam angled his head in the direction of her defaced door, " – might have something to do with your chairman's death?"

"His murder, you mean." She looked into his dark eyes, rimmed by full lashes. "I thought you'd started calling me April."

"What I'd like to keep calling you is safe, April," he retorted. "You and all the rest of the innocent people at Franklin. Please, just tell me – who had issues with Morgenstern?"

Her lips parted. The names were on her tongue. She closed her mouth again.

"We're not talking about your patients, now, are we?"

She swallowed. "No, we're not."

"Who, April?" His voice was soft, but insistent.

She folded her arms, gripping her shoulders protectively. Where did her loyalties lie? If a killer was out there, her colleagues needed more protection than she could give them. She let out a sigh of surrender.

"Stuart Hartman. Clarence McKay. Sandra Chang."

Sam was already writing.

She grabbed his hand to stop the motion of his pen. "Hey,, I'm not implying any of them is guilty of murder. Just that you might want to talk with them. Please don't ask me to say more than that."

He stopped writing and looked at her. "Understood."

She released his hand.

"You know." He put away the notebook. "If you're worried about that patient, the best thing to do is get a restraining order. Go to City Hall tomorrow. I'll give you a copy of my report. There's no evidence that he committed a crime, but the fact that he threatened you should be enough for the judge."

"I'll think about it." She massaged her temples. "What about Boris? My cat?"

Sam reached for her shoulder. "He'll turn up. Post some missing cat flyers. Offer a reward." His fingers closed in a reassuring squeeze. "Cats go missing all the time."

She looked away. "Not mine."

Sam checked his watch. "Getting late. You must be beat. Have you eaten anything?"

"I'm not hungry."

"Well, at least try to get some rest, will you?"

"Uh-huh." Her eyes remained glued to the floor.

"Hey!"

When she looked up, he'd lowered his head, forcing her to look directly into his face.

"Don't give up," he said. "You'll get him back. I'll check in with you tomorrow. Okay?"

She held his steady, brown-eyed gaze a moment longer. "Okay," she whispered.

After he left, she drank herself to sleep.

Ψ

Sam walked to his car, gnawing the inside of his cheek. Despite the pep talk he'd given April, he was worried. Not about the cat, but about her. The whole situation gave him an acidy feeling in his stomach.

He didn't like the missing cat thing, for one; although at least Jenkintown was pretty far from the areas where all those other animals had disappeared. What ate at him was someone scrawling "KILL" in massive, red letters on April's door. Only one day after she had found Morgenstern's body. Sam had too much police experience to believe in that kind of coincidence. A murderer was loose at Franklin and somehow she was caught up in it.

But how? What was her role? Sam's gut, his acid gut, told him she was trustworthy. She'd pointed him in some directions. That had to be a good thing.

Unless it was misdirection, and April Simon was protecting someone else.

So why this feeling that he needed to protect her? Sam started his car, his insides still churning. He preferred not to think too much about his own motives. The hell with the Mayor's office. He had his own reasons to solve this case quickly.

He didn't need to be hanging around with shrinks.

Thursday, September 30

41

The ringing of April's cellphone jolted her awake. It was daylight. Natasha lay curled up against her chest. Boris's absence struck her like a blow. As she reached for the phone, resting on her night table, April glanced at the digital clock. It was 9:37. The sunlight coming through her window meant AM.

She recognized the number for Praxis. "Hello?" she said. A hangover-induced headache kicked in as soon as she sat up.

"Hey, boss, are you okay?" It was Cynthia, the program receptionist.

"Yeah." She felt a wave of nausea. "God, I must have overslept."

"Look, you better get in here, or at least call Dr. McKay, pronto," Cynthia said. "He was down here just now looking for you, and he sure didn't seem happy that you weren't here."

April was already on her feet, fighting off vertigo. "I'm on my way in. Please, call him for me and tell him – "

"I'll tell him you were delayed because you weren't feeling well," Cynthia said, "and that you'll be here in forty-five minutes."

Ψ

"Why didn't you report this incident with Tyrell to me yesterday?" Clarence McKay thundered at April, as soon as she walked into his office. She slunk over to sit in a chair, rather than stand in front of his desk, as if she were in the principal's office.

"You're right, Clarence. I should have." She was going to have to do some appeasing with her supervisor. Recalling that she'd ratted him out to Sam last night made her feel doubly penitent.

"I'm sorry," she said, meaning it. "After Tyrell was taken out to the emergency room, I got caught up trying to get the other patients calmed down, and debriefing the staff, and – "

"And where were you this morning?" Clarence broke in. "I came down there, it was after nine and nobody had even heard from you. You think this kind of behavior helps your prospects for promotion?"

"I know." She lowered her gaze. "I'm sorry," she repeated. She thought of explaining, *my cat is gone*, but stopped herself. It would probably sound to Clarence like, *the dog ate my homework.* Besides, she didn't think she could talk about Boris without crying.

"I was under the weather this morning," she said, which was true enough. "I guess the events of the past two days must have caught up with me."

His features softened an iota and he was silent for a moment. When he spoke, his tone was less harsh.

Morgenstern wouldn't have given so much as an inch.

"April, you assured me this Pacifil group would be no big deal," he said. "Routine med checks, you told me. Now you have one suspended patient wandering around high as the Walt Whitman Bridge and another holding a therapy group hostage at knifepoint."

"Clarence, it's true we've had to do some crisis management," she began.

"With half the study group!" he protested.

"I know." April held up a hand to quell his indignation. "But Tyrell is under control now. And while he's in the hospital, you won't actually need to see him. You could just write the orders for his Pacifil, and – "

"Not a good idea," McKay interrupted. "Look how these patients are acting out. We should discontinue the drug."

She visualized the crude, threatening message left on her door. What if the Pacifil had somehow driven Felipe to do that? Should she say something about it to Clarence? Sam had said there was no real proof.

Clarence sat back in his desk chair. "April, remember how they stopped the Premarin trials when all those women started getting breast cancer? That's called a 'clinical event'. A sign that a treatment is too dangerous to allow the research to continue."

April swallowed her frustration. "Clarence, I know what a clinical event is."

"Then don't you see that the same kind of situation may exist here?" he demanded.

She sighed. "I guess so. I was so sure it was the shock of Lowell's death that was affecting them." She gave Clarence a pointed look. "And if we force any other sudden changes on them, wouldn't we be rocking their boat even more?"

Clarence rubbed his forehead, which made April even more aware of her own headache, now somewhat tamed by Advil.

"All right," he relented. "Here's what we're going to do." He picked up a pencil, twirling it absently as he spoke. "I am going to go back and review Lowell's research proposal, his notes, everything he put together on this project. And after I've done that, I will make a decision, and that decision will be final. Understood?"

"Yes sir."

"And in the meantime, no more crises!"

"There won't be," April assured him, even as she wondered how she could possibly guarantee that. "Chris Willis has offered to be on call for us if we need him," she added.

"All right. We'll let it stand for now," Clarence said. "Make sure you write up an incident report on yesterday."

"I will," she promised, hoping he wouldn't order her to write up her discovery of Morgenstern's body, too.

A spasm of nausea gripped April as she left McKay's office. She barely made it to the ladies room and into a stall before she started gagging. Good thing she hadn't had time for breakfast. She was also grateful that the ladies room was empty.

April rinsed her mouth at the sink, wet a paper towel with cold water and pressed it to her aching head. How much had she drunk last night? She'd rushed out of the apartment so fast this morning that she hadn't surveyed the kitchen for evidence of her debauchery. She'd deal with that tonight.

She wished she were home in bed right now.

It wasn't only the wine, she told herself. It was Boris going missing, Tyrell going crazy, Lowell going dead –the total insanity that suddenly had taken over her life. For God's sake, she was only human.

Not that loss or illness counted for much here in academia. April had watched full professors show up at Franklin, barely able to speak, eyes glazed with fever. They were like the freaking Marines. She understood that the show must go on and the mail must get through. But the next grant proposal?

Please!

Still, despite all she'd been through in the past few days, April had to face up to the fact that she didn't even remember falling asleep last night. Or putting on her pajamas, or anything else after….

After when? She knew what the name for this was. She'd had a blackout. This morning, she'd been so messed up, she hadn't even gotten up for work. Hell, she'd probably killed her chances for promotion. And, she realized with a pang, she hadn't even had time to look any further for poor Boris.

Mortified, she looked up at her reflection in the mirror. Bloodshot eyes stared back at her. You can't do this anymore, she told herself. She had to get sober and be on top of her game, especially now that the world was going crazy around her. No more wine, she resolved, at least not for the next thirty days.

She left the ladies room, with both her stomach and her resolve more settled, and walked to the elevator. As she reached for the button, the elevator arrived. The door opened and she was face-to-face with Sam Perone.

42

Sam peered intently at April, as he stepped off the elevator. "Rough night, huh?"

"I'm okay," she muttered. Once again, he was reading her like an open book. "I appreciate your coming over last night," she added.

"Sorry I couldn't do more." He held her gaze. "You going for that restraining order?"

She hesitated. "You said there's no proof he was there. And taking legal action against a patient could get sticky."

"Why do I get the feeling that you're not the kind to ask for help?"

"I called you last night, didn't I?" she protested.

"For your cat, yeah. I'm talking about you."

Her face felt suddenly warm. How had he picked up on that so quickly?

"If there are any further incidents, I want you tell me right away," he said. "Okay?"

"I will." An unwelcome suspicion occurred to her. "What are you doing here, anyway?"

"Following up on those leads you gave me."

"Leads?" Uh-oh.

"Interviewing some of your colleagues," he replied, glancing at his watch. "Starting with Clarence McKay in five minutes."

"Oh." Her queasiness returned. She wished she could take back the names she'd given him, but obviously it was too late for that. She didn't want his laser vision to pick up her distress, either. "Anyway, thanks again," she said.

He gave her a quick nod of acknowledgement. "You put up those Missing Cat posters yet?"

"I'll do it tonight."

"Don't wait too long. You know what they say – the first twenty-four hours is the critical period." He grinned. "Can't let the trail go cold." With a wave, he was off.

Ψ

"Dr. McKay? Detective Perone is here." Clarence McKay's assistant motioned Sam into his office.

"Thanks for making time for me this morning." Sam extended his hand.

Clarence shook it. "What's this about, Detective?" He gestured at the empty chair.

"Just some routine questions in connection with your late chairman's death." Sam took a seat and looked around. "Nice office." He liked the warm, masculine tones of brown and leather, and a rough-textured fabric that draped one of the walls. Sam also admired some small, primitive sculptures that looked African to his unschooled eye. Plenty of framed degrees and certificates hung above McKay's desk, proclaiming his importance.

"What would you like to know, Detective Perone?" Clarence asked. "I have about twenty minutes before my next appointment."

"Then I'll try not to waste your time. I gather you worked pretty closely with Dr. Morgenstern. What kind of man was he?"

McKay pursed his lips. "Well, brilliant, certainly. Dedicated. I'd say he was," he paused, "quite an intense man."

"Did he have many enemies here at Franklin?"

McKay bristled. "What are you implying, Detective?"

Sam gazed at the ceiling, as if gathering his thoughts. "A brilliant, intense guy in a position of authority. Someone like that is bound to bruise a few egos. I'm hoping you'll tell me whose."

McKay's expression was stony. "And why would I want to do that?"

Sam leaned forward. "Do I need to spell it out for you, Doctor? Because his death was suspicious."

"I'm very distressed to hear that," McKay said. "Particularly because, I assure you, Lowell Morgenstern enjoyed the respect and admiration of everyone who had the privilege of working with him."

The man was delivering a eulogy and Sam thought it rang false. He decided to try provoking a genuine reaction.

"Come on, Dr. McKay. Evidently, Morgenstern liked to throw his weight around. You expect me to believe that none of your colleagues, the doctors and residents you supervise, ever came to you with complaints about him?"

Clarence clenched his jaw so tightly that Sam wondered about the condition of the psychiatrist's tooth enamel.

"You probably know very little about psychiatric residency, Detective."

The arrogance in his voice set Sam's own teeth on edge.

"The training can be quite arduous," Clarence continued. "Dr. Morgenstern was an exceptional and often demanding teacher. If there was some grumbling from time to time, that's only to be expected."

"So, who grumbled to you?"

Clarence raised his chin in defiance. "I'm not going to discuss that with you, Detective. Believe me, nothing I could tell you would have any bearing on your case."

"That's for me to decide, Doctor." Sam studied him. "What about you?"

Clarence looked wary. "What do you mean?"

"Tell me about your own relationship with Morgenstern."

Clarence shrugged. "It was professional."

"Friendly? Cool?" Sam was pushing. "You socialize with him?"

"We had a cordial relationship." McKay's eyes skittered off to the left.

Lying, Sam thought. Time to go fish. "How about conflicts?" he asked. "There must have been times when the two of you disagreed. Maybe about patients? Trainees?"

"When we did, we discussed our differences in a professional manner."

There was that word again, Sam thought. Used to remind me how much more education he has. "Could you give me an example?" he persisted.

"It wouldn't be appropriate for me to get into clinical details regarding patients."

The confidentiality thing again. Shrinks! "How about research?" Sam asked.

Clarence fidgeted the slightest bit in his chair. "What about it?"

Bingo, Sam thought. "Did you two work together on studies? As collaborators?"

"Not really." Clarence reached for a pencil.

"What, never even read each other's articles you wrote for publication? Never bounced ideas off each other? Isn't that the way *professionals* work together?" Sam put some bite into the word.

"Only to a limited extent, Detective. Lowell and I had…" Clarence fingered the pencil eraser. " – different areas of specialization."

It was like talking to a wall. A wall with something to hide, Sam reflected. "Well, I won't take up any more of your time, Dr. McKay." He stood. "This morning," he added pointedly.

Clarence rose as well. "No problem." He sounded cheery, now that the interview was ending. "Happy to cooperate with the police."

One last try, now that his guard was down. "By the way," Sam asked casually, "do you know his wife?"

Clarence's eyebrows shot up. "Sure, I've met Miranda at several faculty parties and university functions. Lovely woman," he added.

"Think she might have killed him?" Sam wanted to rattle McKay, see how he reacted when his buttons were pushed.

"Perone, that's outrageous!" Clarence tossed the pencil onto his desk.

"Was he sleeping around?"

This time Clarence slammed a fist onto the desk. "I don't have time for this nonsense!"

A temper, Sam thought. Worth keeping in mind. "Can you direct me to Dr. Chang's office?" he asked.

"Fifth door down on the left. And Detective?"

"Doctor?"

"Kindly close my door on your way out."

Sam smiled as he did.

43

The psychiatric resident, Sandra Chang, couldn't have been more different from Clarence McKay, the shrink Sam had just interviewed. *Yin yang,* he reflected. One was portly, the other waif-like. One bombastic, the other meek.

One yelled, the other wept.

"Dr. Chang, may I ask why Morgenstern ended it?" Sam inquired, after she'd volunteered the story of their affair.

"I wasn't smart enough for him." Sandra's slender fingers reached for another tissue.

"Or he was too full of himself to appreciate you," Sam suggested gently.

She shook her head, tears streaming down her cheeks.

What a bastard Morgenstern must have been, Sam reflected. Taking advantage of someone who seemed this vulnerable. Could she have taken revenge? She had a compelling motive. On the other hand, her grief seemed deep and genuine. He decided to reserve judgment. Meanwhile, he thought, if handled properly, a jilted mistress could be a good source of information.

"Dr. Chang," he asked, "did Dr. Morgenstern talk to you about his dealings with his colleagues?"

"Sometimes," she sniffled.

"Who did he have conflicts with?"

She looked away from Sam's gaze.

"Sandra," he said. "May I call you that?"

She nodded.

"I'm trying to find his killer. Please, will you help me?"

After a moment, she answered. "There were two people –" She hesitated.

"I need to know."

She drew a breath. "The head of the psychology program, Dr. Hartman. Lowell told him he was about to bring in someone else to be in charge. Lowell told me – " She paused again.

"What?" Sam pressed her.

"He said Stuart made some lame threat about 'consequences.' Lowell laughed him off."

"And the other person?"

She put a hand over her eyes. "He's such a good man," she moaned. "I couldn't believe it when Lowell, when he said he'd caught him committing research fraud."

"Caught who? Tell me, Sandra!"

"Clarence McKay."

Motive, Sam thought.

Ψ

April hurried to retrieve her Missing Cat poster from the printer so no one at Praxis would see how she'd spent her morning. She photocopied the flyer, mentally reviewing her schedule for the day. She was already playing catch-up. What could she cancel?

Not her individual session with Carlee Randall, she decided. She stacked the posters face down as they fed out of the copier. April glanced at her watch. Damn! The session was in ten minutes. She needed to get her energy up. Carlee was tough enough to reach on a good day. Concerned about how she was coping in the aftermath of Morgenstern's death, April wanted to check on her. No special agenda. Just try to develop trust.

Develop trust.

The phrase echoed in April's mind as she carried the flyers back to her office. She was thinking about what Sam Perone had said that morning, about her not liking to ask for help. It rang true. When most in need, she withdrew. She'd done that in her marriage.

How had Sam seen it so soon? He seemed to have great intuition. Probably cops needed that. Still, she'd like to think there was something more to it.

She needed someone to trust.

44

Carlee Randall's long, dark hair hid her face from April's view. Give this woman a pixie cut and you'd strip away one of her major defenses, April thought. She wondered if she could possibly get the girl to open up to her today.

"How are you doing?" she asked. "How have you been dealing with Dr. Morgenstern's death?"

"I don't know," Carlee shrugged. "Better than Tyrell, I guess. I heard about the knife thing yesterday. I had a dental appointment, so I missed all the excitement." She sounded bored.

April debated how to respond. Psychotherapy with someone as guarded as Carlee could be like playing Cat's Cradle. Pick up the string the wrong way, and the whole thing fell apart. She decided to wait her out, and her patience was rewarded.

"Must have been quite a scene," Carlee remarked, sounding as if she were describing a comedy, instead of a knifepoint hostage situation.

April took a chance. "Were you ever in a threatening situation, yourself?"

Carlee snorted. "Only about every other night of my childhood."

"Want to tell me about it?"

Carlee took refuge beneath her hair. "Not particularly."

April sat back, giving her some space. "It was the four of you, right?" she asked. "You, your parents and your half brother."

Carlee nodded.

"How'd your folks get along?"

"Ha!" Carlee gave her a sideways glance, then looked away. "Lousy. He'd come home drunk and slap her around. She cried all the time. Any more questions?"

"What was it like for you to see that?" April asked. This was more than Carlee had shared before.

Tears welled in the young woman's eyes. "I couldn't help her."

"Of course not. You were just a child."

"Sometimes…" Carlee's voice dropped to a whisper.

"Go on."

A tear rolled down her face. "Sometimes I was glad he was hitting her, not me."

April forced herself not to grimace. They were getting into some painful territory. She studied Carlee, noticing the long-sleeved shirt she wore. Were those sleeves hiding the scars of self-injury?

"So he hit you, too?" she ventured.

Carlee nodded, taking full cover under her hair. She folded her arms protectively over her chest. "I don't want to talk about that."

"Okay," April said. "Tell me about your half brother."

"Kit? What about him?"

"His name was Kit?" April smiled.

"It was his nickname. I always called him that." A shy smile flitted across Carlee's elfin features.

"And Kit was – how much older than you?"

"Five years."

"Who was his father?" April asked. "Was your mother married before?"

"No." Carlee's voice sounded flat. "His father was someone she knew in New York. He wouldn't marry her."

Wouldn't, April noted. Carlee no doubt bore the burden of her mother's resentment, along with everything else on her shoulders. "I see," she said. "Did he keep in touch with Kit?"

"Uh-uh. We both missed out in the father department."

April reflected on the remark, wondering what might have become of Kit. "Did your father beat Kit, too?" she asked.

Carlee tossed back her hair, as if defying her memories. "He beat everyone," she said, her voice rising. " Get it?"

April nodded. "Bad scene. A lot for a kid to be angry about."

Carlee rewarded her with a moment of eye contact. "You think?" She looked away again. "I was mostly just scared."

"Who wouldn't be? Carlee, what about your relationship with Kit? How did you two get along?"

She folded her arms again. "When I was little, he was my best friend. The one who used to take care of me." Her voice went high, child-like. "You know, make sure I had breakfast before I went to school, on days Mom didn't get out of bed. Stuff like that. He helped me with my homework. I idolized him." Her tears welled up again.

"And?"

Carlee covered her face with both hands. Evidently her hair wasn't sufficient camouflage for what she was feeling now. "I can't –" A hoarse sob escaped before she choked back what must have been an ocean of grief and rage. She glared at April. "We're done here."

She jumped up and rushed out of April's office.

April rubbed her aching forehead. Carlee had taken a big step, opening up about her family, even that little bit. No surprise that she'd slammed on the brakes. April was amazed Carlee had suddenly begun to disclose her history of abuse, at all. She wondered if Morgenstern's death might have re-traumatized Carlee and weakened her defenses.

Look at Tyrell, she thought, killing that dog, wielding a knife. Behavior utterly unlike him before. And Felipe – what might he have he done? She shuddered to consider the possibilities. At least the fourth subject, Brittany, seemed unchanged.

So far.

A sharp knock on April's open door made her look up.

Stuart Hartman stood in the doorway.

45

Stuart Hartman took a step into April's office.

The tiny hairs at the back of her neck rose, sending her into yellow alert mode.

Stuart stopped in his tracks. "Am I catching you at a bad time?" he asked. "I can come back."

April was tempted to tell him to go, recalling his outburst at the Chuckwagon the other day. The idea of being alone in her office with Stuart made her uneasy.

As if reading her mind, Stuart smiled sheepishly. "Sorry about the other day. I guess we're all a bit on edge this week, huh? And you, finding Lowell's – finding him like that. Must have been rough."

He was letting himself off too easy, she thought, but had no desire to pursue it with him. "I'm fine, Stuart. What can I do for you?" It was rare for Hartman to put in an appearance on this side of Vine Street. April decided not to invite him to take a seat.

"Just checking to see how Kristin's settling in with her practicum placement here."

April felt relieved. He had a legitimate agenda.

"Any concerns so far?" he asked.

"Not at all," April replied. "Kristin's made a good start. She seems eager to learn," she added. "Do you want to touch base with her? She should be free right now. I can take you to her office."

"No need." Hartman held up a hand, signaling April not to get up from her chair. "The place isn't big enough to get lost in."

Ha, ha, April thought.

"Just point me in the direction of her office," Stuart said.

As soon as he left her office, April got up and closed the door. She felt an urge to spray the room with air freshener. She'd never had particularly warm feelings toward Stuart Hartman, but his phony bonhomie, following on the heels of his hissy fit at the Chuckwagon, really frosted her.

She wasn't sorry she'd given his name to Sam.

Ψ

Seated with Kristin in the spare office, Stuart endured an enthusiastic recitation of her initial activities at Praxis.

"So you're getting some good experience here," he interjected, when Kristin finally seemed to come up for air. "Glad it's turning out to be a good match." He looked around, surveying the office. "This is a nice set up," he commented.

Kristin beamed with pride.

"Do you have this office all to yourself?"

"I share it with the psych residents," Kristin admitted. "But two of the days that I'm here, they're not. We only overlap on Tuesdays, and I'm in groups that whole afternoon, anyway."

"That does work out well," Stuart agreed. He sat back and folded his hands behind his head, a study in nonchalance. "Which residents are down here this rotation?" he asked.

He'd already researched it, and knew the answer.

"Mort Abrams and Sandra Chang," Kristin replied. Her expression turned somber. "Poor Sandra," she blurted out.

Stuart gave her his best look of innocent confusion, and Kristin blushed.

"I mean, she really admired Dr. Morgenstern," she said quickly.

"Yes, I'm sure," Stuart agreed. As if anyone at Franklin hadn't known about their supposedly secret affair! "He was a great teacher," he added. "It's a great loss." He assumed a look of profound sorrow.

"Yes." Kristin quickly changed the subject. "So, anyway, we share the desk, but we each have our own drawer."

"Great!" Stuart truly meant it. He stood, smiling. "Well, it all sounds good, Kristin. I'll bring you a copy of that article on group treatment of sexual trauma I was telling you about."

"Thanks, Dr. Hartman. Or I could download it at the library. You said it was the Journal of Group Psychotherapy?"

"No need to bother with that," Stuart said quickly. "I'll drop it off when I come here to meet with Dr. McKay tomorrow."

Stuart smiled to himself as he left Praxis. Mission accomplished..

46

By five o'clock, April was wilted and jonesing for food, sleep and alcohol – not necessarily in that order. She left Praxis, clutching her folder of cat posters, eager to get home and post them around Briar Hill before collapsing for the night.

"Hey!" Chris Willis greeted her as he exited the outpatient clinic. "All quiet on the Praxis front today?"

"Hi, Chris. Yes, back to normal. Normal as a psychiatric program ever gets, at any rate."

He gestured at the file folder. "Taking work home?"

"Not exactly." She checked her customary reticence and said: "My cat's gone missing." She held up the folder. "I'm going to put up some posters in my building."

"Aw, too bad." He gave her a sympathetic smile. "Hope it turns up. I like cats. Hey!" he added. "Sounds like you could use some cheering up. Buy you a drink?"

April had been waiting for an invitation like this. But not tonight. "Thanks, Chris. Can I get a rain check? I really need to get these posters up before – "

"Hi!" Sam Perone joined them. "So you made up the posters. Let's see."

April opened the folder to show him the flyers.

Sam nodded approvingly. "Nice job."

A moment of awkward silence followed.

"I guess you two haven't met," April said. "Detective Sam Perone, Dr. Chris Willis."

While they shook hands, April studied the two men, each attractive in a distinctive way. Tall and lean, Chris had the wiry body of a tennis player. There was an elegance to his angular features, and, once again, he reminded her of someone – she couldn't say whom. A few inches shorter, Sam was more solidly built. Shaggy brown hair grazed his collar and his brown eyes glanced her way.

Suppose she had to choose between them…?.

"You investigating her missing cat, Detective?" Chris asked.

The brown eyes narrowed. "Among other matters."

"Of course!" Chris said. "The mysterious death of our illustrious chairman. You're working the case."

"Getting the lay of the land," Sam responded. "What do you do around here, Dr. Willis?"

Sensing an undercurrent building between the two men, April wanted to break the tension. "Chris directs the psych emergency service," she interjected.

"Guess you're a good man in a crisis, huh?" Sam observed.

"He is." Anxiety kept April talking. "Yesterday he talked down a patient with a knife."

"That so?" Sam asked.

Chris shrugged, indifferent. "All in a day's work."

Sam's expression remained equally impassive. "I would think that's a job best left to law enforcement."

"Like the police have a great track record at dealing with the mentally ill?" Chris shot back.

April didn't like where this was heading.

"Maybe not," Sam acknowledged. "But I wouldn't say that therapists know much about violence prevention."

"Well," April intervened, "we all have a lot to learn on that subject. Right?"

Both men turned to look at her. Suddenly April wanted to get out of there.

"Well, I'd better get going," she said.

"Need a ride?" Sam asked.

A drink, a ride. She was up to her eyeballs in offers tonight, but just wanted to get home.

"I have my car," she said.

"Good luck with your cat," Chris called out as she headed toward the parking lot.

April's stomach was in knots. And, worse, she still had an evening of sobriety to get through.

Ψ

Luck smiled on Stuart Hartman.

Behind the locked entrance to Praxis, the lights were on and he heard the sound of a vacuum cleaner running. The janitor could let him in. In a moment, the man himself came into view, pushing the noisy machine. Stuart rapped on the glass door, but the cleaning guy didn't look up from his work. Stuart could see now that the man was wearing ear pods.

Stuart tapped louder, his ring clanking against the glass. At that moment, the janitor looked up and saw him.

He turned off the vacuum cleaner, removed his ear pods and unlocked the entrance from inside, opening the door just enough to allow communication.

"Help you, man?"

Stuart stood up straighter, determined to appear official. "Dr. Hartman, director of the psychology program," he announced. "I came to drop off this article for Kristin, the psychology student here."

The janitor shrugged. "You know where her office at?"

"Yes. I won't be a minute."

"Awright." He replaced his ear pods and resumed vacuuming.

Quickly, Stuart walked down the corridor to Kristin's office, closing the door part way behind him. He positioned the envelope, with Kristin's name written on it, upon the desk. He glanced through the open door before he began opening desk drawers.

In the middle drawer, Stuart struck gold. A red and gold paisley scarf lay folded there. He remembered Sandra Chang wearing it at the last Grand Rounds.

With his thumb and index finger, Stuart pulled the scarf from the drawer, then partly unfolded it across the desk. He stole another glance at the door. He could hear the vacuum cleaner running down the hall.

Stuart used his handkerchief to remove the two vials he'd placed in his breast pocket. He took care to wipe each one before wrapping it in the scarf. He replaced the package in the drawer and closed it quietly. For good measure, he wiped the handle of the drawer before returning the handkerchief to his pocket.

He waved at the janitor on his way out.

47

Why on earth did Stuart want those Botox vials? At the wet bar in her great room, Miranda Morgenstern mixed herself a very dry martini. She carried it over to the sofa, where she curled up among the plush cushions. Removing the toothpick from her glass, she used her teeth to pull off one of the two green olives and chewed it as she thought.

Miranda had a feeling – call it women's intuition, that she was better off not knowing what Stuart might be up to. She hoped he wouldn't do anything stupid. For a Ph.D., Stuart wasn't quite as smart as he liked to think he was. At any rate, he'd better return her Botox soon. She had an appointment scheduled with her plastic surgeon next week.

Ψ

Sam popped open a bottle of beer. Snooty academics, he reflected. What was that phrase – "effete intellectual snobs?" Not that Sam had any fondness for Spiro Agnew, but his encounters today with those shrinks at Franklin had left a sour taste in his mouth. At least the cold beer was helping with that.

It was the men who'd pissed him off – Clarence McKay and Chris Willis. So far, Sam liked McKay for Morgenstern's murder, especially because of that business about the research fraud. Could Morgenstern have been blackmailing him? Sam decided he'd go confront McKay first thing in the morning, see what he could shake out of the man. He took another swallow of beer.

And Chris Willis! What an arrogant, condescending prick. Sam sniffed with disdain. Psychiatrists had no business trying to talk down people with weapons. They didn't understand the criminal mind. If anything, they made excuses for criminals – bad childhoods, trauma, fucking food allergies. Shrinks should stick to something they understood, like pushing pills.

No, he thought. Don't go there. Dangerous to probe old wounds – they might not be fully healed. Yet, Sam admitted to himself, those scars had been aggravated tonight by a fresh injury – the sight of that creep Chris Willis looking so cozy with April.

Ψ

April eyed the bottle of wine in her refrigerator – about a third full. Enough for one very large glass, or two small ones. It beckoned to her, a siren song, undermining the resolution she'd made that morning.

She reached for the wine. It felt deliciously cold in her hands, a promise of blissful refreshment, a balm for her anxiety and distress. She carried the bottle to the countertop, set it down and pulled out the cork.

The moment of truth.

Taking a deep breath, she poured the last of the wine into the sink, watching regretfully as the golden liquid disappeared down the drain like a faithless lover.

Not tonight.

April filled a kettle with water and took a mug from the cabinet. Rooting through the pantry closet, she found a nearly empty box of herbal tea. It would have to do. She'd get some fresh tomorrow, maybe a different flavor. She hadn't drunk this stuff in ages.

When the tea was ready, April took it into the living room and sat on the couch, where Natasha promptly jumped onto her lap, purring contentedly. If she missed her litter-mate, the orange tabby wasn't showing it. Boris was the alpha cat. Probably Natasha was enjoying her temporary monopoly on April's attention.

Let's hope it's temporary, April reflected. She'd hung the Missing Cat flyers in the mail rooms of all three buildings at Briar Hill, conducted another sweep of the outdoor grounds, and checked in with Ed, the doorman. No sign, no news, no Boris. She forced herself to interrupt the downward spiral of her thoughts about what might have happened to him. The idea of him suffering or alone out there in the dark was unbearable.

She focused on her breathing. Inhale to a count of two, exhale to a count of four. Concentrate only on the breath. No stray thoughts of cats, or wine, or –

Breathe!

She did, for a while, before her mind drifted again – this time, back to her encounter with Chris and Sam earlier that evening. She must have sounded like a dope, prattling on about Chris. Then he was so condescending to Sam.

What must Sam think of us, she wondered, with our degrees and our attitudes? The detective struck her as quite astute – street smart, perhaps. She wondered if he was married. It must be tough being married to a cop.

But perhaps no tougher than being alone, with a missing cat and no wine.

April tickled Natasha's ears, which set the cat to purring again. "How about we rustle up some dinner?" she asked the tabby. "Tuna for you, chicken salad for me." She sighed. "And water for both of us tonight."

Friday, October 1

48

"Back already, Detective?" Clarence McKay looked up from his desk and frowned. "What can I do for you this morning?"

Sam strode into the psychiatrist's office and closed the door behind him. "Start telling the truth."

McKay glared at him. "You're implying I haven't?"

"No, I'm saying it," Sam retorted. "When you told me about your cordial relationship with Morgenstern, you left out the part about blackmail, didn't you?"

McKay barked out a harsh laugh, which rang hollow to Sam's ear. "I assure you, Perone, I was not blackmailing Lowell Morgenstern. Or anyone else," he added.

Sam approached the desk, leaned over and braced his hands on it, invading McKay's space.

"Cut the crap. Morgenstern knew you were committing some kind of research fraud – no, don't deny it, Doc," he said, as McKay gave another fake laugh, "because it's a fact. The question is whether he was using the information to extort something from you. Was he?"

McKay's face reddened.

Sam braced himself for a verbal attack – or worse. He stood his ground as the psychiatrist abruptly pushed his chair away from the desk and paced to his office window. He stood, looking out, his back to Sam, who could read the tension in McKay's hunched shoulders. As Sam watched, something inside the psychiatrist seemed to break. His shoulders slumped. When he turned to face Sam, his features were slack with defeat.

"There was no blackmail, Detective. Lowell did threaten to inform my funding source that some of my data was – "

"Faked?"

McKay grimaced. "Exaggerated." He shook his head. "I'm not proud of it. I'm going to rectify it. You can believe that or not."

"What I believe is that you had a motive to kill him."

Clarence met Sam's gaze. "I didn't murder Lowell Morgenstern. I'm no killer."

"I'm going to prove otherwise."

"Are you planning to arrest me?"

"You'll be the first to know."

McKay sighed. "I'm not going anywhere. You obviously know where to find me."

Sam turned to go.

"Detective," McKay called out, "who told you about all this? Dr. Simon?"

Sam wheeled around to face him. "Why do you think it was her?"

McKay shrugged. "Who else could have known? April was right outside my office door when Lowell and I were – discussing the matter. I certainly didn't tell anyone else."

"I don't reveal my sources." Sam kept his tone level, careful not to betray a hint of the turmoil he felt inside. "But I'm sure I don't have to explain the concept of confidentiality to you, Dr. McKay."

April had been holding out on him, Sam reflected as he left. And he'd thought she was someone he could trust.

Ψ

It was the psychiatric resident's turn to use the spare office at Praxis, and Mort Abrams was preparing to write a prescription for his patient, Denise.

"Another go-go-goner," he stuttered in annoyance, tossing a second empty ballpoint pen into the wastebasket. "You'd think a pres-pres-tig-ious university hospital would k-keep pens in supply." Mort's stammer invariably worsened with even minor stress. Talking slowly and articulating each syllable sometimes helped.

He shoved the top desk drawer closed and opened the middle one. A red and gold scarf covered the drawer's contents and he lifted it out.

"Wha – what?" Two glass vials – one empty, one full – slid free of the scarf and tumbled to the floor. Mort picked up the full vial and inspected it. "Huh! What the – ?"

"What is it?" Denise leaned in for a look.

"N-nothing." Mort frowned. This wasn't looking good. "Uh, Denise, could you ru-ru-run down to Dr. Simon's office and s-see if she can come in here? I'll write your pre-pre – your scrip – while you go."

Denise headed down the corridor.

Mort rooted through the drawer until he found a pack of ballpoint pens. He scribbled out Denise's prescription.

"Mort?" April stood at the door, flanked by Denise.

Mort raised a finger, signaling her to wait, and handed the scrip to Denise.

"See you l-l-later," he said, as she opened her mouth to speak. Denise closed her mouth and left.

"What's going on?" April demanded. "Denise said you found drugs in the desk."

"Have a l-l-look." He held up the full vial.

"That was in the desk?" April asked, dumbfounded. "What is it?"

"B-b-botulinum t-t-t-toxin type A."

"Botulism?" she cried in disbelief.

"Bo-Bo-Botox."

April gaped at him.

"And here's another one." Mort picked up the empty vial, where it lay on the industrial carpeting. "They were wrapped in this." He showed her the scarf. "Whose is this, anyway?"

April stared at the brightly colored scarf. "Oh no," she murmured.

49

Her thoughts racing, April stared at the red and gold scarf Mort Abrams held in his hand. She knew it was Sandra Chang's. But Sandra, humiliated and pregnant, couldn't possibly be a killer. Instinctively, April reached for the scarf.

"I'll take that," she said to Mort.

He drew back his arm, holding the scarf away from her. "But it's S-Sandra's, isn't it?"

April's mouth went dry. "I'll return it to her." Even as she said it, an alarm went off in her head. What was she doing?

Mort stared at her as if she were crazy. "You can't d-d-do that!" he protested. "It m-might be evidence!"

"What might?"

April and Mort turned.

Sam Perone stood at the office door, his gaze fixed on April's outstretched hand. "Your secretary said I'd find you in here. What's going on?"

April's eyes darted to Mort. She opened her mouth to caution him, but closed it again. With a deep sigh, she looked back at Sam.

"There's something here you need to see," she said.

Ψ

April felt tense enough to climb the walls of her office.

After they'd shown Sam the Botox vials and scarf, he'd sent her out of the residents' office so he could interview Abrams. Now the minutes ticked by while April awaited her turn, her dread steadily mounting. The detective had caught her red-handed, trying to conceal evidence. She wondered if he would arrest her.

Asking Mort to give her the scarf had been a foolish mistake. April had acted on an impulse to protect Sandra Chang, without stopping to weigh other considerations – obstructing justice, for instance. And now it dawned on her – why was she even so certain that Sandra was innocent? After all, Morgenstern had –

"All right. Now I have a few questions for you."

Sam breezed into April's office. In one hand, he held the Botox vials, bagged in Ziplocs, which he placed on her desk. The red and gold paisley scarf dangled from his other hand.

The sight of it made April queasy.

"Let's start with an easy one," he said, pulling up the extra chair. He positioned it so close to April's that he was sitting practically on top of her. "Where's your buddy, Sandra Chang?"

April leaned back in her chair, trying to put more space between them. "Isn't she upstairs in the outpatient clinic?"

The detective leaned forward, closing the gap. "According to the clinic secretary, Sandra didn't come in this morning, didn't call to cancel her patients and hasn't answered her phone. In other words," he concluded, "she's AWOL. Since you're so chummy, I thought you might have an idea where she is."

April was speechless. Had Sandra run away? What could that mean?

"Next question." He gave her no time to ponder. "Did you plant that stuff in her scarf?" Sam angled his head at the Botox vials on the desk.

"What?" The question hit April like a gut punch.

"This is your program. Your territory down here." His gaze was steely. "You strike me as a logical candidate to have set her up." Sam sat back, contemplating her. "Especially since you pointed me at her in the first place."

"That's crazy!" April protested. "Why would I have tried to take her scarf – to protect her – if I wanted to set her up?" Her face felt hot. "And what reason would I have to incriminate her, anyway?"

"Maybe she was competition."

April was completely at sea. "For what?"

"Your chairman's attentions?"

"That's absurd!" Her lip curled with scorn. "The only attention I ever got from Lowell Morgenstern was his bullying me. The only attention I paid to him was trying to convince him to promote me and let me hire more staff for my program."

Sam leaned forward again, crowding her. "Maybe by fucking him?"

"I'd slap you," she muttered through clenched teeth, "if I didn't think you'd arrest me for assaulting an officer."

"Before or after I arrest you for tampering with evidence?" he shot back.

She took a breath to slow her racing heartbeat. Her hands were ice cold. It felt as if they were both racing headlong toward a cliff. One step further, and the drop would be fatally steep.

"Detective." She softened her voice. "Sam, I'm sorry. I did a stupid thing, or tried to, but only because I care about Sandra and wanted to protect her. If that's a crime, I guess I'm guilty." She drew her arms around herself protectively. "But I swear to you," she held his gaze, "I didn't have anything going on with Lowell Morgenstern, I didn't kill him, and I didn't try to incriminate anyone else."

She saw Sam's jaw working. Had she managed to pull them back from the cliff?

"I was trying to help you," she went on. "I steered you in the direction of three of my colleagues. And I felt like shit for doing it," she said bitterly.

He stared back at her silently. "You didn't give me much of a map," he finally said. "You knew Morgenstern had nailed Clarence McKay for research fraud. Didn't you?"

She nodded ever so slightly.

"And you held back on me."

She caught the hint of disappointment in his tone. "I guess I felt protective of him, too," she admitted. "I have to work with these people. You can't expect me to go around airing their dirty laundry."

"They seem to have a lot of it," he said dryly.

"Besides, I have a promotion on the line."

He sneered. "What? More letters after your name? I'm trying to figure out who killed a man."

"You sound pretty self-righteous," April retorted. They were heading back toward the precipice, but this time she couldn't seem to stop. "I suppose you don't care about promotions."

"Not all that much."

His reply surprised her into silence.

"Climbing ladders isn't my definition of success," he said.

"Then what is?"

"Learning who you are," he replied. "Figuring out how to go out and be that, in the world."

April was stunned. This cop was deep. "Now you sound more like a psychologist."

He gave her a half-smile. "Hey, there's no need to insult me."

April chuckled ruefully. *"Touché!"* Psychologists tended to take themselves too seriously. They didn't hold the patent on wisdom. "But I still don't believe Clarence is any more capable of murder than Sandra," she insisted. Remember, I know these people, Sam."

"And I thought I was starting to know you." His tone was sour.

April couldn't think of a decent response. Nor could she explain why his disapproval should fill her with so much regret.

"Are you going to charge me with anything?" she asked miserably.

He stood and reached for the bag of Botox. "Not yet."

She should have felt relieved. Instead, her heart sank as he walked out of her office.

50

April listened to Sam's footsteps retreating down the hall. She wanted to call out to him, beg him not to go away. How had he done that to her – gotten so deeply under her skin that she felt more upset about disappointing him than she did about becoming a murder suspect?

Her phone rang and she stood and left her office to get away from it, not even caring where she was going. She stopped at the office where Mort had discovered the Botox and went in, closing the door behind her. She sat at the desk and let her eyes travel over the books and papers there. A neon-green Post-It, stuck to the corner of a manila envelope, caught her attention. Pulling the envelope closer, April read the note:

Kristin – Here's the article we discussed. S. H.

Stuart Hartman?

April hesitated for a moment, then opened the envelope's clasp. Given all the ways she'd already screwed up, peeking at Kristin's unsealed mail seemed like a pretty innocuous transgression. She pulled some papers out of the envelope – a journal article. *Group Psychotherapy for Trauma Survivors.*

Stuart must have given this to Kristin – but when? April tried to remember whether he'd been carrying anything when he came yesterday. His hands were empty when she pictured them – no attaché case, no envelope. Nor would Stuart have known of Kristin's interest in the topic until they spoke about her experience here, April realized. He could have given the article to Kristin later.

Or returned to deliver it.

Did Stuart plant the Botox vials – in order to frame Sandra? Deep in thought, April replaced the article inside the envelope and closed the clasp.

Maybe she'd do a little detective work of her own this evening.

Ψ

Sam walked straight to his car in the lot next door, without looking back. He'd had enough of Franklin for one day. He was sick of the place, sick of the case.

Sick of shrinks.

He started the engine and backed his car out of the parking space. Sam flashed his badge at the attendant, who waved him out of the lot, and turned right onto Vine Street.

He'd been so sure of his instincts about Clarence McKay – and maybe he was the killer. Sam made another right onto 15th Street, heading for Race. But he'd trusted his instincts about April Simon, too. Now Sam wondered if that made him a first-class sap.

She had steered him toward three possible suspects, he reminded himself, and maybe it wasn't fair to expect more than that. So why was he so pissed off that she hadn't told him about the research fraud?

Get real, he told himself.

Still, he couldn't block out the image of April reaching for that scarf, with every obvious intention of concealing it.

She's only human, he argued with himself. Hell, she might not even have realized the scarf could be evidence. Sam turned on Race Street.

Crap.

The truth, he admitted, was that he'd wanted to trust April Simon, still did. He needed something from her, and didn't want to think too much about what it was.

Shrinks. Maybe he really did need one, after all.

51

The Survivors' Group required April's full attention that afternoon, and she resolutely pushed all thoughts of murder, scarves and Botox out of her mind. Not that the group wasn't an attention grabber in its own right. The four women were snapping away at thick rubber bands encircling their wrists, practicing their first session of Self-Mutilation Lite.

Like some kinky string band concert, April reflected. The ladies were clearly digging it – giggling and comparing techniques – as they competed to see who could pull her rubber band out the furthest before releasing it for a stinging slap.

"I'm liking this!" Danielle worked the band around her plump wrist. "The only thing better would be putting the band around my uncle's thing and snapping the shit out of it."

She was rewarded by a chorus of laughter.

"Hey," Denise said, "I got something I want to talk about."

The rubber bands came to rest as the group gave her their attention.

"The other night, I was hanging out with my girlfriend, Charlene, and the guy she goes with?" Denise continued. "So, she goes to the bathroom? And her dickhead boyfriend starts trying to feel me up, right there, while she's in the next room!"

"Asshole," Danielle commented.

Kristin, the psych student, turned to Denise. "So what did you do?"

Denise sat up straighter and looked around at her audience. "Shoved his hand off me." She glowed with pride. "Stood up, told him if he ever messed with me again I'd tell Charlene and we'd both kick his ass!"

"All *right!*" Danielle crowed.

"What happened next, when Charlene came back?" April asked.

Denise shook her head, her large earrings jangling. "Nothing. Everyone acted like nothing happened."

"And that bothered you," April observed.

"Yeah, 'cause I don't know what's right. Should I say something to Charlene, or what?"

There was silence as the group pondered her question.

Angela frowned. "She might not believe you, if you told her."

"Right," Danielle agreed. "She might turn on you for badmouthing her guy."

"Well, see, that's what I was afraid of," Denise said. "He's cheated on her before, but she just ain't dealing with it."

"It's a tough call," April agreed. "You can't open someone's eyes when she wants to keep them closed. But the important thing is that you acted and set a limit with this guy."

"I did," Denise agreed, beaming. "And, you know? It felt good."

"It *is* a good feeling to stand up to someone who tries to hurt you," April said.

"No it isn't." Carlee's voice was almost a whisper, which made her words even more compelling. All eyes turned to her, and she looked at the floor.

"Carlee?" Kristin, who sat next to her, leaned slightly toward her.

A tear ran down Carlee's cheek.

Denise, sitting on Carlee's other side, placed a hand on her shoulder. "Come on, girl," she said, "you got to *talk* about it."

Carlee sat, silent tears streaming down her delicate face. Suddenly, she looked up, her features twisted in anguish. "I *stabbed* him!"

"You mean – Kit?" April asked softly.

Carlee nodded.

"Who's Kit?" Angela asked.

"I. Stabbed. My. *Brother!*" Carlee's voice rose with each word.

April gave her a few moments. This was a breakthrough.

"What happened?" She hoped Carlee would share what she'd kept buried for so long.

"I didn't mean to hurt him," Carlee gasped. "I loved him! When things were so crazy in my family, Kit was the only one who looked after me." She paused to accept a Kleenex from Kristin and wiped her eyes. "But then he started – doing things with me. First just fooling around, you know, tickling me and play wrestling. But then he would touch me –" She paused, taking a deep breath. "On my breasts, at first. Then – he would – he put his hand – " She motioned toward her abdomen. "Down my pants. And he got me to – " She shook her head, crying harder.

"To what?" April pressed her gently. Could Carlee push past the shame?

"To suck on him."

"How old were you?" April asked.

"The first time? Ten."

April cringed inside. So young. "And he was?"

"Fifteen." Carlee twisted the Kleenex in her hand. "I hated it. But I – I couldn't say no to him."

"Did you say anything to your parents?" April guessed the answer.

Carlee gave a sharp laugh. "Lot of good that would have done!" She drew a breath. "It went on for almost two years. It got so I didn't want to be alone in the house with him. But I didn't have that many friends I could go out with. That's when I started – going outside myself.

When he would do things to me, it was like I was watching and it wasn't happening to me."

"You dissociated," April said. They'd used the word before in this group.

Carlee shrugged. "I guess. But it wasn't enough, because I was getting more and more upset. I couldn't sleep at night. Had trouble in school. So then that one day, Kit followed me into the kitchen and came up behind me. He reached around me and started to unzip my pants. And I was watching myself again, but this time –" She swallowed, struggling with the words. "This time I watched myself take a knife from the rack on the counter, a small, sharp one, and the next thing I knew, his hand was bleeding. A lot. We were both really scared."

"What happened next?" April asked.

Carlee's gaze looked far away. "I'm not sure. I think I started screaming and Kit ran out of the room. I remember later, when Mom came home, she took him to the emergency room and he had to get some stitches. He told her some story about how he accidently cut himself. When it healed, he had a scar on that hand, his right hand. A crescent shaped scar." She sighed. "He didn't touch me again after that. He hardly talked to me anymore. It was like nothing had happened." She shook her head. "Except that I lost the one person I cared about. A year later he went away to college. I haven't seen or heard from him in years."

The group sat in silence.

"Do you know where he is?" Kristin asked.

"No. He went to school in upstate New York. The last time I saw him was when he came down for Mom's funeral. After she killed herself. He didn't come back again after that. Then I started having problems, and went into the hospital, and – I lost track." Carlee's gaze dropped to the floor.

"Carlee," April asked, "is this the first time you've told anyone about this?"

Carlee looked up at her. "Yes." She sounded surprised.

"How do you feel?"

Carlee looked around the group, as though registering their presence for the first time. The women smiled tentatively at her as she met their eyes. "I feel – okay." She drew a deep breath, slowly exhaled. "I feel okay."

Amen, April told herself. Maybe this was one Pacifil subject who would turn out all right.

52

April tried to keep busy at her desk while she ran down the clock, waiting for her staff to leave. It was a good chance to catch up on her paperwork – or would have been, if she could have concentrated. When her phone rang at four-thirty, she was glad for the distraction.

"Hi, it's me," Larissa Lewis greeted her. "It's Friday!" she announced cheerfully. "Wanna go for a drink?"

Great, April thought. The week she'd resolved to get sober, everybody was inviting her to go out drinking. Besides, she had another agenda for the evening.

"Thanks, but I can't tonight. I – ah – " She hesitated, trying to come up with an excuse. "I have to meet with someone."

"A date?" Larissa's radar was instantly engaged. "Who with?" Her voice dropped about a half-octave toward the sultry range. "You got something going on with that sexy detective?"

"Of course not!" April responded. "Why would you think that?" She realized she probably sounded defensive. "No, I – uh – promised a friend I'd talk to her niece about psychology graduate school. You know, one of those informational interviews." April was pleased with her impromptu alibi. It was sufficiently boring to deter further questions.

Sure enough, Larissa lost interest. "Oh, well, another time then." She giggled. "But if you don't want that detective, mind if I play with him?"

April caught her breath. "Has he asked you to?" she blurted out, before remembering she was trying to steer clear of the subject.

"Hah! I wish," Larissa said.

Now, April couldn't help herself. "He does seem like an interesting guy."

"Interesting?" Larissa echoed. "I said 'sexy.' How could a cop be interesting? What would you talk about – handcuffs? Guns?" She sniffed. "Maybe he'd make a good boy toy, April, but if you want a real relationship, you need to find someone who's on your professional level. Why don't you make a move on Chris Willis, already?"

April clenched her jaw, but not enough to stop her response. "Why do we all have to make such a big thing about graduate degrees?" she exploded. "What makes a professor or psychiatrist better than – than a businessman who builds an enterprise? Or a carpenter who builds a beautiful house? Or –?"

"A plumber who designs a better toilet," Larissa interjected. "Good luck with that! Anyway, you certainly sound ready to discuss the merits of grad school with your friend's niece. Have fun, girlfriend."

"Yeah," April mumbled. "You, too." She hung up, feeling an uncomfortable mix of embarrassment and annoyance. What had Sam said? It's not about climbing ladders?

She checked her watch. It was after five. Her staff usually cleared out pretty promptly on Fridays. She decided to stay put in her office and wait.

Ten minutes later, she heard the sound of a vacuum cleaner. She peered out of her office door. Bingo! There he was.

Stepping into the corridor, she approached the janitor. With his back turned to her, his industrial-size machine running and his ear pods in place, he probably couldn't have heard a marching band come up behind him.

He jumped when April tapped him lightly on the shoulder. Turning to face her, he yanked out his ear pods and turned off the vacuum cleaner.

"Damn, babe, you startled me!"

"That's Doctor babe. Can I ask you something, Joe?"

"Seems to me you just did that."

April rolled her eyes. "Last night, when you were cleaning, did anyone come in here?"

Joe shrugged. "Nobody comes around here at night."

A non-answer. She thought he looked uneasy, his gaze anywhere but meeting hers. "Please, Joe, try to remember. It's important."

"Look, I know better than to be lettin' strangers in here. 'Specially now that there's been a killing. I always lock up when I'm cleanin'. Go check the door, you don't believe me."

"I know how careful you are, Joe. You're almost like a security guard for us. That's why I need your help – because this is actually a security issue, in a way."

She paused for effect, looking around as if to make sure they were alone, then leaned closer to the janitor. "Did a tall, thin guy – say, in his fifties and wearing a grey suit – show up here last night?" When he still hesitated, she added: "Please, Joe. I know you didn't do anything wrong. But you're the only one who can help me with this."

He cleared his throat. "Matter of fact, yeah. Some professor, wantin' to drop off somethin' for Kristin. I thought it was okay to let him in, seein' he had a Franklin ID."

"Fine, Joe. This is a big help. Tell me, did he give you an envelope for Kristin, or did he go into her office himself?"

"He went himself."

"Did you happen to notice what he was doing in there?"

"Nah, I was busy cleanin'. He wasn't in there but a minute or two."

April nodded. "Thanks, Joe. And let's keep this between you and me, okay?"

"Hey, no problem, babe."

"That's Doctor babe. 'Night, Joe."

Nodding, he replaced his ear pods and restarted his noisy machine. April quickly collected her jacket and briefcase from her office. Stepping carefully around the vacuum cleaner cord, she walked down the corridor and out the door onto the darkening street.

"Dr. April?"

"Felipe!" The sight of him sent waves of adrenaline coursing through her. Fight or flight? She thought of Boris and stepped forward to face Felipe. "Do you have him? My cat?" she demanded. "Tell me!"

"What? No way!"

"You were there, weren't you? At my apartment. You wrote that message on my door, and somehow you got inside and took Boris."

"I didn't take no cat! I heard him inside, and then I wrote that stuff. But I never went in. I swear!"

"So you admit you wrote that threat on my door?"

He folded his arms and looked at the sidewalk. "Look, I've been so messed up, Dr. April, like you don't know. I – I waited for you tonight to ask you to please let me back into the program."

His distress was so apparent that she had to restrain an impulse to reach out and comfort him. "Why, Felipe?"

He stared at his feet, as though something were happening there. "That's where my friends are."

He looked like a lost boy. She reminded herself that she'd suspended him for dealing drugs. "I hope you'll be back with your friends soon, Felipe. But first you need to prove you're ready to be a friend."

He rolled his eyes. "Aww, c'mon!"

"Don't you see? Trying to sell drugs at Praxis is no act of friendship. People there are trying to get clean and sober." Including me, she reflected. "Go to Freedom House, start your own recovery and then we'll talk about you coming back."

"I don' like the staff at Freedom House! They boss people around." He shifted from one foot to another, twitchy.

"Those are the rules, Felipe."

"Shit!" He kicked the ground with his sneaker.

April turned to walk away, then stopped. "Felipe?" She turned back to face him. "Please tell me the truth. Did you really not take my cat?"

He glared at her. "Not yet."

She turned and walked quickly away.

53

All the way to the train station, April ruminated over her confrontation with Felipe. Had she been too hard on him? Or too easy? Addicts often lied and manipulated, yet she could see that Felipe was suffering and needed help.

He'd denied taking her cat. She wanted to believe him. But if Felipe hadn't taken Boris, then where was he? For the first time, it dawned on April how odd it was that Boris, rather than Natasha, had gone missing. He was bigger than his littermate, but a true fraidy-cat. Anytime someone unfamiliar came into the apartment, Natasha presented herself, front and center, while Boris hid under the bed. So why was he the one who'd disappeared?

April's thoughts returned to Felipe. All she'd accomplished was to antagonize him – a big mistake, she realized, since he knew where she lived. She considered changing the lock on her apartment door. But if Felipe hadn't been inside, what was the point? She couldn't make sense of it. And poor Boris was still missing.

She reached Suburban Station and boarded the train to Jenkintown. As she rode home, April replayed her interview with Joe, the janitor. Stuart could have planted the Botox vials last night. But why would he have tried to frame Sandra? It seemed farfetched to think that Stuart had killed Lowell Morgenstern in an effort to hold onto his status within the department. Did people commit murder over stuff like that? Over climbing ladders, as Sam had called it?

The thought of Sam made April's mouth go dry. Their encounter that morning still troubled her. Where was her allegiance in this mess? She'd automatically moved to circle the wagons around her colleagues, but now she questioned her reaction. The detective had a point – a man had been murdered, even if it was a man she hadn't liked. Didn't she have a responsibility to help him find the killer?

Or did her impulse to assist him spring from more personal, less high-minded motives?

Still deliberating, April pulled out her cellphone and found Sam's number. She composed a brief text, telling herself she wouldn't send it. What was the right thing to do? She pictured the anger and disappointment she'd seen on Sam's face, heard his words.

I thought I was starting to know you.

She hit Send.

Darkness had fallen by the time the train pulled into April's station. She trekked up the hill to her apartment building, bracing herself to face the absence of her missing cat.

Ed, the doorman, held the door open for her. "Evening, Doctress."

"Thanks, Ed. Any news about my cat? Any reactions to those flyers I posted?" If Felipe had told the truth, maybe there was still hope for Boris.

"Afraid not, Doctress. But did you hear about Mrs. Lipman?"

"No. Why, what happened?" April's elderly neighbor lived down the hall and sometimes cat-sat for Boris and Natasha.

"She's in the hospital." Ed told her. "Abington Memorial. Had a mild heart attack the other day."

April's eyes widened. "Oh, my God! Is she all right?"

"I hear she's doing better. Her daughter came in from Chicago last night. She said Mrs. L. is coming home tomorrow."

"That's good. Thanks for telling me, Ed." A thought occurred to April. "Do you know if her daughter is staying in Mrs. Lipman's apartment? I'd like to stop over."

"Yes, she is, Doctress."

April stopped at her apartment to feed Natasha and write a short note to leave on Mrs. Lipman's door, in case her daughter was still at the hospital. She headed down the hallway and rang her neighbor's bell. No footsteps or human voice responded. But April heard another sound. A faint meow inside the apartment.

Mrs. Lipman did not have a cat.

This time, April knocked. "Hello?"

Again, the meow – louder, more insistent. Familiar.

"Boris?" she cried. "Boris, is that you?"

54

"What did you say?" Sam looked up at his partner, sitting across the table from him in a South Street pizza joint.

"I asked whether you want another beer." Justin raised his own nearly empty glass.

Sam shook his head. "I'm good." He'd lapsed into thoughts of chasing Botox vials down blind alleys.

"Hello?" Justin interrupted Sam's ruminations again. "I said, do you have any suspects?"

Sam frowned. "Maybe too many. Seems like everyone hated this guy." He drained the last of his beer. "There's this one shrink the victim threatened to expose for research fraud."

"That's a solid motive," Justin observed.

"For sure," Sam agreed. "But how do I prove he spiked the nasal spray? Or that anyone did?" Sam shook his head in disgust. "This has cold case file stamped all over it."

"Hey, you'll figure it out. You always do." Justin drained the last of his beer. "Wanna catch a movie?"

Once again, his partner was trying to rescue him from morose thoughts. Before Sam could reply, his phone chirped. He pulled it from his jacket and read the text he'd just received.

FOUND SOMETHING YOU SHOULD KNOW. APRIL.

The corners of his mouth curved upwards. "Better pass on the movie," he said. "I need to follow up on this."

"Hot lead or a hot date?" Justin chuckled. "You're grinning like a cat with a mouse, partner."

Ψ

April reveled in the raucous sounds of two cats arguing. Far from welcoming the return of her litter-mate, Natasha yowled and hissed at Boris, who undoubtedly smelled of the unfamiliar territory of Mrs. Lipman's apartment. Boris himself appeared none the worse for his sojourn, especially after licking the sauce off his favorite Nine Lives beef entree.

Mrs. Lipman's daughter had arrived before April was forced to resort to breaking and entering. She'd effusively apologized for not calling about Boris right away – understandably, April assured her, with her mother in the hospital. Ecstatic at his return, April thanked her profusely and accepted a towel to swathe Boris, preventing another escape during his trip down the hall.

Now, as April savored the sight of her cats, a craving crept over her. A glass of wine – the perfect way to celebrate Boris's return. She'd spilled out the last of the Pinot Grigio yesterday, but could go buy another bottle.

Sure, do it, the voice of temptation whispered. She pulled a jacket from the coat closet and reached for her purse.

April froze at the door, reminding herself of her promise to do thirty days. How easy to come up with an excuse to break that vow. She knew addiction had a cunning, insidious voice, and now she'd heard it.

Not that she considered herself an addict. But she found it sobering (ha!) – and humbling – to learn how seductive the craving could be.

She thought of Felipe. He was an addict. What must he be feeling? No doubt he wrestled with his own powerful cravings, isolated and alone. He'd messed up, no question, but he was only human. April had accused him of stealing her cat, and knew now that he was innocent, as he'd claimed. There must be something more she could do for him than shunt him off to Freedom House.

She sure as hell wouldn't want to go there.

A ringtone sounded from April's purse and she pulled out her phone. Sam.

"Hey," she said. Natasha yowled.

"Hey, yourself," he replied. "What's going on there? Is someone strangling your cat?"

"No, Boris is back."

"Great, but the other one doesn't sound too happy about it."

"They'll work it out." April let her purse drop to the floor. "They're like an old married couple." She leaned back against the wall.

Sam chuckled. "Yeah, they sound like my parents. So how did you get him back?"

"He got out when I left for work the other day and a neighbor, who cat sits for me, took him to her apartment. Then she was hospitalized – she's okay now," April quickly added. "Anyway, her daughter was there and returned him this evening."

"So he's okay?"

"He's fine. They were feeding him solid white albacore – human-quality tuna."

"Lucky cat. Glad it worked out."

An awkward pause descended and April's mind filled it with ugly memories of their argument.

Sam broke the silence. "So, was that the – uh – information you wanted me to know?"

"Oh! No," she said. "I sent that text before I got him back." She took a breath, steeling herself. "It's about those Botox vials." April relayed the story of Stuart's presence in the residents' office the previous night. "I'm not sure what it means," she concluded. "But I thought you should know." After a moment, she added, "and not just so I can get myself off the hook."

"I appreciate it," he said. "But what made you decide to tell me? This seems like an amendment to the No Dirty Laundry policy."

"I know," she said. "I was wrong to think I owed my colleagues some kind of blind loyalty. It's not Mount Olympus over there. I'd like to help you find the killer."

When Sam replied, his voice was softer than usual. "That's excellent. In fact, you are. Welcome to the side of the angels."

She smiled, twisting a lock of her hair. "Is that where we are?" Her tone turned more serious. "Does this mean you no longer consider me a suspect?"

He chuckled. "Oh, but I do! I suspect you of being a stand-up person and a genuine sweetheart. I hope I'll get a chance to confirm that."

She smiled again.

"Go take care of your cats," he said. "Good night."

"Good night." April ended the call, glowing inside. Her craving for wine was gone.

Saturday, September 25

55

At an uncivilly early hour on Saturday morning, Sam leaned against the doorbell of a Society Hill condo. The detective wouldn't have minded dragging the occupant out of bed. The sound of slippers swishing on carpeting was followed by a man's voice.

"Marcy? What's the matter? Forget your key?"

As soon as Stuart Hartman opened the door, Sam thrust his gold detective shield at his face.

Hartman's mouth fell open. "What – what is it?"

"Detective Perone, Philadelphia PD." Sam pocketed his badge. "May I come in?"

Stuart held his position in the doorway. "Why?"

"To discuss the murder of your department chairman."

Hartman froze. "Here? Now? It's eight o'clock in the morning! Is this really necessary?"

"No," Sam replied mildly. "We can do it over at the police station, if you prefer."

Sighing, Stuart stepped back to allow Sam through the door. "I was making coffee. Would you like some?"

"Thanks."

As Hartman led him to the kitchen, Sam took the chance to look around the pricey apartment. He found the heavy Restoration Hardware-style furniture a bit much for the modest space, but Sam had never particularly gone in for the whole massive furniture bit.

Stuart motioned him to a stool at the granite table top. "How do you take your coffee, Detective – uh?"

"Perone. Milk, no sugar, thanks."

Stuart joined him at the table, bearing two steaming mugs. "So, what is it you want to know, Detective Perone?"

"To begin with, what you were doing in the residents' office at Praxis on Thursday night."

Stuart let out a bray of laughter. "You're busting me for dropping off a journal article for one of my students?"

"Why assume you're being busted?"

Stuart stopped laughing. "Look, what is this all about?"

"What else did you drop off in the office that night, Dr. Hartman?"

Stuart's eyes went bug-wide. "Whaat? Nothing!"

Sam pulled out a baggie, holding the folded red and gold scarf, from his jacket pocket. He removed the scarf and placed it on the table in front of Hartman.

"You know who this belongs to," he said – a statement, not a question.

Stuart shrugged. "Why would I?"

Reaching into his jacket pocket, Sam produced the Ziploc bag containing the Botox vials. He carefully positioned the bag on top of the scarf, and fixed his gaze on Hartman. "Because you wouldn't have taken the trouble to plant these in the scarf unless you knew whose it was."

"That's ridiculous!" Stuart's laugh rang hollow. "Where would I get Botox, anyway?"

Sam grinned. He had him.

Hartman froze, a deer in the headlights. He eyed Sam warily. "What, Detective?" he demanded. He pointed down at the Ziploc bag.

"It says Botox, right there on the labels. What's that supposed to prove?" Stuart glanced down and blanched. Sam had positioned the bagged vials so their labels faced the table, hidden from view.

"So, professor," the detective said, "you've got a choice here. Either I can arrest you for obstruction of justice, or – "

"Whoa! Whoa!" Stuart held up his hands. "I'm calling my lawyer right now."

"Fine. I'll read you your rights." Sam pulled out his Miranda card. Not that he needed it to jog his memory, but he found it always made a nice visual impact. The handcuffs would come next.

"Or what?" Stuart's face went ashen.

Sam raised his eyebrows in a silent question.

"You said you could arrest me, or – ?"

"Oh." Sam tapped the Miranda card on the table, holding Stuart's gaze. "Or you can tell me why you planted those vials. And I mean the complete, unabridged version, Dr. Hartman."

Stuart groaned, leaning forward his head sinking into his hands.

Sam waited. Arresting the psychologist for obstruction wouldn't necessarily lead to a homicide charge, he knew. What he was really seeking from Hartman was information.

Finally Stuart looked up, his face slack with resignation. "All right. I'll talk to you. But, please – can we leave my wife out of this? She went out for bagels. She'll be back any minute. Couldn't we get out of here? We could go across the street and talk in the park," he added hopefully.

"No, but my offer to take you to the station still stands," Sam replied. He sat back and casually sipped his coffee, before adding, "or you can tell me the truth and we can probably wrap this up before she gets back." Sam winked at Stuart. "Keeping a few secrets from the missus?"

Stuart grimaced. "A few."

"Let me guess," Sam said, "like the prospect of your career going into a tailspin because of Morgenstern's planned departmental changes?"

Stuart gaped at him. "How do you know about that?"

"I've been learning quite a bit this week about academic life," Sam said. "Not exactly the ivory tower it's cracked up to be, is it? Seems to me you had a pretty good motive to kill Morgenstern."

"I didn't, Detective, I swear!" Stuart's voice rose. "Give me a lie detector test, if you want."

"Then you must have planted that Botox to implicate someone else," Sam observed.

Stuart's lips tightened.

"What did you do with the contents of the empty vial?" Sam asked.

Stuart gulped. "I flushed it down the toilet."

"Why?"

"So it would look – you know – like it had been used."

Sam shook his head, eying the empty vial, its rubber stopper twisted open, the seal broken. He looked back at Hartman, almost pitying the man. How had he managed to complete a doctoral program and rise to a prominent academic position? Perhaps he believed you could mix Botox powder into water as if it were Kool-Aid. Then again, Sam acknowledged, he'd have thought the same thing himself until a few days ago.

"Look, Hartman." Sam's tone betrayed his impatience. "Talk to me now, or I'm arresting you. Take your choice."

Stuart looked over at the kitchen clock. He raised his hands to his head, fingers raking through his hair. Then his hands dropped to his sides, his shoulders sagging, as if Sam had dropped weights on them.

"Okay, I did put the stuff in Sandra Chang's scarf," he sighed. "I admit it."

"Why?"

Hartman's eyes skittered about like nervous hamsters. "I – I thought it might create some – confusion. You know, slow things down."

Sam stared, waiting him out.

"Look, I was just trying to help her out," Stuart said.

"Her?"

"Miranda." Stuart's gaze dropped to the table.

"Morgenstern's widow?"

"Yeah."

"Why would you be so concerned on her behalf?" Sam asked.

"Because – " Stuart looked fleetingly at Sam, then glanced away. "We're, involved."

"You mean, having an affair?"

"Please," Stuart begged, sneaking another glance at the clock, "my wife will be here any minute."

Sam folded his arms. "Then don't waste time. Tell me about it."

"It hasn't been going on that long." Stuart spoke rapidly now. "Only about six months. We met at a faculty function."

Sam listened in silence.

"Look, I care about her, Detective. Or I wouldn't have put myself in jeopardy like this." He wrung his hands. "In some ways, Miranda is a very vulnerable woman," he added.

About as vulnerable as a piranha, Sam thought skeptically. "So, did she murder him?"

Stuart squirmed.

"Did she tell you she murdered him?"

"No! Never," Stuart insisted.

"But you thought she did."

"No." A line of perspiration broke out across Stuart's forehead. "I don't know."

"You planted that Botox to throw suspicion onto Sandra Chang because you knew Miranda Morgenstern killed her husband." Sam leaned into him. "You knew she had access to Botox and to her husband's nasal spray."

Stuart shook his head frantically.

"What was her motive?" Sam persisted. "Simply to get out of an unhappy marriage? Or was she looking at a nice estate?" He leaned in still closer. "Were you in it together?"

"I swear, I had nothing to do with Lowell's death. Nothing!" Stuart whined. "And neither did Miranda. I thought – I was afraid she might look guilty. She was so upset on the phone, because Chad Klein wanted his Botox back, and the police were asking questions." Stuart took a breath. "I mean, it's like you said. She had reasons to kill him." His lip curled. "You cops always suspect the spouse in these situations, right?"

"Did Morgenstern leave a big estate?" Sam repeated.

"I guess so," Stuart admitted.

"And maybe you liked the idea of hooking up with a rich widow?"

Stuart's face reddened. "I told you, Detective, I care about Miranda. I didn't kill Morgenstern and I wasn't part of any plot to kill him. I was just trying to protect her." He sighed. "Obviously, in hindsight, it looks like a pretty dumb move."

"Certainly does," Sam agreed.

The sound of a key turning came from the front door.

56

April jogged to the rhythm of her breathing on a perfect morning in Valley Green. Dewdrops on the foliage sparkled in the sunlight. A tang of autumn crisped the air. The rushing of the creek and the clamor of birds accompanied her along the bike path, and she savored the sensations – her heartbeat, respiration, and the fresh sweat that slicked her body.
Sobriety felt good.

Her cellphone rang and she zipped open her fanny pack to retrieve it, as she slowed to a halt. She checked the display and headed for a nearby bench to take the call.

"Hi. It's me," her ex said.

"I know." She'd barely thought of Mark in days.

"What are you doing?" he asked.

"Taking a run in the park. It's beautiful out."

"Great." He paused. "Hey, I'm sorry I was such a jerk. I shouldn't have hung up on you Tuesday, and I shouldn't have given you a hard time about coming down there."

He was apologizing? That was different.

"So," he continued, "I'll come to Philly, if you want me to. I mean *I* want to, April. Tomorrow, okay?"

She didn't know whether to laugh or cry. Poor Mark. Too little, too late. "I can't," she told him. "I have to go to a funeral tomorrow. Remember, I told you about my department chairman?"

"Oh, right." Disappointment in his voice. "Why don't I come with you? We could do something together after the funeral."

April imagined walking into the service with Mark, her colleagues seeing them together. It felt wrong. She pictured who else might be there tomorrow. Chris Willis. Maybe even Sam Perone? A ripple of excitement, tinged with guilt, passed through her. Suddenly her boring life was becoming interesting.

"Thanks, Mark, but I think I'd better go by myself."

"How about next weekend?" he persisted.

Not long ago, this would have worked, April realized. But not now. "Mark, I don't think it's a good idea for us to start dating."

"Hey, I didn't ask you to get married again!" His laugh sounded uncomfortable. "I just wanted us to spend some time together."

"I know. But that would be going backwards. I need to move forward now."

He was silent. "So there's someone else?"

"No," she said, even as she thought fleetingly of the detective. "But I might be ready for that," she added, realizing it was true. "And it took a while to get here." Her voice grew stronger. "I think we should both move on." A relief to say it, to finally mean it.

"You're sure, April?" Mark sounded wistful. "You don't think we owe each other a second chance?"

She'd moved beyond the reach of guilt trips. "Thanks for giving me the chance to reconsider, Mark. But it's time to let go."

"So, I guess that's it, huh?"

"Guess so." A pang of nostalgia caught her off guard. "Let's not be enemies, okay? If there's anything I can do for you – "

"Sure. Same here. So, ah, take care, huh?"

"You, too, Mark."

"Bye."

April replaced the phone in her pack. She listened to the call of birds, felt her moist skin cooling in the morning breeze. Was this recovery? She liked the feeling.

57

Sam and Stuart turned and stared as the Hartman's apartment door opened. A petite, mousy woman, carrying a large brown paper bag, walked into the entryway. As she turned to drop her key on the side table, she looked across to the kitchen.

"Oh!" she said. "I didn't know we had company." She moved to put the paper bag on the side table, but appeared to change her mind and carried it to the kitchen.

Stuart jumped up and took the bag from her.

"The bagels are hot," she said, her eyes traveling from Stuart to Sam, her smile uncertain.

Sam stood and extended his hand. "I'm Sam Perone." They shook hands. "I'm with the police," he added, looking over at Stuart.

"The police!" she gasped. "What's happened?"

"I just wanted a few words with your husband," Sam said. "But we're finished, for now." He nodded at Stuart. "I'm sure he'll fill you in." Stuart's shoulders slumped.

"Nice meeting you, Mrs. Hartman." Sam smiled. "I'll be in touch," he told Stuart.

"Stuart? What's going on?" Marcy Hartman demanded as soon as Sam walked out of the apartment. "Why did that detective come here? And so early, on Saturday morning? What did he want?"

"Nothing much." Stuart opened the bag. "The bagels smell great. Why don't you take off your jacket and sit down?"

"Stuart!" Marcy's voice was shrill. "Tell me!"

Hartman closed the bag and turned to face his wife. "It's just a routine investigation. He's looking into Lowell Morgenstern's death. You know," he added, "interviewing the faculty, and all that."

"But – why?" She stepped into the kitchen and stood in front of Stuart.

"I really don't know." He patted her shoulder. "I'm sure it's nothing to be concerned about."

"But then why would he come here on a weekend like that?" Marcy's eyes went wide. "My God! Stuart, does he think you're a suspect or something?"

"Marcy, don't be ridiculous! I told you, there's nothing to worry about." He gripped her shoulders and steered her toward the closet. "Now, go put away your jacket and let's have breakfast."

His wife reluctantly went to hang up her coat.

Stuart exhaled. Now what? He'd dodged a bullet with his wife, but he'd managed to wade into a deep swamp, and the alligators would be closing in – Miranda, for one. He debated calling to warn her about what he'd told the detective, but couldn't summon the nerve. Anyway, the police were probably monitoring his calls. Not to mention how suspicious it would look to Marcy if he suddenly grabbed his cellphone and slipped out of the apartment right after a visit from a cop. No, he'd have to find an opportunity to take Miranda aside tomorrow, after the funeral service.

What a mess. Who the hell put that detective on his trail?

Ψ

"You again!" Miranda Morgenstern fumed, clearly displeased to open her door and find Sam Perone standing on her front deck. "Do you realize my husband's funeral is tomorrow?"

Sam gave her a look of mock surprise. "You want us to find your husband's killer, don't you, Mrs. Morgenstern?"

She rolled her eyes and let him in, leading him to the living room. The furnishings glowed in the soft morning light. Miranda sat on the sofa this time, motioning Sam to a seat on the opposite side of the cocktail table. Sam settled into a chair. He removed the bagged Botox vials and placed them on the table in front of Miranda.

"I believe these are yours."

Miranda glared at him, still indignant. "Where did you get that?" She leaned forward and peered at the vials. "And why is one of them empty?"

"Were they both full when you gave them to Stuart Hartman?" Sam asked.

Her expression became wary. "What's that supposed to mean?"

"Hartman told me all about your relationship," Sam replied. "I also know you gave him two vials of Botox powder the other day."

"So? What if I did?"

"Why did you?"

Miranda shrugged. "I don't know. He wanted them." Her eyes narrowed. "But what are you doing with them?"

Sam smiled. "It's kind of an interesting story."

"Detective Perone, I told you, my husband's funeral is tomorrow. I don't have time for stories."

"Do you know a woman named Sandra Chang?" He fired the question at her.

"No. Who is she?"

Sam pulled out the scarf and tossed it onto the table. "The owner of that. Your Botox vials were folded inside it and left in her desk"

"Then she killed Lowell?" Miranda pumped her fist. "Good work, Detective!"

"Thanks," he said. "But there's a couple of problems." He watched her forehead remain smooth as she raised her brows. "For one thing, Hartman admitted planting the Botox in her scarf."

She gaped at him.

"And, for another, how exactly did you figure out that Botox was the cause of your husband's death?"

Miranda sat bolt upright. "Shit!" She smashed a fist into one of the sofa cushions. "That idiot!"

"Uh-huh," Sam agreed. "So." He sat back in the chair. "Let's start at the beginning."

An hour later, when he left, Sam felt like spitting out the nails he pictured digging into the inside of his stomach. This damned case! The deeper he dug, the murkier things became. How could he pin down the killer?

He walked slowly to his car, mulling it over. Miranda's story jibed with Hartman's. She admitted giving him two full Botox vials on Wednesday, claiming she had no idea what he planned to do with them.

Her anger over the empty vial seemed convincing, leading Sam to believe it was Stuart's idea to flush the Botox powder.

Yet all Stuart had accomplished by that was to prove the contents of the empty vial couldn't have been used to spike Morgenstern's nasal spray. Sam now knew that saline had to be injected into a sealed vial to reconstitute the Botox powder. Stuart had broken the seal.

But when? Sam stopped in his tracks. Could Stuart have broken the seal after injecting saline into the vial?

He hurried the rest of the way to his car. Sam jumped into the driver's seat and pulled out the bagged Botox vials. He studied the empty one. A couple of grains of powder still clung to the inside. Unlikely anyone had injected saline into that vial and mixed its contents into solution.

Sam flung the Ziploc onto the passenger seat. Was Stuart Hartman really that stupid? Or that brilliant? He pounded the steering wheel before starting the engine.

Back to square one.

Sunday, October 3

58

It was a lovely day for a funeral.

Flanked by Larissa Lewis and Chris Willis, April concentrated on looking solemn as the family and other mourners completed their final rituals at Lowell Morgenstern's graveside. At least it was sunny and dry. Muddy, wet cemeteries were the pits. She wondered if she could discreetly slip away after the burial, or should put in an appearance at the Morgenstern residence to console the family and eat catered food. To her disappointment, Sam Perone hadn't turned up at the funeral, and she doubted he'd intrude on the gathering afterward.

Larissa's elbow poked April in the ribs. "See that?"

April looked over in the direction where Larissa's chin pointed. Standing back from the assembled group, Sandra Chang stood, weeping.

Chris Willis leaned in. "At least we know she's alive."

"Shhh!"

They resumed a respectful silence in response to the harsh whisper behind them.

April kept her gaze fixed on Sandra. Would she show up at the Morgensterns' house? Should she go talk with Sandra as soon as the service ended?

But April didn't get the chance. Clutching a handkerchief to her eyes, Sandra turned and hurried away. When the service ended minutes later, she was gone.

April followed the other mourners heading for their cars. Now what? Slip away? Or commit to the condolence visit? She glanced at her companions.

"You guys going to the house?"

Larissa shrugged. "Sure."

"For a while, anyway," Chris said.

"Okay." She resigned herself to the condolence call. "How about I follow you there?"

After a short drive from the cemetery, Larissa and Chris secured parking spaces across from the Morgenstern's colonial. April settled for a spot a little way down the street. She walked back up the block, admiring the large homes, widely spaced by lawns and neatly groomed shrubbery. She found the front door ajar, walked in and followed the sounds of conversation. At the central stairway, the action divided between the dining room, where people helped themselves from a long table laden with platters of cold cuts, bread and rolls, salads and condiments – not quite the lavish spread she'd anticipated – and the large living room, where guests chatted in groups. Her stomach rumbled at the sight of the food, so April started with the dining room. As she filled a plate with veggies and small scoops of tuna and egg salad, Larissa appeared at her elbow, carrying a plate of her own.

"I guess Sandra won't be coming to the house." Larissa reached for a roll.

"Did you expect her to?" April asked.

"I didn't even expect her to be at the service." As the crowd at the table pressed in on them, Larissa said: "C'mon, let's go to the living room."

"In a sec," April replied. "I want to get something to drink."

She was relieved to find the beverage selections all non-alcoholic, sparing her any temptations. She poured sparkling water into a plastic glass and added a twist of lime.

She worked her way to the living room, where Miranda Morgenstern stood talking with a tall, tanned man with a shaved head. He looked familiar, although April couldn't quite place him. Drawing closer, she studied Miranda with admiration. Her toned body hinted at sessions with a personal trainer and her medium-length, swept back hair gleamed with soft highlights. Well tended, April thought. She approved of Miranda's black and grey dress – soft and subtly fitted, combining the smartness of a day dress with the ease of a sweat suit. If she ever needed a coach on graceful aging, April thought Miranda would be a good choice.

And yet Lowell had cheated on her.

April wondered if Miranda knew. She herself had failed to pick up on Mark's infidelity until he'd confessed. She found it oddly comforting to realize that she and Miranda had been in the same leaky boat.

A thought struck her. Could Miranda have killed Lowell?

Curious, April edged closer to Miranda and her bald companion. She stood sideways to the couple, so as not to make her interest too obvious.

The man was speaking. "… Really sorry I acted like such an insensitive jerk. That detective totally freaked me out."

Detective? Did he mean Sam?

"So you only thought of covering your own butt, Chad?" Miranda's tone was caustic.

He winced. "Look, I hope you'll accept my apology, along with my condolences, Miranda. And keep those last two Botox vials. I should never have asked you to return them."

Botox? Chad? That must be Chad Klein, chair of the dermatology department, April realized.

"Hah!" Miranda sniffed. "A lot of good that does me now."

"I don't even have them anymore. That damned detective is holding them as evidence."

Startled, April whirled to face Miranda. Was she referring to the vials Sam took from Praxis? But if Stuart planted those, how did Miranda Morgenstern fit into the picture?

Suddenly aware of Miranda staring at her, April blushed. "I'm so sorry for your loss, Mrs. Morgenstern," she exclaimed. Horror dawning on her, she thought: Oh God, will she think I meant the Botox vials?

Miranda nodded coolly. "Thank you, Miss – uh?"

"Oh, it's April Simon. I was a colleague of your husband's." Her hands were full with her plate and plastic drinking glass, so April nodded, instead of offering a handshake. "Lowell was an extraordinary man," she added.

"Thank you." Miranda looked her over, her gaze traveling from head to toe. "April Simon," she repeated thoughtfully. Her eyes widened in recognition. "You're the one who found Lowell!"

April shifted, wishing she weren't holding a plate of food. "Ah, yes, I'm afraid that's true." Should she apologize or something? What was the etiquette for a situation like this?

Miranda continued to stare. She took a step closer to April.

"Miranda?" Chad Klein reached toward her.

April involuntarily took a step backwards. Her shoulder brushed a wall.

Miranda pushed her face close enough for April to smell her Chanel. "Exactly what was going on between you and my husband?" she demanded.

59

April recoiled from Miranda's accusing question. "My relationship with Lowell?" she repeated. "We were just colleagues! He hired me. That's all." Her eyes darted from side to side – searching for an escape from the crazed widow whose nose was now inches from April's face.

"Miranda!" Chad Klein kept his grip on her arm. He pulled her back just enough to give April breathing room. "Please!" He muttered into Miranda's ear. "You shouldn't upset yourself like that."

Miranda turned to face him.

April seized the opportunity and broke toward Miranda's left. Sensing April's motion, Miranda spun around and lurched toward her. As April twisted away from her, the plate of food balanced in her hand tilted, spilling tuna, egg salad, olives and more – most of it landing on Miranda's Manolo Blahnik-clad foot.

"Oh my God!" April cried out. "I'm so sorry!"

"Are you crazy?" Miranda snarled. Chad Klein clutched her elbow, restraining her.

"Please," April whispered, desperate to prevent a scene. "Let me get some paper towels and clean this up."

"No, I'll get it." Stuart Hartman materialized at Miranda's side. "Come on, Miranda. Let's go to the kitchen and you can show me where the paper towels are."

To April's relief and amazement, Miranda's wrath immediately shifted to Stuart. She glared at him, as if she'd forgotten all about April.

"Oh, thank you, Dr. Hartman," she said through clenched teeth. "Right this way." She spun on her heels and marched off.

Stuart trailed after her, like a man on the way to a firing squad.

April glanced over at Chad Klein. He stared back at her as if she'd sprouted suppurating lesions all over her body.

"Excuse me," she murmured, and took off. She wove her way through the crowded living room, intent on escape. She looked around for Larissa Lewis. A tap on her shoulder made her turn around.

Clarence McKay stood there. "Just a minute, April."

"Oh," she said. "Hello, Clarence."

He stared at her in silence.

Now what?

Finally, he spoke. "What did you tell that cop about me?"

"Huh?"

"Someone tipped him off that Lowell accused me of research fraud. I'm thinking it was you."

She gaped at him. "I didn't tell him any such thing!"

"Who else knew? You were standing right outside my office while he and I argued about it. Weren't you?"

"I admit I was there, but I didn't mean to overhear," she said. "I never said a word to Detective Perone." She'd had enough accusations for one funeral. "Or anybody else."

"Then who did?" Clarence demanded.

In the kitchen, Miranda ignored the mess on her shoe and pounced on Stuart. "What did you tell that detective?"

"He – he spoke to you?"

"He came here yesterday! He had my Botox, or somebody's, anyway." Her voice rose shrilly. "And one of the vials was empty! "

Stuart cleared his throat. "I, uh – " His guilty gaze was fixed on the bamboo floor.

"He asked me all these questions! I think he actually believes I killed Lowell. And he knew about us! What the hell did you tell him, Stuart?"

Stuart hunched his shoulders. "Nothing, really. Not much."

"What did you tell him about me?" she demanded.

"He was going to arrest me!"

"Arrest you? For what?"

"Miranda, I – "

"Stuart, what?"

"I only wanted to help you. You know, throw suspicion off you."

"Goddamnit, Stuart, tell me what you did!"

He rubbed his forehead. "I planted the Botox."

"What the fuck do you mean, you planted it?" She folded her arms across her chest.

"I – I put it with someone else's things, in her desk."

"You mean, in Sandra Chang's desk."

His mouth hung open. "How did you know that?"

"The detective told me. Who the hell is she?"

"Just a woman. Someone Lowell was, uh, friendly with."

"You idiot!" Miranda shouted. Raising a hand to her lips, she looked around to make sure no one else was within earshot. "You idiot," she repeated in a harsh whisper.

"Look, maybe it wasn't such a great move, all right?" Stuart conceded. "But I was frightened for you. For us." Using his scholarly lecture voice, he added, "They always suspect the spouse in these situations, you know."

"So you acted out of concern for my welfare," she sneered.

"Out of concern for both of us." He sighed. "Anyway, he didn't arrest me, and obviously he didn't arrest you, either. So – "

"Any more Diet Coke in here, Mom?"

They broke off abruptly, as Miranda's daughter walked into the kitchen.

"Right there in the fridge, dear." Both Miranda and Stuart fixed smiles onto their faces.

"Mom!" Miranda's daughter pointed at her shoe. "What's that gunk all over your Manolos?" She reached for the paper towels. "Here, let me clean that up."

Miranda rushed over to intercept her. "No, dear, I've got it. Go ahead and get your Diet Coke."

"But – "

Miranda opened the refrigerator door and waited until her daughter took out a can of soda. "I'll be out in a minute, sweetheart," she said. She kept her smile in place.

"So, Stuart." Miranda dropped the smile as soon as her daughter left. "Thanks to you, the police are now hovering around me." She stared icicles at him. "You and I need to cool it for a while. Not see each other.

I can't afford to arouse any further suspicions."

"But Miranda!" Stuart halted as a woman in a purple dress walked into the kitchen.

"Miranda, is there any more rye bread?"

"Sure, Joan." Miranda took the woman's arm. "Let's go grab the bread basket and refill it." They walked out of the kitchen before Stuart could say another word.

In the living room, April stared at Clarence McKay's retreating back. Who did tell the detective about the confrontation between Clarence and Lowell? Since she certainly hadn't, April had assumed Clarence himself must have admitted it. But if he didn't tell Sam, then…

Lost in her thoughts, she looked up to see Stuart Hartman glaring at her from across the room. Take a number, she thought, her stomach sinking.

Stuart stomped over to her, scowling. Inches from April's face – *she should sell real estate there!*—He pointed a finger at her.

"You! You're the one who put that detective onto me!"

April kept silent. This time, it was true.

"I also happen to know you're looking for a promotion." His voice dropped into a low, menacing tone. "And you're going to need my recommendation, aren't you?" He smirked. "Well, don't hold your breath!" He stalked off.

April's heart thumped in her chest. Beam me up, she wished. As if responding to her distress call, Chris Willis appeared.

"Where's Larissa?" she asked him.

"She left. She said you were busy talking to Miranda Morgenstern. Hey," he asked, "you okay? Want to go outside for some air?" He took her elbow. "C'mon, I'll walk you to your car."

She flashed him a look of gratitude. "Thanks, Chris. Yeah, let's go."

"No problem," he said. "Funerals can be so draining."

60

The fresh air cooled April's face as she and Chris stepped out the door onto the Morgensterns' front deck. The quiet street was a balm to her ears. She inhaled deeply, released the breath slowly.

"I wasn't sure I'd get out of there alive," she said. "My car's right over there."

They ambled in that direction.

"Pretty classy neighborhood," Chris observed. "Lowell did all right for himself. What do you think that house is worth?"

April shrugged. "Whatever the price, it's worth more to me to be out of there."

Chris stopped walking, reached over and clasped the nape of her neck. Rattled by the confrontations she'd just experienced, April nearly jumped away. As he massaged her tight muscles gently at first, then with more pressure – she relaxed and gave herself over to his touch. She sighed with relief as the knots in her shoulders eased.

"Mmm! Thank you, doctor!"

"My pleasure."

He released April's neck and draped his hand over her shoulder. They continued walking.

"You know," Chris said, "I overheard what Stuart said to you in there."

She stopped and turned to face him.

"Maybe it's none of my business, April, but do you think it's a good idea to get chummy with that detective?"

She stiffened, wriggling her shoulder free. "What made you think I was?"

Chris held up his hands, palms toward her. "Hey! No harm meant. But lots of people seem to be getting that impression."

Waste of a good massage. The muscles in April's neck and shoulders knotted up again. "Including you, apparently."

"Wait, I'm on your side, remember?"

There were sides, now? Before she could come up with a response, Chris continued.

"But I'll say this, April, the other evening after work, you and he seemed pretty friendly."

Did she even know who her friends were anymore? "He helped me when my cat went missing," she said. "That's all." The denial left a sour taste of guilt in her mouth.

Chris smiled and took her arm. "Glad to hear it." He steered her toward her car. "I'm not looking for competition."

He was flirting with her again. Only now April wasn't experiencing the usual frisson of excitement. Instead, she felt an undercurrent of mistrust she couldn't quite explain

They reached the Mini and April used her remote to open the door. She gave Chris a tight smile.

"Thanks again." As she started to get in the car, he pulled her toward him. He leaned down and kissed her lightly.

"Take care of yourself."

From the look of things, she'd better. "Bye, Chris." She got into her car.

April merged into the expressway traffic, driving on autopilot. She was feeling distinctly paranoid. Her colleagues considered her a confidential informant, and she'd lost their trust. That wouldn't do her career at Franklin any good. Confiding in Sam had cost her.

But she wasn't the one who told him about Clarence McKay.

She exited the expressway. Then who did tell Sam about Lowell's allegations and threats to Clarence? Who else would have known? Surely, Clarence wouldn't have told anyone. Who might Lowell have talked to? Sandra.

It made sense – Lowell crowing to his girlfriend about having the goods on Clarence. But she was sure Sandra respected Clarence. So why would she rat him out?

April turned onto Broad Street, heading toward Jenkintown. What if Sandra really believed Clarence killed him? A chill shuddered down April's spine. What if he had? She remembered the fury she'd seen on Clarence's face in the living room. Maybe he wasn't the teddy bear she'd thought he was. But was he really a killer?

She thought of Sandra again, remembered her weeping at the funeral home. Bereaved, pregnant and so vulnerable right now. Sam Perone was so very skillful at drawing people out.

Especially women. Had he played Sandra as cleverly as he'd played her?

61

PACIFIL SUBJECT: Brittany Jacobs

The most together of the four Pacifil research subjects wasn't so together tonight. Fact was, Brittany felt worse than she could remember ever feeling – which was saying a lot, given her personal history.

She couldn't say why, but she'd had an overwhelming sense of wrongness, since the death of her psychiatrist. Before Dr. Morgenstern started treating her, she used to cut herself when she felt this kind of despair, but she couldn't do that anymore. It wasn't an option – why? Her head was filled with fog.

So now, here she stood in her little brother's room, staring at Harvey, his pet rat. Harvey stared back at her from inside his cage, twitching his tiny pink nose. His fur was pure white and his beady, little rat eyes, red.

Rodents were disgusting.

She opened the cage. Harvey rushed forward and sniffed eagerly at her outstretched hand, probably expecting food. She picked him up. Completely tame, the rat offered no resistance.

She carried Harvey out of the room and down the hall to the bathroom. What an ugly, little snow-white, and red-eyed rat. She dropped him into the toilet and flushed. Harvey's tiny paws skittered against the porcelain, struggling for a grip, but the rushing water overpowered him. His mouth opened, water surging inside and muffling his squeal.

She giggled.

Brittany watched Harvey disappear, then flushed two more times, for good measure. She studied the empty toilet bowl for a few moments. Looking up, she turned and caught her reflection in the mirror over the sink. Haunted eyes stared back at her.

She moved over to the sink and regarded her reflection, watching her eyes fill with tears. When she couldn't bear the sight any longer, she pulled the mirror, opening the medicine cabinet.

She rifled through the contents, tossing bottles, brushes and other useless items into the sink. Finally, she pulled out three amber prescription medicine containers. Brittany studied the labels, and put two of the bottles back into the cabinet. She opened the third and spilled the contents into her open palm.

About twenty pills. Enough.

Monday, October 4

62

April sank into the chair at her desk, already exhausted at the start of the work week. Sleep had eluded her. She'd tossed about for hours on end, ruminating over who might be a killer and who would be the next to tear into her on sight. The only positive thing she could say about last night was that she'd kept sober. That much, at least, she could control.

She yawned and checked her voicemail. One message, already.

It wasn't good news. Calls from the psychiatric emergency service rarely are.

"April." The voice of Chris Willis played. "One of your patients was admitted last night."

Carlee? April called him back right away.

"Who was it?" she asked as soon as Chris picked up.

"A young woman, Brittany Jacobs."

"Brittany!" She'd been doing so well! "What happened?"

"Her father called 911 and the paramedics brought her to the ER. She got hold of his blood pressure pills and overdosed. The ER pumped her stomach and cleared her, medically. Then the on-duty psychiatrist evaluated her and admitted her to the involuntary psych unit."

So she hadn't even signed herself in. That sounded bad. "How is she?"

"On suicide watch."

"I don't understand. She was so positive about things. She planned to go back to college in January."

"Guess she got cold feet," Chris said.

"Maybe." April didn't believe it. "Will they let me see her if I come over around lunch time?"

"Probably."

"Thanks, Chris."

"Sure." He hesitated. "Hey, about yesterday…"

April had no stomach for rehashing all that. "No worries," she said. "You helped me out and I appreciate it."

She hung up, her thoughts turning back to Brittany. Another Pacifil subject in crisis. First Felipe dealing drugs, then Tyrell, and now this. They'd need to keep a close watch on Carlee Randall, the fourth subject. The only one still attending Praxis, April realized. Tension building in her jaws and forehead signaled a headache on the way, and the cause was no mystery. After her encounter yesterday with Clarence McKay, he was one of the last people April wanted to talk to this morning. But they had to discuss the Pacifil project and figure out what to do next.

She got up to go break the news to him, made her way down the corridor preparing herself for the confrontation. When April reached the Praxis reception area, to her surprise, Sandra Chang walked in.

"Sandra! Are you all right?" she exclaimed. "I saw you at the funeral yesterday, but you left before I could talk to you. We've all been worried about you," she added, observing how pale the resident appeared.

"I'm all right now," Sandra said. "But –" She looked around nervously, then took April by the elbow and pulled her aside. "I – I had a miscarriage," she murmured.

"Oh, Sandra! I'm sorry." April regarded her with concern.

"No." Sandra shook her head. "Don't be." Her eyes welled up. "God took care of me," she whispered. "It wasn't meant to be."

Sandra patted April's arm as if she were the one doing the consoling. "I have to go see my patients now, before I meet with the detective later."

April was stricken – the scarf! The Botox vials! What should she tell Sandra?

But Sandra didn't give her a chance. She smiled and swiped away a tear. "I just came down to tell you I'm okay," she said, and hurried off.

Ψ

Sam waited outside Chris Willis's office door. When he heard Chris wrapping up a telephone conversation, he knocked sharply.

"What?" The voice barked from inside.

Sam opened the door. "Your assistant said you were free."

Chris replaced his telephone receiver and scowled. "I'll give you ten minutes. I have a seminar with the residents at nine."

Sam pulled a chair over to the side of Willis's desk and sat.

Chris dropped a hand onto his desk with a loud thwack. "So, what do you want, Detective?"

"To talk about Morgenstern."

Chris swiveled his chair and gazed up at the ceiling. "Sorry, I don't have any insights to offer you."

Sam clenched his teeth. Cheeky son of a bitch. Willis had acted the same way the other night, when Sam interrupted his conversation with April.

"Who do you think killed him?"

"Huh!" Chris snorted. "Shouldn't I be asking you that, Detective?"

Sam leaned back, stretched and folded his hands behind his head. "But your perspective interests me, Doctor."

Willis straightened an already orderly stack of charts on his desk. "I'm too busy to give a forensic psychiatry lecture this morning," he said. "Figure it out for yourself."

Sam took his time retrieving a notebook and pen from his jacket pocket. "Okay," he said, "we'll come back to that." He turned the notebook to a fresh page, pausing to scan the contents of the ones he'd already written on.

Chris drummed his fingers on the desk top.

Finally, Sam looked up from his notebook. "How well did you know Morgenstern?"

Chris shrugged. "Not that well. I've only been here for eight months. Can't say I worked all that closely with him." He sniffed. "Managing a psychiatric emergency room doesn't leave me much time for shooting the breeze with colleagues."

Sam recalled that Morgenstern hadn't been at Franklin all that long either. He played a hunch. "Did you know him before you came here?" Chris opened his mouth, then snapped it shut. He eyed Sam coldly. "Why would I have?"

An interesting non-answer. "I thought, perhaps, as a relatively new chairman, Morgenstern might have recruited you, or something," Sam replied.

"He didn't. The position was advertised and I applied." Chris glanced at his watch.

"How did you two get along?"

"Famously."

Sam raised an eyebrow at the flippant retort.

"In a cordial professional manner, okay, Detective?"

Evidently that was the party line at Franklin. Nodding, Sam jotted a note on his pad – reminding himself to pick up a quart of milk on the way home.

"A lot of people here seemed to have issues with Morgenstern," he commented while he wrote.

"Hardly unusual in academic circles." Willis folded his arms across his chest.

Quite the cool customer, Sam thought. Still, he had no real justification to take up more of the man's time. Unless he counted his own curiosity about Willis's relationship with April. But that topic was off limits for an official interview.

Sam pocketed his notebook and stood.

"So that's it?" Willis asked.

"Yup. Except you still haven't told me who you think killed him," Sam added. "You strike me as a man who'd have a theory."

"Buttering me up, Perone?" Chris squinted at him. *"Cherchez la femme."*

"Huh?"

"Dr. Morgenstern liked the ladies." Chris winked. "I wouldn't be surprised if one of them got angry." He scooped up some papers from his desk and put them into a briefcase. "You know what they say about a woman scorned, right?"

"So you do have a theory. Any particular woman you have in mind?"

Chris snapped his briefcase closed. "Nope. Just a hunch."

"Okay, then. I won't keep you from your seminar." Sam turned to go.

"By the way, Detective, did you ever solve the case of the missing cat?"

Sam turned back and caught Willis smirking. "If you're talking about Dr. Simon, she did get her cat back, yes." He stifled his irritation at the man's sarcasm.

"But you're not taking credit for the solve?" Chris taunted him. "Why so modest, Detective? I got the sense that you were eager to – " he grinned, "get into the good graces of the lovely Dr. Simon."

Sam's face grew hot.

"But I wouldn't get my hopes up if I were you," Chris went on. "I doubt a woman like April goes out with cops."

Sam's hand curled into a fist at his side. He swallowed. Stay in control, don't let that shrink play head games with you.

"I see what you mean about those academic turf battles, Doc." Sam raised his chin and stared at Chris Willis. "Personally, I try to stay out of pissing contests." He bared his teeth in an unfriendly smile. "Have a nice day," he said, as he left.

63

April braced herself and knocked lightly on Clarence McKay's open office door.

Clarence looked up from his desk and frowned. "What is it?"

"Another Pacifil casualty." No point in beating around the bush.

Clarence pursed his lips and motioned her to a chair. "Who now?"

April gave him a quick summary of Brittany's overdose and hospitalization the previous evening.

"That's it for the Pacifil trial," he announced.

"I still don't understand it," April said. "They were doing well – especially Brittany."

Clarence sniffed. "They certainly aren't now. What about Carlee? Any signs of trouble with her?"

"No, but we'll keep close tabs on her," April said. "I'm afraid she's the most vulnerable of the four. She's begun to open up about her sexual abuse history." April's eyes widened as a thought struck her. "Doesn't it seem strange that three out of the four subjects started unraveling right after Lowell's death?"

"No." His tone was brusque. "Why wouldn't their psychiatrist's sudden death be stressful for them?"

"But these patients are always stressed out," April protested. "Felipe abuses drugs, Carlee and Tyrell have histories of self injury – "

"Exactly my point. They all lack coping skills. Now, I really must _"

"But they were coping better on the Pacifil," April interrupted.

He shrugged. "Only as long as things were on an even keel."

April bit back another rebuttal. Was she way off base in sensing a pattern here, or was Clarence simply determined to give her a hard time? She felt certain there was something going on that they were missing.

"Clarence," she ventured, "you were going to review all of Lowell's notes."

"And I did."

"Did you find anything at all that seemed, I don't know, unusual? Confusing?"

"Not at all." He picked up the document from a pile on his desk. "You've read it."

April nodded.

"I also checked some handwritten notes Lowell left in the project file."

She sat up. "I never saw those."

Clarence reached for a briefcase next to his desk. "Not much to them." He rifled through the bag, pulled out a folder and looked through its contents. "Here, see for yourself." He tossed a stack of handwritten pages from a yellow legal pad onto the desk in front of her.

April gathered up the scattered sheets. At least he might have passed them instead of throwing them at her. The notes were in Morgenstern's bold handwriting and the familiar blue ink of his fountain pen. She scanned through the pages. Nothing striking there, only his initial ideas for the research project. When she turned another page, an underlined sentence caught her eye:

"Treatment compliance must be strongly suggested."

A rather innocuous statement, she thought. Why had it been underlined? She looked up at Clarence, who was already studying his appointment book.

"What do you think this means: 'Treatment compliance must be strongly suggested'?"

Clarence snapped the book closed, clearly losing patience. "I suppose he wanted to make sure they'd show up for med visits, maybe for their Praxis schedules. Borderlines can be pretty inconsistent."

Like she didn't know that. "But it's the only part he underlined like this."

"Evidently he thought it was important. So, if we're finished…"

She ignored the prompt, still puzzling over Lowell's notation. "I don't remember anything in the proposal about how he planned to address this compliance issue. Do you?"

Clarence waved dismissively toward the printed document on his desk. "No, there's nothing."

"But doesn't that seem strange?" April persisted. "I mean, for Lowell to underline this point about compliance in his notes, then not even mention it in the proposal?"

Clarence scowled. "April, what are you getting at?"

"I don't know, Clarence." She frowned. "He wrote that compliance must be 'strongly suggested'."

"So?"

"Wouldn't you say 'suggested' is a pretty weak word, especially for Lowell? If he thought something was important, he'd have said 'required,' or 'mandated,' or –"

"Dammit, April! Get to the point!"

A thought hovered at the edge of her awareness, just out of reach, tantalizing. She took a breath, tried to quiet her mind and allow the idea to float into consciousness.

And suddenly, there it was. Her eyes opened wide. "Could 'suggested' mean hypnosis?" she whispered.

"What?" Clarence demanded. "You think he was talking about giving them some kind of hypnotic suggestion about treatment compliance? That's crazy!"

"But it's possible, isn't it?" she insisted, the notion becoming more plausible as she considered it. "Wasn't Lowell certified in hypnosis?"

"Yes, but there was nothing about that in the research proposal. No consent forms for hypnotherapy. If Lowell was inducing trance states in these subjects, it would have been highly unethical, and – "

Clarence fell silent and they stared at each other. The subject of professional ethics had put them on thin ice.

"But he still might have done it," April said.

Clarence sighed. Silence descended again. Finally, he said, "I guess none of us are immune to bad judgment."

Lines in his face suddenly made him appear years older. April resisted an impulse to reach across the desk and touch his hand.

He cleared his throat. "Borderline patients live on the verge of fantasy, as it is." His tone was professorial. "If Lowell planted some sort of post-hypnotic suggestion that they must continue to take the meds, or keep their appointments – "

"Or come to Praxis." April felt a jolt of excitement. "Suppose he did, Clarence. Think of what might happen when they couldn't comply because their psychiatrist died."

Clarence stroked his white beard. "If his suggestion wasn't specific, I suppose each patient might express distress in his or her own way."

"Like a suicide attempt?" April's voice rose. "Drug abuse? Even holding a therapy group hostage at knifepoint?"

"Maybe," he conceded. "We don't know what kind of suggestions Lowell might have planted."

"Clarence, are you trained in hypnosis?" April asked.

"No." His eyes narrowed. "Are you?"

"Actually, yes. I had a course in grad school and some supervision in hypnosis during my internship," she said. "If Lowell did give them a post-hypnotic suggestion, maybe I can undo it."

"What?"

"He probably created amnesia for the suggestion," April went on, too charged up to heed the edge in Clarence's curt response, "to make it more powerful. If I could remove the amnesia and get one of the subjects to disclose what the suggestion was, I bet I could reverse it."

"Out of the question!" Clarence smacked the desk.

"But – "

"It's too risky. A little training in graduate school doesn't make you an expert in hypnosis, April. Besides, you have no real evidence to support this whole crackpot theory."

"I disagree!"

"And even if you did, this is hardly the time to engage in dangerous experiments with unstable patients."

"Why not?" She stared at him, baffled.

"Because Michael Giametti, the new Ph.D. director, is coming here tomorrow."

"He is? But –"

"There's been more than enough drama at Franklin in the past week without you stirring up trouble," Clarence said. "We need Giametti here more than ever, and you're not going to mess up his visit with – with your half-baked voodoo!" He stood. "I forbid you to attempt any hypnosis with those patients. Understood?"

She rose from her chair, white-faced with fury. "I understand, Dr. McKay."

She turned and stalked out of his office. What she understood was that he wasn't the man she'd looked up to. She closed the door behind her, not as hard as she wanted to.

He wasn't going to stop her from helping those patients.

64

Promptly at noon, April rang the bell outside the locked door of the involuntary inpatient unit.

"Yes?" A scratchy voice came through the intercom.

"It's Dr. Simon, from Praxis. I'm here to see one of my patients."

"Which one?"

"Brittany." April knew better than to use a last name and violate the privacy regulations. The bleat of a buzzer told her the door was unlocked. She entered the unit and showed her Franklin ID to the attendant at the reception desk.

At least a coded password and secret handshake weren't required.

"She's in her room," the attendant said. "But don't stay too long. Lunch will be served in about twenty minutes." She directed April to Brittany's room.

April headed past the TV room, where a game show was blasting at top volume. That in itself could cause mental illness, she reflected. Still, the unit wasn't bad, as such facilities went. At least the furniture was relatively new and the paint wasn't peeling off the walls. Thank God they no longer allowed smoking in the hospital. The ban might be hard on some of the patients, but at least the air smelled of nothing worse than a faint tinge of body odor.

She continued down the corridor, nodding to a vacant-eyed woman who shuffled past her in slippers. The patient ignored her greeting, but smiled into space, either at a private joke or a remark from a voice only she could hear.

April found Brittany in her room. Alone, fortunately. The young woman looked pale and thin. She sat, rocking, in a chair – not a rocking chair.

"Brittany?"

Large blue eyes turned in response to April's voice. They welled with tears. "Dr. April! It's good to see you." A choked sob broke from her throat and she covered her face with her hands. "What am I going to do?" she wailed.

April rushed over and knelt beside the chair. "You're going to let me help you," she murmured.

Brittany stared down at her face. "How?"

Quickly, April explained what she intended to do. Ideally, she should have brought a consent form for Brittany to sign. But she was already breaking plenty of rules.

"Okay, Brittany?" she asked when she finished her explanation.

The pale young woman nodded.

"Good." April took a deep breath to steady herself. She didn't want to rush this, but there was no guarantee of privacy on a locked psychiatric unit. Brittany's room, like all others, had no door to close. Anyone could come by and catch her in the act of hypnotizing a patient – a suicidal one, at that. And if Clarence McKay discovered she'd violated his orders – she didn't even want to think about the consequences.

April pulled a silver pen from her handbag. "All right, Brittany. I want you to sit back and rest comfortably. Concentrate on your breathing and feel it become slow and deep. Notice how your muscles begin to relax and grow heavy – heavier." April watched Brittany's chest rise and fall with slow, regular breaths. She held up the pen.

"Now, look at the pen, Brittany. Your eyes follow it as I move it, up and down, side to side."

Exposed as she felt hypnotizing Brittany here, April believed it was the safest choice. On an inpatient unit, Brittany could be monitored and treated in the event of an adverse reaction. Anyway, waiting wasn't an option. She clearly needed relief from the inner demons driving her.

April watched her eyes tracking the pen. "Now your eyelids are growing heavy – so heavy that you want to close them."

She did.

April's eyes darted quickly to the doorway. No sign of any intruder. "You are resting comfortably," she said to Brittany, "and will hear and respond only to the sound of my voice. Do you understand? Raise your right index finger, if you do."

Brittany raised her finger.

April inhaled, willing her own body to relax as she breathed out. Time for the next step. "Brittany, I want you to picture an elevator – your own private elevator. It will take you down to your secret safe place." She paused, observing Brittany's calm face and even breathing. "Now the elevator doors are opening and you step in. The doors close behind you and it's very quiet." April kept her voice low and soothing.

"Now the elevator begins descending. With each floor, you grow more relaxed. When you reach the bottom floor, you will be completely safe and at peace." April took her down, floor by floor, to the bottom level. "And now, the elevator doors open and you're at your secret place, safe and at peace," she concluded.

A face appeared in the doorway – a skinny young man, with bad skin. He looked in, and April's spirits sank. Please, she thought, go away. Rather than risk engaging him, she looked away from his silent gaze. After a few moments, which felt like an hour, he walked off.

His brief visit impressed on April the need to create some back-up, in case of a more serious disturbance. Focusing back on Brittany, she instructed her: "If we're interrupted at any time, I want you to return to your safe place and wait for me there. Understand?"

Brittany raised and lowered her finger.

"Good. Now you're taking the elevator back up one floor. When the doors open, you will be in a session with Dr. Morgenstern, in his office. If you become too uncomfortable there, you can go back down to your safe place." April took another deep breath, wishing for a safe place of her own. "Now, the doors open and you are in Dr. Morgenstern's office, having a session with him. Raise your finger if you're there, Brittany."

Brittany raised her index finger again.

"Good. Even though you are still deeply asleep, you can talk now, and I want you to describe what is happening."

Brittany's voice was calm and clear. "I'm sitting back in the big reclining chair. I hear the clock ticking. It's so loud, but I can hear Dr. Morgenstern's voice at the same time."

"And what is he saying?"

"That I'm growing more and more relaxed. My arms and legs are getting heavy. When I try to raise my arm, I can't."

So Morgenstern had used hypnosis! April kept the excitement out of her voice as she continued. "Yes, that's right. And then, after you're very, very relaxed, does Dr. Morgenstern give you some instructions?"

She frowned for a moment, then brightened. "I must take the medication exactly as he prescribes it."

"The Pacifil?"

"Yes."

"What else does he tell you, Brittany?"

"To keep coming to Praxis."

This was the treatment compliance suggestion she had expected. But April was sure there was more. "And what else?"

Brittany screwed up her face. "I have to – "

"Yes?"

She relaxed again. "I have to see him every two weeks, and never miss an appointment."

April contained her impatience. "Or what will happen, Brittany?"

Her voice rose. "I have to! He says so."

The sound of footsteps caused April to look up as someone appeared in the doorway. She wore an ID tag – a staff member.

"Everything all right in here?"

"Fine!" April smiled. "We're having a nice talk."

"Lunch in ten." The woman left.

April looked at Brittany, who appeared calmer now. "Are you back in your safe place?"

Again, the raised finger.

Good to know the default plan worked. But what to do now? April didn't want to risk traumatizing Brittany any further, but she was sure the girl's agitation was significant. Her intuition told her that Morgenstern had planted a deeper compulsion and she wanted to find and undo it. Which posed the greater threat to Brittany? To stop now, or continue?

April made her choice.

"All right, Brittany. Now you are returning to your session with Dr. Morgenstern. The elevator takes you up. You are calm and relaxed. You can remember everything Dr. Morgenstern tells you. Is there something else he instructs you to do?"

"Yes." A tear trickled from the corner of Brittany's closed eye.

"It's all right," April told her. "You're safe. Tell me what he says."

Brittany's voice was childlike. "He says – he says I should never hurt myself again." More tears.

"And does he tell you to do anything else?"

"Do I have to say?" she whimpered.

"Yes, Brittany," April said softly. "Tell me now."

The young woman's breathing grew rapid and shallow. "Please? I don't want to!" Her voice was high with fear.

"I know you're afraid. Tell me and you'll feel better, Brittany."

"He says – he tells me I should hurt an animal instead."

April choked back a gasp. "Instead of hurting yourself?"

"Yes." Brittany let out a hoarse sob. "Whenever I feel like cutting or hurting myself, he said I should do it to – I should use an animal."

My God! April shuddered with a sudden chill. No wonder Tyrell killed that dog! She remembered Felipe's threat to her cats. She swallowed.

"Tell me, Brittany, did you follow his instructions? Did you hurt an animal?"

"I didn't mean to!" she wailed. "I couldn't help it!"

"No, you couldn't," April said. The poor girl! "What did you do?"

"I drowned him!"

April wiped her sweaty palms against her pants. She wasn't sure she wanted to hear the rest. But they had to get through this if Brittany was going to be free of Morgenstern's suggestion.

"Tell me exactly what you did," she urged gently.

Tears streamed from Brittany's closed eyes. "I killed Harvey, my brother's pet rat. I flushed him down the toilet last night."

April let out a breath. "Was that when you took the pills? After you drowned Harvey?"

Brittany nodded. "I was supposed to feel better!" she sobbed. "But I didn't. My brother – " Grief choked her voice. "My brother loved Harvey! Dr. April, how could I do something so bad and hurtful?"

"It wasn't your fault, Brittany. It wasn't your idea. When you feel better, you can get your brother a new pet."

"Can I?" Brittany's face brightened.

"Yes," April said. "You're going back down to your safe place now. And when you get there, you'll never have to hurt any animals again."

Brittany smiled. "Good."

"Dr. Simon!" April jerked her head up to see Clarence McKay glaring at her from the doorway.

"What do you think you're doing?" he demanded.

"Brittany," she whispered. "You know what to do?"

She raised her finger.

65

"But you saw it, Clarence! You heard her!" April protested.

"I can't say what I heard, April. What I do know is that you deliberately defied my order not to hypnotize any Pacifil subjects. That's insubordination, and I won't stand for it!"

They stood, squared off across the desk from each other, in McKay's office. He'd sent April back to Praxis after catching her red-handed with Brittany, but ordered her to report to him at the end of the day.

Now his face was beet red with fury.

"What you did was completely unethical!" he thundered. "Do you realize that?"

She held up her hands, palms out, in a placating gesture. "I know I went behind your back. Believe me, I didn't want to do it that way, but she'd already been hypnotized. Lowell gave her the suggestion to kill animals, Clarence! He probably gave all of them that suggestion. And they've been doing it! For all we know, they could escalate to killing people. We can't leave them that way. How is that ethical? For God's sake, let me go back and make sure Brittany's suggestion has been reversed before – "

He interrupted her. "For all I know, you gave Brittany that suggestion and I caught you in the act."

April recoiled as if he'd punched her in the gut. "Clarence! You can't mean that. You know me!"

He shook his head, curling his lip in disdain. "I thought I did. Now I see how untrustworthy and unprofessional you really are." Before she could respond, he continued. "As of right now, I am placing you on probation.

If you try any further hypnosis on those research subjects, or on anyone – or even commit one more act of insubordinate or unprofessional behavior…" He paused, either to choose his ultimatum, or for dramatic effect. "I will terminate your employment at Franklin," he concluded. "Is that understood?"

Her hands trembled, but April's voice remained steady. "I understood you, Dr. McKay. And I'm going to find out what steps I can take to file a grievance."

He slammed a hand down on his desk. "Damnit! If you make any more trouble around here, Dr. Simon, I will report you to the state psychology licensing board. Now get out of my office!"

She rushed out.

Wishing she were invisible, April sped down the hall, eyes lowered to avoid meeting anyone's gaze. She made it to the elevator without an encounter. She pressed the "down" button, which struck her as particularly apt.

Alone in the elevator, she prayed she could make it to her office without having to face anyone. She was too angry and mortified. If she didn't have to say a word to anybody, maybe she could pretend the whole thing wasn't real.

With no husband to support her anymore, April couldn't afford to lose her job. If Clarence made good on his threat to report her to the licensure board, he could derail her career as a psychologist. An ethical violation didn't have to be true to cause professional and financial damages. A board inquiry could drag on indefinitely, without affording her the due process of a court of law. Clarence's outlandish accusations could torpedo her.

The elevator opened on the ground floor. A pang of remorse hit her. Despite all her anxiety over her own situation, April realized that the other three Pacifil subjects had even more at stake. They were ticking bombs. If their distress became too great, their compulsion to hurt animals could transfer to people. She had to find a way to help them, no matter how great the personal risks might be.

To April's surprise, Cynthia was waiting at the reception desk when she entered Praxis. It was well past the time her secretary normally left for the day and she looked none too pleased.

"Finally!" Cynthia scooped up her purse. "Another two minutes and I was going to split and leave him in your office."

"Him?"

Cynthia was already heading for the door. "That detective. He's been waiting for you."

"But why…?"

"Better ask him that." The door closed behind her.

April approached her office, her heart pounding. Sam Perone was the last person she wanted to see.

Yet he was the only one she wanted to see.

Sam stood as she entered her office. "What's wrong?" he asked.

She took a step toward him and froze. How could she even begin to answer? "I hate this place!" she blurted out.

Without saying a word, Sam scooped her into his arms. April's closed around him instinctively, and they held each other. Like Brittany, she'd taken the elevator all the way down to her secret, safe place.

Later, April would remember the way he'd stroked her hair, the feel of his lips pressed to her temple, the warmth of his solid body against hers, and his scent – an intoxicating mix of spice and male sweat.

The sound of Joe's vacuum cleaner coming from the hallway made her stiffen. Sam released her slowly, reluctant to let go. Cupping her chin, he gently raised her face so that they locked eyes. He kissed her once, and she wanted more.

"Bad place, bad time." His brown eyes were soft as he regarded her. "But I'm here if you need me."

She smiled, amazed she could, after all that had happened that day.

"I have to go," Sam said. "The captain is waiting for me to brief him."

"But why did you come?"

"Oh, that." He hesitated. "I met with Sandra Chang today."

April eyes opened wide.

"I just wanted to tell you, I think you were right. I don't believe she had anything to do with Morgenstern's death."

She was astonished. He'd confided something to her about his case. "But, why…?"

His lips grazed her forehead. "I didn't want you worrying about her, or about that business with the scarf."

His concern touched her. She was tempted to confide in him about Morgenstern's hypnosis experiment, her struggle to help the Pacifil subjects. But he already had so much to deal with. Why burden him with that?

Before she could decide, Sam spoke. "But, April, remember." He looked at her intently. "There's still a killer out there. Please, be careful."

Too late for that, she thought. "I will," she said.

He left.

April listened to his footsteps going down the corridor. They were still strangers, she reminded herself. They'd known each other less than a week. Intense as it felt, the current flowing between them was probably just a pseudo-intimacy – a product of infatuation and wishful thinking.

Still, it might help her make it through the night.

66

The Captain hadn't exactly been pleased with Sam's report. The Inspector was breathing down his neck about the Franklin case, and the Mayor was breathing down the Inspector's neck, so the finer points of Botox poisoning were not particularly relevant.

Solving the frigging case – and quickly – that was relevant.

Sam had assured the Captain he had things in hand. Now, driving home from the meeting, he wished he actually felt that confident. He was going to have to lean harder on his suspects. He mentally ticked them off.

Clarence McKay, with a volatile temper and Morgenstern threatening to expose his research fraud. Stuart Hartman, his career also endangered by Morgenstern and in cahoots with his widow. The widow herself. The two of them together struck Sam as prime suspects. Maybe he could pit them against each other.

He'd already ruled out Sandra Chang, even if she was a jilted mistress. She'd been so utterly transparent with him, confiding about her pregnancy and miscarriage. Unless she was a world-class actress, there was no way she was a murderer. Chris Willis? No obvious motive for him, but Sam had a funny feeling about the guy. Although maybe that was because he was such an obnoxious asshole. Still, Sam had learned to trust his gut – trust, but verify, as the saying went.

And what about April Simon?

Did she still belong on the list? She'd been in Morgenstern's office with the body. That proved nothing though, because he'd most likely died before she got there. She'd been perfectly situated to frame Sandra Chang, but then tried to protect her.

And how would April benefit from Morgenstern's death? Unless she, too, was a spurned lover seeking revenge.

Sam didn't want to think of her that way. Right now, all he wanted to think about was the way she'd felt in his arms. And he wanted to trust that, too. Part of him felt lighter, hopeful for the first time in three years. Yet another part pulled him down like a lead weight tied to his heart.

It wasn't only that he couldn't entirely rule her out as a suspect. Shame was at the root of his despair. He'd told April he'd be there if she needed him, but he hadn't been there for Toni. How could April possibly care for him if she knew how he'd failed his wife?

Ψ

It was already dark out on the street and Felipe Diaz was crawling out of his skin. He needed something, man. Even a little pot to take the edge off – that would do the trick.

If he had any *dinero.*

Carlee Randall was a righteous *amiga* for letting him crash at her place, no question. Still, Felipe wished she wasn't so uptight, especially about weed. Shit, you'd think someone as messed up as Carlee would want to get high, right?

He shivered, and buttoned his jacket. He'd better get back to her apartment before he froze. It was time to get more persuasive with Carlee. She had money, he'd looked in her purse. More important, she still went to Praxis, where Felipe knew some folks who weren't such solid twelve-steppers that they wouldn't supply him.

Carlee had better come through for him. He'd go to her place right now and explain things to her.

Tuesday, October 5

67

April rooted through her desk drawer for the container of acetomenophen. She had two groups to lead this morning. Not to mention that Mike Giametti, the new psychology program director, was coming to Franklin today. She'd have to be on her toes. She shook out a couple of tablets and washed them down with her coffee. What good was being sober if her life felt like a killer hangover?

"Dr. April?" Carlee Randall stood at the office door, her face pale and drawn. Trouble, April thought. "Come in, Carlee."

The young woman edged into the office and stood beside April's desk, her eyes filled with pain.

"What's wrong?" What had Morgenstern's suggestion driven her to do?

"I shouldn't have told about Kit the other day." Carlee picked at a hangnail as if her salvation depended on it.

Not what April had expected. "Why not, Carlee?"

"I – it was wrong, that's all."

"What Kit did to you was wrong. Talking about it in group wasn't. It's part of healing."

"Then why do I feel so bad today?" Carlee moaned. "Why did I have nightmares again last night?"

You and me both, April thought, but Carlee with even more reason. "Because the session in group stirred up some powerful emotions. Tell me, what was your nightmare about?"

Carlee cringed. "I was stabbing Kit – again and again. And he wouldn't stop bleeding." She shuddered. "Don't you see? It proves what I did was evil." She covered her face with her hands.

"Carlee? Can you look at me for a moment?"

Reluctantly, the girl lowered her hands and met April's gaze.

"You took an important step in group and it triggered feelings you've kept locked up for a long time. I'm not surprised you had nightmares. People often react that way when they deal with traumatic memories. You feel worse, but you're getting better."

Carlee considered this in silence, but stroked, rather than picked at her nail. "Maybe."

"Try to accept your feelings," April encouraged her. "Let them pass through you, without allowing them to frighten you. Imagine them as clouds blowing across the sky."

Carlee's face relaxed. "Okay." She hesitated. "Can I ask you something else?"

"What's that?"

"It's about Felipe."

April's eyebrows shot up. "What about him?" What awful thing might he have done?

"I – I was just wondering when you'd let him back in the program."

Her question caught April off guard. "Are you in touch with Felipe?" She wouldn't have expected Carlee to be friends with a drug dealer. Could the Pacifil subjects have formed a bond?

Carlee shrugged and looked away. "Not really, I just thought he might be missing this place."

Although April suspected Carlee was lying about her contact with Felipe, she was probably right about him missing Praxis. Recalling her aborted hypnosis session with Brittany yesterday, April realized Felipe must be struggling with the same induced compulsion to attend the program. And she had barred him from coming.

"Carlee," she said, "if you should happen to hear from Felipe?"

"Yes?" The girl looked at her eagerly.

"Tell him to call me."

"I will, Dr. April. Thanks!"

As Carlee left her office, April felt sick at heart. Those poor tortured souls – Felipe, Tyrell, Brittany, Carlee. They must be wracked with impulses they could barely control. How could she sit back and let it go on? No matter what Clarence had threatened her with, she had to do something. April pushed aside her half finished coffee. She made a decision.

She got up and walked out of her office, heading down the corridor toward the reception area. When she came to James's office, his door was open and she poked her head in.

"Can you run community meeting? There's something I need to do."

"Actually, I – "

"Thanks." She rushed out the door before James could finish.

Outside, April crossed Vine Street, glancing around nervously. It wouldn't do to run into Clarence McKay. She reached the main entrance to the hospital and walked through the lobby to the elevators.

On the eleventh floor, she looked around again before approaching the locked inpatient unit. She pushed the buzzer.

"Yes?" The voice from the intercom was encased in static.

"It's Dr. Simon from Praxis. I need to see Brittany."

"Just a moment."

April used the brief wait to mentally prepare to resume the session Clarence had interrupted yesterday, to ensure that Brittany was free of Morgenstern's suggestions.

"Dr. Simon?" The voice broke in on April's reflections. "Dr. McKay has instructed us that you are not allowed to speak with Brittany or enter the unit. I'm sorry, but I can't let you in."

68

"Damn this case!" Sam tossed his empty coffee cup at the wastebasket.

"The Captain wasn't happy with your briefing, huh?" Justin, his partner, watched the cup bounce off the rim and land on the floor

"To put it mildly." Sam shrugged. "Shit flows downstream. I'm sure he got his share from the Inspector."

"So what's the plan?"

"I think it's Hartman, but I've gotta find a way to nail him." Sam picked up a stapler from his desk, examined it and put it down again. "Maybe play them off against each other somehow."

"Hartman and the widow?"

Sam nodded slowly. "If I can lead him on, make him think she's incriminated him, he might get rattled enough to spill something."

"How you gonna do that?" Justin asked.

Sam stood and pulled his jacket off the back of his desk chair. "Damned if I know." He flung the jacket over his shoulder. "But I'd better come up with something today."

Ψ

Stuart Hartman contemplated his reflection in the mirror above the sink in the men's room. Was that a gray hair? He angled his head for a better look.

It was.

Wrapping the offending strand around his index finger, he yanked it out, feeling noble at the small twinge of pain. He frowned at the silvery evidence of his distress, rinsing it off his finger and down the drain. He pressed the button on the automatic soap dispenser with a wet finger.

Nothing happened. Sighing, he turned off the faucet and moved over to the next sink. Everything was going wrong.

The past two days had been the worst of his life. His wife, Marcy, was still giving him cold, suspicious looks when she thought he couldn't see. He'd failed to convince her that the detective's visit on Saturday was routine. Maybe it would be better if Marcy came right out and accused him, instead of hiding behind her icy wall.

But accused him of what? Did she suspect him of killing Lowell Morgenstern? Of screwing Morgenstern's wife? Stuart pushed on the new soap dispenser and a stream of pink liquid shot out, splattering his tie. Cursing, he yanked several paper towels from the dispenser on the wall, wet them and began scrubbing at his tie. He cursed again, louder, as the soap blossomed into pink foam.

No doubt Marcy suspected him of lying to her. He had been, for quite some time, he reflected miserably, as he worked on his now sopping wet tie. He hadn't told her about Morgenstern's plan to bring in Mike Giametti and give him Stuart's job. And now, this very day, the man himself was here at Franklin to survey his new fiefdom.

Tossing a large wad of wet paper towels into the trash, Stuart looked at his watch. He was scheduled to meet Giametti in five minutes. He walked over to the automatic hand dryer mounted beside the sinks, pushed the button and held his wet tie under the flowing hot air.

He dreaded that meeting. If only he had the nerve to blow off the whole thing and not show up. But Stuart still needed his job, even if it did come with a functional demotion. He wished he could stay here in the men's room, hide in one of the stalls if anybody came in. He wished there were someone else who felt as sorry for him as he did.

With a pang, he thought of Miranda. Would she get past her anger enough to see him later? Should he risk calling her, even though she'd ordered him not to? It was never only about her money, the way that detective had implied. Miranda was sleek as a mink. Stuart felt a stirring in his pants, thinking about her.

The door to the men's room flew open and Stuart turned, startled. One of his graduate students walked in.

"Hi, Dr. Hartman!" He smiled and his gaze dropped to the conspicuous bulge at the front of Stuart's trousers.

"Hello, John – er, Jim." Stuart quickly turned away. He buttoned his jacket over his still-damp tie and rapidly subsiding erection.

"Hear Dr. Giametti is coming today." John or Jim sounded obscenely cheerful.

It was too much.

Grunting in response, Stuart hurried out of the men's room. Without slowing his pace, he shot down the hall.

"Dr. Hartman?" His assistant's voice followed Stuart down the stairs. "What should I tell Dr. Giametti? He'll be here any minute!"

Stuart muttered an inaudible expletive and raced out of the building. In moments, he reached the parking garage, jumped into his Volvo and peeled out onto the street. Entering the traffic on Vine Street recklessly enough to elicit a few angry horn blasts, Stuart hit the speed dial on his car phone.

"I'm on my way over," he said. "We have to talk." He disconnected without waiting for a response.

Ψ

Seething over being barred from the inpatient unit, April stormed out of the hospital onto Vine Street. How dare McKay bar her from seeing her own patient! She'd had enough of his domineering and bullying...

She froze in her tracks as McKay himself approached her. He glared, probably suspecting where April had just been. She was past the point of being intimidated, a pot ready to boil over.

"Dr. McKay, I demand to know – " She fell silent at a slight motion of Clarence's head toward the stranger standing beside him. The small, gnome-like man smiled pleasantly at her.

"Dr. Michael Giametti." Clarence nodded at his companion. "Dr. April Simon." His stern eyes and tight jaw warned her against any further display of anger.

April gulped back her unspoken tirade. "I – it's a pleasure to meet you, Dr. Giametti." This was the famous creator of psychological assessment instruments? The wizard was hardly what she'd expected. He looked more like a Yoda than a Gandalf.

Giametti shook her extended hand. "Please – it's Mike. And I'm happy to meet you, April. I'm looking forward to hearing about the program you've developed."

April bit down to keep her jaw from dropping. Giametti had heard of her?

Before she could reply, Clarence grasped Giametti's elbow. "You'll have a chance to discuss Praxis with her later. Right now we're due to meet with Dr. Hartman."

Giametti threw April a finger wave as Clarence led him away.

"Who was that?" A familiar voice came from behind her.

She whirled and saw Sam. Her heartbeat quickened. His smile went all the way up to his eyes, and all the way into her heart.

"Hi. What're you doing here?" She felt shy, standing next to him on the crowded sidewalk, after yesterday's intimacy. Without waiting for his answer, she launched into an explanation of Giametti's visit. "They're on their way over to see Stuart Hartman," she concluded.

"To answer your question, I'm on my way to see him, myself," Sam said. "But if Hartman's going to be busy for a while, why don't you and I go grab a coffee?"

"I'd like that." Maybe this was the time to tell him about the hypnosis. He might have some...

"Whoa!" A sudden squealing of tires on pavement made Sam turn toward the traffic. "That guy is burning some rubber!" he exclaimed, as a dark blue Volvo roared past them.

April caught a glimpse of the license plate – 1PHD. She gasped.

"Oh, my God, that was Stuart! That's his car. He's supposed to be meeting with Dr. Giametti. Where could he be going?"

When she looked back, Sam was already racing away.

69

Had everyone she knew gone crazy? April stood in front of the hospital on Vine Street, utterly perplexed. Clarence McKay, former teddy bear, had turned into a snarling grizzly. Stuart Hartman was tearing away, fleeing his interview with Mike Giametti, at considerable risk to his career, and Sam had just zipped off like the Road Runner in those old cartoons. At least Giametti seemed friendly enough.

April decided to head back to Praxis. Her patients might offer a welcome dose of sanity.

But the scene she walked in on was sheer hysteria.

In the Praxis lobby, James struggled to calm Carlee Randall, who, crying and shrieking, resisted his efforts to coax her out of the reception area into his office. Another therapist was shooing away the other patients who had gathered to observe the commotion.

"But I saw him! I know I did!" Carlee cried.

"What happened?" April approached Carlee and James, who looked at her as if she were the cavalry riding to the rescue.

"Let's talk about it in my office," he said. "Carlee, why don't you come in and tell April what's going on?"

"Yes, let's do that," April said, picking up the hint. She positioned herself alongside Carlee and opposite James, teaming up like a pair of border collies so they could herd her toward his office. As they worked her through the doorway, Carlee turned to April with wide eyes and an anguished expression.

"He's here! I saw him!"

"Saw who?" April motioned her toward a chair, but Carlee was nearly dancing with agitation.

"Him! Kit!"

"Your brother?" April was dumbfounded. "Where?"

"Right here. Outside on Vine Street!"

"When?"

"Now! A minute ago. I went out for coffee and saw him crossing the street." Terror twisted Carlee's features. She looked like the painting, The Scream. "My God, why is he here?"

April exchanged glances with James. Was Carlee hallucinating?

"Did he see you?" James asked.

She shook her head. "No, I – I turned around and came right back here as soon as I spotted him."

"Are you sure it was him?" April asked. "You said it's been a long time since you saw him."

"I know it was Kit!" Carlee's eyes darted around the office. "I can't stay here. I've gotta get away."

"Carlee –" April found it difficult to believe the girl's story could be true, but Carlee obviously believed it. "You've been under a lot of stress. We talked about reactions people have to reliving traumatic memories. It's possible you were having a flashback. They can be very realistic."

Carlee's eyes narrowed. "You don't believe me!"

"No, I believe you saw him," April reassured her. Saw something, at any rate. The girl was obviously terrified.

"He wasn't a flashback!" Carlee shouted. "He was there."

April exchanged another anxious glance with James. Could Carlee possibly have seen her brother? Whatever was going on, she was on the verge of hysteria.

"Carlee?" April ventured. "Would you feel safer in the hospital?"

"You think I'm crazy!" Carlee looked at April, then at James, her face contorted with panic.

"No!" April insisted. "No, we just want you safe."

A soft knock startled all three of them. The door opened and Cynthia peered in, a grim look on her face.

"This isn't a good time," April told her.

"Think I don't know that?" Cynthia muttered. "Dr. McKay called. He said Dr. Giametti's meeting with Dr. Hartman got postponed. He wants you to meet with Dr. Giametti instead, and give him a tour of Praxis." Cynthia rolled her eyes. "He's bringing him over here right now."

70

Da Da Da DAH!

The opening notes of Beethoven's Fifth reverberated as Stuart Hartman repeatedly pressed Miranda Morgenstern's doorbell. He accompanied the symphony with percussion, pounding on the door until it was yanked open and Miranda stood there glaring at him.

"What do you want?"

"We have to talk."

"We do not, Stuart. There's nothing to say."

"Miranda, please! Give me five minutes. My goddamned life is falling apart."

Sighing, she stepped back, letting him into the entryway. She left the front door open. Hands on her hips, she regarded him with a stony expression.

"Can't we at least go inside and sit down?" he begged.

She didn't budge. "Say what you came to say, then go."

"Miranda –" Stuart gulped. "I came to ask you to go away with me."

She brayed a harsh laugh. "What?"

"Now – anywhere. We can afford it now that you've inherited." He reached out for her. "There's nothing to keep us here."

She backed away. "Are you crazy? Why the hell would I leave with you?"

Stuart froze. His face darkened with anger. He took a step toward her. "You used me," he muttered through clenched teeth.

"I used you? You thought I'd be your meal ticket." She stared at him, wide-eyed. "You killed him, didn't you?"

"Me? I've been the one protecting you! I put myself in hot water with the police, my wife, probably ruined my goddamned career. And now – " He took another step toward her.

Neither of them turned to look at the car pulling up in front of the house, tires screeching.

Miranda pulled back and pointed at the open door. "Get out, or I'll call the police."

A car door slammed.

"Damn you, Miranda!" Stuart lunged at her. She crouched, eluding his grasp.

The sound of running footsteps was followed by a shout: "Hold it right there!"

Stuart turned toward the voice. As he did, Miranda uttered a guttural cry, kicked out with her right foot, and nailed him squarely in the crotch. He groaned and fell to his knees, as Sam Perone ran through the door, gun drawn.

"Arrest him, Detective!" Miranda pointed at Stuart, on the floor. "He tried to strangle me. You saw it!"

Stuart, on his knees, retched, a thin stream of vomit drooling from his mouth. "Shit!" Miranda fumed. "Look what he's done to my hardwood floor!"

"All right, Hartman." Sam pointed his gun at him. "Face down on the floor. Now!"

Whimpering, Stuart crawled a few inches away from the mess he'd made and gingerly lowered himself into a prostrate position.

"Thank God you're here, Detective!" Miranda said. "He could have killed me."

Sam regarded her with skepticism. "You don't seem exactly helpless, Mrs. Morgenstern."

She shrugged. "Kickboxing class."

"Detective?" Stuart whined from the floor. "I wasn't going to hurt her, I swear!"

"He was! He threatened me!" Miranda cut off Sam's reply. "And he killed my husband! I'm sure of it."

"Miranda!" Stuart wailed.

"What makes you say that?" Sam asked, holstering his gun.

"He planted my Botox, right? He begged me to go away with him, now that he thinks I'm rich. And Lowell was threatening his career." She crossed her arms and glared triumphantly at Sam. "What more do you need?"

Sam pulled out his handcuffs. "A confession would be nice," he muttered under his breath.

71

"No!" Carlee shouted. "I won't go into the hospital!"

Anxiety knotted April's stomach. Clarence would arrive at Praxis with Mike Giametti any minute. Their guest of honor was about to walk in on a crisis.

"It's okay." James waved April off. "You handle Giametti. I'll take care of this."

April hesitated. She trusted James implicitly, but also felt responsible for Carlee. Before she could reply, James took matters into his own hands.

"You don't have to go into the hospital if you don't want to." He gave Carlee a reassuring smile. "Where do you think you'd feel safe?"

Carlee wrung her hands. "Nowhere!"

"Then where would you feel the least vulnerable?" April asked, still reluctant to walk away from the situation.

Carlee chewed a fingernail, pondering the question. Finally she looked up at April, then James. "Home, I guess. As long as I can make it back there without seeing him again." Her eyes fixed James with a silent plea. "Could you walk me to the bus and make sure I get on?"

James looked at April, who nodded. "Maybe that's a good idea." Any moment now, Clarence and Giametti would walk in. April turned to Carlee: "How about using the Emergency Service here as your backup tonight? We can alert them, so they'll know what's going on if you call."

"Good plan," James agreed.

Carlee thought for a moment. "Okay."

Footsteps sounded from the reception area. Cynthia called out: "Dr. Simon?"

They were here.

"Go!" James murmured. "I'll have Carlee sign a release, give her the number for the ER and get her on the bus." He gave April a thumbs up. "Break a leg."

"Thanks." She turned and composed her face into a welcoming smile.

Ψ

"You arrested Hartman?" Justin caught up with Sam at the coffee maker. The thick brown sludge Sam was pouring into a mug looked like it might dissolve the ceramic before he could swallow it.

Sam took a sip and grimaced. "For all the good it'll do. He's been charged with assault and obstruction of justice. He immediately lawyered up." He blew on the hot coffee. "I don't have enough evidence to go after him for homicide."

"So why the bust?"

Sam took another sip, coughed and spilled the contents of the mug into the sink. "At least it should slow him down. He was trying to get Miranda Morgenstern to run off with him. He'll probably make bail, but it might make him think twice about skipping town." He rinsed the mug and left it on the drainer. Frustration wrinkled his face. "Are those two that smart? Or am I dropping IQ points?"

"What do you mean?" Justin asked.

Sam held up his index finger. "One, Morgenstern was killed by a lethal dose of Botox injected into his inhaler. According to the ME, that required at least two vials." He raised a second finger. "Two, Miranda Morgenstern acknowledged receiving two vials of Botox from her husband and admitted she gave them to Hartman."

Justin shook his head in puzzlement. "So?"

"Hartman planted two vials in Sandra Chang's desk, but only one was empty. And even the empty one didn't look like it had been properly mixed into solution."

"Meaning Morgenstern wasn't killed with the vials from the desk."

"Exactly." Sam held up a third finger. "And three, Dr. Klein, the dermatologist, said that besides the two vials of Botox he gave Morgenstern, two more vials from his fridge are unaccounted for."

"Oh, man."

"But we didn't find any other vials in Hartman's apartment or office, or at the Morgensterns' house." Sam frowned. "Which proves nothing."

"Sure," Justin said eagerly, "because they could have used them, or tossed them, or whatever." He was intrigued by the puzzle now. "So where does that leave you?"

"Hartman did such a half-assed job of planting those vials that he couldn't not get nailed for it," Sam mused. "So, is he a jerk? Or did he deliberately bungle the Botox plant in Sandra Chang's desk to convince me that he and his girlfriend didn't kill Morgenstern?"

Justin nodded. "That's deep. But maybe Hartman is a jerk and the widow is your mastermind. She could have killed Morgenstern and used Hartman as her fall guy."

"Could be." Sam paused. "But there's another possibility."

"Which is?"

"That someone else took the other two vials and killed Morgenstern. And I still don't have a clue who it was."

And April might still be in danger.

72

"Very impressive!" Mike Giametti applauded as April concluded her impromptu presentation. "You've combined the major state-of-the-art elements of psychiatric rehabilitation: skill development, medication management, relapse prevention, dialectical behavior therapy. Praxis is an exciting program." He picked up the papers resting on his lap. "And I look forward to reviewing your research proposal, April."

"Thanks, Mike. I'll be eager to hear your feedback." April was elated. Even if she ended up in more hot water with Clarence for giving out a copy of her proposal, she didn't care. Dr. Michael Giametti, a certified VIP, "got" her program and appreciated her work. She soaked up his praise like a parched houseplant abandoned by a family on vacation.

Giametti glanced at the clock on April's desk. "I'd better run. I'm already late for my wrap-up with Clarence McKay." He shook a finger at her playfully. "Got caught up in your siren song, my dear."

Blushing, April lowered her head. Giametti stood, and she rose to shake his hand.

"Look forward to working with you," he said.

"It'll be great to have you here," she replied, meaning it.

She walked him from her office to the reception area, waving as he left. The hour she'd spent with this kind little man felt like a rest stop at a desert oasis.

"You look like you hit one out of the park, Red." James stepped out of his office to join her.

She smiled. "It did go well. What happened with Carlee?" So much for the oasis.

"Got her on the bus," James said. "She seemed calmer."

"Did she sign the release for us to brief the ER staff?"

"Yup. It's in her chart. I wrote up everything in a progress note."

"Good." She patted his shoulder. "You're the best."

"All part of the Praxis five-star service." James grinned. "Want me to call the ER?"

"No, I'll do it," April said. "Pack up, go home and kiss your kids."

At a few minutes after five, April phoned the Emergency Service. Chris Willis was still there.

"Hi, Chris, it's April Simon. I'm calling to – "

Chris chuckled. "You need to give me your last name? How many Aprils do you think I know? Besides, we have caller ID, remember?"

"Point taken." She laughed, too. It was a relief to let go of some of the day's tension. "Anyway, I called to give you a heads up about one of our patients who might be in contact with your staff tonight."

"Okay."

"She was very distressed this afternoon, and we encouraged her to call if she needs to talk or go into the hospital."

"What's the situation?"

"A thirty year-old, single, white female. Diagnosis of PTSD in response to sexual abuse by her half-brother during adolescence. Kind of borderline, with a history of depression and cutting herself. Recently started talking about the abuse in group therapy and it seems to have triggered her. Now she's having either a flashback or a delusion."

"What's the content?" he asked.

"She reported nightmares last night about stabbing her brother, told us she did cut him once when he came after her. This afternoon, she claimed she'd actually seen him out on Vine Street."

"Think there's any chance she did?"

"Unlikely. She said he left Philadelphia years ago for college and then she lost track of him," April said. "What are the odds of running into him the day after she disclosed the abuse? More likely, she's reliving the trauma."

"Can't argue with your logic there," Chris said. "What's the patient's name?"

"Carlee Randall."

There was silence for a moment.

"Chris?"

"Sorry, someone here distracted me. You said 'Randall'?"

"Right. Do you want her chart?" April asked. "It might help in case you need to admit her tonight."

"Good idea. Want me to send someone over for it?"

"No, that's okay, I'll drop it off on my way home."

"Okay. Anything else?"

Should she tell Chris that Carlee might be under the influence of a post-hypnotic suggestion? Explaining her theory about Morgenstern's experiment would be complicated and, if she did, it might get back to Clarence McKay, making a bad situation even worse.

"No," she said, "I guess that's it."

"See you later, then. Hey!" His voice dropped to a conspiratorial tone. "Hell of a thing about Stuart Hartman, huh? Bolting like that. Guess you heard?" He hooted. "If you have his chart, maybe you ought to bring that one over, too!"

"You're bad!"

She hung up. Why had Stuart run off? Had he wanted to avoid meeting Giametti, or was there more to it? Maybe Sam knew, and might clue her in. He'd taken off pretty quickly himself. She hoped he'd call her later, to explain. The thought made her smile.

April finished up a few notes and put her desk into her customary end-of-the-day order. Then she reached for Carlee's chart – one of medium thickness, by Praxis standards. She leafed absently through treatment plans, progress notes, and records from Carlee's previous hospitalizations. Turning to the admission summary from Carlee's last hospitalization, April began reading. Usually, these reports were pretty thorough. There might be more information about Carlee's family history and her relationship with Kit.

"Ahem!"

The abrupt sound of a man's throat clearing yanked April's attention from Carlee's chart. She stared as Clarence McKay walked into her office, his face set in a deep frown. Foreboding rippled through her. Her staff was gone, the cleaning man hadn't arrived.

She was alone with Clarence.

He walked right up to where April sat at her desk, towering over her and blocking her way out of the office. "You and I need to have a talk," he announced.

73

Clarence McKay loomed over April. Trapped at her desk, her heart pounding, she awaited his next words. She was frightened of this man, of whom she'd been so fond. She no longer knew what to expect from him.

Again, Clarence surprised her.

Heaving a sigh, he sank into the chair beside her desk. "First," he said, "I want to thank you."

April exhaled and let the tension drain from her body.

"Mike Giametti was singing your praises this afternoon. You did a great job bailing us out when Stuart was unavailable today."

She nodded, her pulse slowing back to normal. "Glad I could help."

"You sure sold Mike on Praxis."

"I could talk about Praxis in my sleep," April said. "In fact, I probably do."

Clarence smiled, the first time she'd seen him do so in weeks. His gaze dropped to the floor and when he looked back at April, his face was full of sorrow.

"I owe you an apology." When April remained silent, he continued. "IT gave me access to Lowell's computer and I went through his files." He sighed. "You were right. He had notes about the Pacifil project, protocols for hypnosis and, worse." His lip curled. "He had a folder of e-mail correspondence with someone he was chummy with at BAFF, his funding source. Lowell wrote about giving the subjects a suggestion to harm animals." Clarence laughed bitterly. "Called it a temporary measure. Obviously he didn't plan on dying before he could make a change."

"My God!" She'd known it was true, but hearing the proof sickened her.

"Please." His eyes beseeched her. "Go ahead with the hypnosis. Help those patients."

April nodded. "Thank you." She paused, still feeling unfinished with Clarence. "So that's what you wanted to apologize for? For not believing me?"

"No." Again, Clarence sighed. "I want to apologize for taking out my shame on you."

Her eyes widened. "What do you mean?"

He remained silent for a moment. "Lowell did a terrible thing, but so did I. It's easy to convince yourself to cut corners when you get too invested in your own research." He grimaced. "In your own sense of importance."

"The end justifies the means?"

"It's a mistake for any of us to think we're above such beliefs." He peered at her intently. "That day, when Lowell interrupted our meeting and you came back for your phone, you heard everything he said to me, didn't you? His accusations."

She held his gaze. "I did."

"He was right." Clarence looked away. "I fudged some of my data. Way beyond what's acceptable." He bit his lip. "I lied. I was under so much pressure. Too many deadlines, too much on my plate." His mouth set in a hard line. "But that's no excuse." He took a breath. "Anyway, there are two other things I want you to know."

She sat up, curious.

"One is that I've told my funding source there were – errors – in my data, and asked for an extension to correct them. If they refuse, I'm going to return the grant money. I'm not submitting fraudulent results."

April nodded. "What's the second thing?"

"I've withdrawn from consideration for the department chairmanship on a permanent basis. I'll fill in until Lowell's successor is appointed, and then – "

"Clarence, no!" She knew him well enough to understand what the appointment meant to him.

He held up a hand to silence her protest. "I've thought about this. I don't want to be in a position where I'd end up treating people the way Lowell did." He looked her squarely in the eyes. "The way I've been treating you."

"But, Clarence! You could bring exactly that kind of understanding and humility to the position. Just what's been lacking. Please, think about it some more." Hearing her own words, April realized that her respect and trust for Clarence had returned – or never really gone.

He smiled. "Thank you for that. It's more than I deserve. But I'm sure about this. It's a weight off my shoulders. Maybe I'll be able to sleep nights again and stop snapping at my wife." He stood. "I'd better let you go now. It's been a long day."

She got up and took a step toward him, impelled by a flood of affection for the man. She hugged him. He was her teddy bear again.

As they moved apart, he raised a finger to his lips. "Just between you and me," he stage whispered, "our next chairman is going to be someone who's a big fan of yours."

She stared at him in confusion.

"Mike Giametti."

"But he's a psychologist! Doesn't the chairman have to be a medical doctor?"

"There's going to be a special arrangement here at Franklin. Giametti as chairman, McKay as medical director." He winked. "And I'd say your prospects for promotion are excellent."

She watched him walk out, relieved, yet strangely numb. The promise of finally getting her promotion to the tenure track should thrill her. Yet it didn't. What had Sam told her about happiness? That it didn't come from climbing ladders, but from learning who you really were.

Maybe he had a point. She was starting to get the hang of being April Simon. And she liked it.

74

The roar of Joe's vacuum cleaner from the hallway followed Clarence's departure. Eager to escape the noise, and any potentially tedious conversation with the cleaning man, April scooped up Carlee's chart. She waved to Joe on her way out the door and made her way across Vine Street to the Psychiatric Emergency Service.

At the front desk she asked for Chris Willis. The receptionist pointed her through to his office, while she switched back and forth between calls without missing a beat. April found Chris at his desk, wrapping up a phone call of his own.

"Phew!" He blew out a breath as he hung up the phone. "I hereby declare that to be my last call of the day."

"No more emergencies allowed until tomorrow?" she teased.

"Not for me. The night shift just took over." He leaned back in his chair, folding his hands behind his head, and regarded her with a roguish half-smile. "Wanna go have a drink and celebrate surviving another day at Franklin?"

April was hit by a swift pang of craving. A glass of wine would be so nice! She had a right to celebrate, after her meeting with Giametti and her talk with Clarence. But the weight of Carlee's file, clutched in her hand, pulled her back from the precipice. "Thanks, Chris, but I can't. I have to go up and see a patient on the involuntary unit."

"Too bad. Guess I can't compete with company like that. Another time?"

"Sure." Not a lie. Eventually she'd be able to drink again. "Anyway, I stopped by to give you this." She held out Carlee's medical record, then pulled it back. "But if you're leaving, maybe there's someone else I should give it to?"

He reached for the chart. "No, I'll take care of briefing them before I go."

She handed him the records. "Thanks, Chris." She rose to leave.

Chris stood, too, patting the chart in his hand. "Don't worry. We'll take care of her tonight."

April hurried up to the inpatient unit.

No longer persona non grata she sat with Brittany in her hospital room a few minutes later. April swiftly guided Brittany into a trance state. As she took Brittany back down in the imaginary elevator, the young woman grew progressively calmer and more receptive to suggestion.

"Three, two, one," April concluded. "Now you are back in your secret place, totally safe and at peace."

Brittany smiled. "I was waiting for you here. And I haven't had to hurt any animals while you were gone."

April smiled back, even though Brittany's eyes were closed. "And now you won't have to ever again."

Her limbs heavy with a pleasant tiredness, April stepped back out onto Vine Street. One down, three to go. Next, she would repeat the hypnotic reversal with the other Pacifil subjects. She resolved to stop by the voluntary inpatient unit in the morning and take care of Tyrell before she went to Praxis. Hopefully, Carlee would return tomorrow and April could rid her of Morgenstern's suggestion, too. Felipe was another matter.

She hoped Carlee would relay her message and he would call her. If she could restore the four Pacifil subjects to their baselines, then…

The musical ringtone of her cellphone interrupted April's thoughts. She retrieved the phone from her purse and smiled at the now-familiar number that appeared on its screen.

"Hey!"

"Hey yourself," Sam replied. "Sorry I had to run off like that."

"You were really flying. Were you trying to catch Stuart's car, or what?"

"Something like that."

"So did you catch him?"

"Well…" Sam hesitated. "Let's say I slowed him down. But, April…"

"What?"

"The same thing I told you yesterday. Be careful."

"Of what? Who?"

"Hartman. Clarence McKay. Anyone at Franklin who's acting strangely these days."

"That doesn't exactly narrow it down. Everyone around here is wacko right now." A man walking nearby glanced at her with amusement, and April ducked her head like an ostrich in search of privacy.

"I know, but watch your back. And so will I."

"Mine or yours?" She grinned, turning the corner onto Fifteenth Street.

"Huh?"

"I meant, whose back will you be watching?"

He laughed. "Yours is definitely more fun!"

She laughed, too. "More of the community relations program?"

"Yeah, a whole new initiative. I'll fill you in when this case is finally solved."

"Thank you, Detective."

"You're welcome, Doc. See ya."

April ended the call and walked up Fifteenth Street, smiling to herself as she recalled her banter with Sam – but not his warning.

Wednesday, October 6

75

Compared with the drama entailed in hypnotizing Brittany, April's early morning session with Tyrell was a breeze. Not having to sneak around the hospital and conduct hypnosis in secret made all the difference. Like Brittany, Tyrell proved highly suggestible and April had no difficulty placing him into a trance and removing Morgenstern's suggestion. Knowing what she was looking for this time made things easier, as well.

Cynthia was already at the reception desk when April arrived at Praxis.

"Any word from Carlee?" she asked.

"Nope," Cynthia replied, "but Dr. Willis dropped off her chart about ten minutes ago. I put it on your desk."

"Did he say whether she called the ER last night?"

"Uh-uh."

"'Uh-uh' he didn't say, or 'uh-uh' she didn't call?" April asked impatiently.

Cynthia's phone rang. "Didn't say." She picked up the call.

April waited a moment, eyebrows raised in a wordless query: Was that Carlee?

Cynthia shook her head.

April went to her office and found Carlee's chart on her desk. She opened it to the progress notes section. The last entry was her own note from yesterday. If Carlee had contacted the ER last night, there was no record of it. What did that mean? That Carlee was okay? Or that she was alone and in trouble?

April was tempted to call the ER to ask whether Carlee had been in touch. But it might be insulting to imply that they'd been remiss in documenting a patient contact. She decided to wait and see if Carlee showed up at Praxis.

Voices and footsteps signaled the arrival of patients and the start of morning activities. Caught up in the bustle of the Praxis routine, April led community meeting and ran a therapy group before she found time to check in again with Cynthia.

"Any word from her?"

Cynthia shook her head.

"Damn." April spotted James walking into his office and followed him in.

"S'up?" he asked.

"I'm worried about Carlee. She hasn't come in or called, and I don't think she got in touch with the ER last night. Maybe we shouldn't have let her go home by herself yesterday."

"We didn't have grounds to hospitalize her against her will."

"I know." April rubbed her forehead, trying to ease the tension there. "I just think we should have done something more."

"Did you try calling her?" James asked.

"I was about to."

"Let me know what happens," he said.

April went back to her office and checked her voicemail – a message! She hoped it was from Carlee. But the voice that played back when she retrieved it was her friend Larissa's.

"Hey! We haven't talked since the funeral. I heard Sandra's back. Have you seen her? Let's have lunch and catch up."

April had no appetite for lunch or gossip. She selected the Reply option to Larissa's message, knowing it would take her directly to her friend's voicemail. She recorded a cryptic response, saying she couldn't make it today. Then April closed her office door and opened Carlee's chart. Her contact information included a cellphone number, but no residential line. April's call went straight to voicemail, not the outcome she'd hoped for this time.

"Hi Carlee, it's April Simon," she said, after the beep. "I wanted to make sure you're okay. Please call me at Praxis when you get this message."

By mid-afternoon there was still no word from Carlee.

April took a late lunch break at her desk, nervously shuffling through the papers in her in-box. Her mounting anxiety left her too distracted to deal with them, or manage more than a few bites of the sandwich she'd picked up from the deli. She looked again at the identifying information in Carlee's chart. In the space for "Person to Contact in Case of Emergency," there was a woman's name, with the relationship listed as "neighbor." Instead of her sandwich, April chewed the inside of her cheek. Was this an emergency?

She called the number. It rang three times, and she waited for voicemail, trying to decide what kind of message she could leave without violating Carlee's confidentiality. Meanwhile, the line continued to ring. After twelve rings, April slammed down the phone receiver in exasperation. She picked up the phone again and dialed the Psychiatric ER.

"Emergency Services, can I help you?"

"This is Dr. Simon from Praxis. I spoke with Dr. Willis yesterday about one of our patients who might have called last night, and – "

"Just a moment, Dr. Simon. I'll transfer you to Dr. Willis."

"No, I – " She heard a click and Chris picked up. She felt awkward about appearing to second guess his staff, but was too worried to drop the matter. She quickly explained her concerns about Carlee's absence.

"We never heard from her," Chris said. "I checked the night log myself when I came in early this morning because I knew you were concerned about her. Did you try calling her?"

"I left her a message, but she hasn't called back."

"Probably she needs some space."

"Maybe." April didn't believe space would help Carlee. "Thanks, Chris."

At three in the afternoon, Praxis members began filing past April's office, leaving for the day. She'd left her door open so she could see them off, meanwhile paging through Carlee's chart. She was searching for some hint, anything to guide her toward what to do. Turning to the hospital admission summary she'd started reading yesterday, something teased at the edge of her awareness.

"Dr. April?" Denise stood in the doorway. "I left Carlee at least six messages today and I still haven't heard from her. Have you?"

"No, Denise. I left her a message, too."

"That's not like her. We're tight and she always returns my calls."

April's stomach knotted. "I'm worried about her, too."

"Did she really see Kit yesterday?"

"I don't know, Denise. She says she did."

"She seemed so scared."

"Yes, she was." A thought occurred to April. "Did Carlee ever tell you why she called him 'Kit'?"

Denise scratched her head, causing her braids to move up and down. "She said her mother gave him the nickname, after some famous English playwright. Shakespeare, or something."

"Hmm." April didn't get the allusion.

Denise frowned. "Damn. I'd go to her place and check it out, but I got an appointment over at the Disability Office with my caseworker in twenty minutes. If I blow her off, they'll stop my checks."

"Keep your appointment, Denise. I'll – I don't know. I'll find a way to check on Carlee."

When Denise left, April turned back to the identifying information sheet in Carlee's chart. Her home address was nearby in North Philadelphia. Not a great neighborhood. April's fingers tapped a drumbeat on the page. She didn't relish the idea of going there, but at least it was still afternoon, with plenty of daylight left. Her car was in the lot next door.

Should she go? A frisson of anxiety tickled the back of her neck. The neighborhood intimidated her. But the thought of Denise, wanting to go check on her friend, caused April a twinge of shame. Was she herself too good – too middle class – to go there? On the other hand, was it even appropriate to show up at Carlee's apartment, like some suspicious welfare worker?

Maybe James would come with her, she thought, but immediately dismissed the idea. Someone needed to stay and debrief with the staff over progress notes. Besides, if Carlee was home, holed up and frightened, two visitors might be more threatening to her than one.

She was tempted to call Sam. Maybe he'd drive there with her.

No, she thought. Showing up with a detective in tow would probably frighten and anger Carlee. But suppose Sam waited in the car while she went in?

No. Sam had a murder to solve and who knows what else to deal with. He wasn't her personal bodyguard. Carlee was her responsibility.

Quickly, before she could change her mind, April entered Carlee's address into the GPS app on her cellphone. She reached for her bag.

She was going.

76

Afraid she might lose her nerve, April rushed out of Praxis, claiming she had a faculty meeting. She didn't tell any of her staff where she was really going because they'd have tried to talk her out of it – and possibly succeeded. Having decided to go check on Carlee, April was committed to the mission. Still, as she turned off Broad Street onto Carlee's block, she almost hoped she wouldn't find a parking space. The neighborhood was as rundown and scary as she'd feared. When she spotted a rusted yellow Beetle pulling out of a space half a block up from Carlee's building, April wasn't sure whether to feel relieved or disappointed.

She navigated her Mini into the space and locked the car behind her. The residential street was lined with aging row houses. A few sported colorful flower pots on their front steps and weathered porches, defying the wear and tear surrounding them.

Her eyes darted about as she made her way back to Carlee's building. Empty beer bottles littered the sidewalk in front of the house next door, where three young men lounged on the steps. Shirtless, their tattoos were on full display. Their baseball caps were worn fashionably backwards, and the cigarette they passed back and forth had the distinctive sweet aroma of pot. April avoided their stares as she walked past. Murmurs and laughter followed her. Cold sweat trickled down her back.

She approached the apartment building.

The front door was unlocked and April stepped into the entryway. A table on her left was piled with circulars. On her right, the wall was lined with doorbells and mail boxes. She counted fifteen apartments in the three-story building.

Scanning the doorbells, she found the one labeled "Randall," number 302, and pushed the button.

Nothing.

April's anxiety mounted. As frightened as Carlee had been, it seemed unlikely she'd be out and about. She rang again. Maybe the bell was broken.

Maybe she should leave.

She swallowed her fear. Carlee might be in trouble up there. Besides, if she left now, she'd have to walk back past the three guys next door. April rang two other doorbells. After a few moments, a buzzer sounded. She pushed open the inner door.

There was no elevator. April began trotting up the stairs, eager to avoid any curious tenants. She reached the second floor. A door opened and an elderly woman, her hair in pink foam curlers, peered out at her. April smiled and nodded at the woman, who frowned and retreated to her apartment.

Continuing up to the third floor, April found apartment 302 to the left of the stairs. She raised her hand to knock, and saw that the door was open a crack. She hesitated, her throat tightening with fear, and knocked softly.

No response.

April's reptile brain screamed at her to retreat, but she fought the impulse. She hadn't come this far to give up now. She pushed the door open a little wider.

"Carlee? Are you there?"

No answer.

Listening intently, April thought she heard running footsteps within the apartment. "Carlee, it's April Simon. Are you all right? I'm coming in."

She pushed the door open.

Amid a scene of chaos – an overturned chair, a broken lamp, a red throw pillow on the floor – she saw Carlee splayed stiffly on a sofa, her lifeless face blue and swollen. Flies buzzed around the body. Even though she'd never smelled this sickly odor before, April knew what it was.

She screamed and groped inside her purse for her cellphone. As she pulled it out, a slender figure darted out of the kitchen, making for the door. Felipe Diaz.

"No!" April shouted. Automatically, she stepped forward to block his path.

"Out of my way!" He moved to evade her. Suddenly he froze, his expression anguished. "I didn't do it!" he cried. "I came in and found her like that."

"I don't believe you! I'm calling the police." She raised her phone, but Felipe lunged and knocked it out of her hand. She reached for it, and he shoved her, sending her sprawling to the floor. Felipe raced out the door, and she heard his footsteps pounding down the stairs.

"Help!" she shouted, crawling over to retrieve her phone. "Help! Stop him!" She found the phone, inches from Carlee's body. The battery had fallen out. The odor of death made her stomach lurch. "Help, please!" She pushed the battery back into the phone. Would it still work?

The footsteps grew faint, then disappeared. Voices drifted up from the floor below and more footsteps pounded up the stairs. Her cellphone was dead, but she hit "send" and it came back to life.

Two faces appeared in the doorway, the woman in pink curlers and a middle-aged Latino man in a white tee shirt and cardigan, suspenders dangling from his trousers. At the sight of the body on the couch, the woman began to scream.

The man glared at April and took a step toward her. "What the hell happened here?" he rumbled. "Who are you?"

"I – I'm her doctor."

"You don't look like no doctor." The man frowned. "And this don't look like no house call."

"Wait!" April cried. "I'm calling the police." She scrolled quickly and pressed a key on her phone.

The man eyed her suspiciously. "You got 911 on speed dial?"

"Not exactly," April admitted. "But there's a detective I know."

77

Once again, April watched Sam take charge of a crime scene. He showed up at Carlee's apartment within minutes of April's call, along with two uniformed police officers and a crime scene technician – the same one who'd been at Morgenstern's office. Sam quickly sent the suspicious neighbors off with the officers to give their statements, clearing the apartment for scrutiny by the technician, who now combed his way through Carlee's living room.

In the course of the hour she spent recounting to Sam her discovery of Carlee's body and subsequent tussle with Felipe, April's emotions went from panic to numbness to exhaustion. Now, as Sam studied his notes, April saw the corners of his mouth turn down, as if he didn't like what he was reading. He looked back at her, his expression impassive.

"Sooo," he drew out the syllable. "This guy Felipe is the same one who wrote that threat on your apartment door."

"Uh-huh."

"Both he and Carlee were in Morgenstern's research study."

"Right."

"And Morgenstern gave them some kind of post-hypnotic suggestion to kill whenever they felt bad."

"To kill animals, right," April said. "But who knows whether the suggestion might have generalized to people."

"But the guy Carlee was so afraid of was her brother, Kit."

"Half brother, yes."

Sam's pencil tapped a drumbeat on the notepad. "Whose last name you don't know."

"Right. But he'd have Carlee's mother's maiden name."

"And he'd be how much older than Carlee?"

She thought for a moment. "Five years, I think. I can check it in her chart."

Sam closed his notepad with a sharp snap. "Anything else you can tell me?"

"No," April said, "that's everything."

"Not quite everything." He shoved the notepad into his jacket pocket.

"What do you mean?"

"I mean what the hell were you doing, coming here by yourself?" he exploded. "Was that your idea of being careful?"

She almost jumped at his abrupt change in tone. The glare in his brown eyes made her mind go blank. "I – I was worried about Carlee. And obviously with good reason."

"And that's also a reason to abandon common sense? You had no business coming here alone."

She'd never seen him so angry.

"You should have called me before walking into this, not after." Sam shook his head in disbelief. "I mean, entering this apartment when you found the door open? Trying to tackle a suspected killer? Have you gone freaking crazy, or what?"

April looked away, fighting for composure. He was right. She hadn't even told anyone she was coming here. But she hated having him yell at her. She glanced over and noticed the crime scene technician staring at them. The man arched an eyebrow when their eyes met, and April's face grew warm with embarrassment.

"And why the hell are you only now telling me about this whole hypnosis thing?" Sam demanded.

"I didn't think it was relevant to – "

"Relevant?" he shouted. "You're in the middle of an unsolved murder and you presume to decide for me what's relevant?"

April clenched her jaw. He could only push her so far before she started shoving back. "There was also the matter of patient confidentiality here, and – "

"Ahem!" The crime scene tech cleared his throat. "Uh, Detective?"

"Yeah?" Sam turned to face the man and April took the opportunity to steady her breathing.

"Let me show you a couple of things over here." The technician motioned Sam over to the body.

"Okay." Sam turned back to April and frowned. "Wait right there."

She silently raised her hands in a gesture of surrender. Inside, she was fuming. She was sick and tired of men yelling at her.

"Take a look at this." The technician pointed at the red throw pillow on the floor next to Carlee's body. "These look like makeup smudges here. Same color as her lipstick. And here –" He indicated Carlee's right hand. "Two broken nails, probably defensive wounds. I'll bet she was suffocated with this pillow. Might get a partial print off it. I'll dust the doorknob and other surfaces around. Just thought you'd want to see this."

"Yeah, thanks, Marty," Sam said. "Any guesses on time of death?"

He shrugged. "Probably late last night or early this morning."

Sam nodded.

"Sorry to interrupt your speech to the lady, Detective," the technician deadpanned.

Sam narrowed his eyes. "Go dust something, Marty." He walked back to April. "She's been dead too long for Felipe to have killed her just now." As April opened her mouth to reply, he quickly added: "Which doesn't mean he didn't kill her earlier, or that he isn't dangerous." He waited for her response, but she didn't answer. "Okay," he said. "We're done here. I'll drive you home."

April had no stomach for any more lectures. "That's not necessary." Her tone was icy. "My car is just down the block."

"Then I'll drive your car and have a patrol car pick me up after I get you home."

"I prefer to drive myself."

Sam's face twisted with irritation. "Don't be ridiculous. You've had a shock. You shouldn't be driving."

"I'm fine." April folded her arms across her chest. "You want to give me a sobriety test, or something?"

"Hey, don't cop an attitude." He pronounced the word like a typical Philadelphian atty-tood.

Although April had even heard professors here say it that way, it still grated on her. "Detective Perone, am I under arrest?"

"What?"

"Because unless you're taking me into custody, I have the right to leave on my own, no?"

Sam's face flushed and April was afraid she'd pushed him too far.

He sighed and pushed his hair back from his forehead. "Doc, you are some piece of work. All right, let's go. I need to check on the interviews with the other tenants, but first I'm walking you to your car." Over her protests, he added: "For all we know, the killer is still out there.

We're going to your car, and if you give me any grief, I will bust your ass."

April shrugged wordlessly.

"Marty, I'll be right back," Sam called to the technician, who waved a hand in response. April avoided looking at the man, but thought she caught him smirking out of the corner of her eye.

They walked out of the building in a silence that continued for the half block it took to reach April's car. She unlocked the door with her remote and started to get into the Mini.

"April –" Sam reached for her arm, and she shook him off.

"I'm tired." She refused to look at him. "I want to go home."

Ψ

After running the first few blocks from Carlee's apartment, Felipe slowed to a walk and finally, a dead stop. Where could he go? *Mamita* wasn't going to take him back – especially now that the police would be hunting for him. Dr. April must have called them. She thought he'd killed Carlee.

He was totally fucked. He had about two bucks left in his pocket and he'd burned all his bridges – his mother, Carlee, Praxis.

Praxis.

They'd tried to help him there and he'd blown it, big time. Felipe walked to the intersection and checked a street sign to see where he was. Not so far from Vine Street. He could make it to Praxis from here. He didn't know what time it was, but he figured the program must be over for the day. Maybe Dr. April would go back there from Carlee's. He knew the staff stayed there until five or later, so she'd have to return to work, right?

Felipe started walking. He'd talk to her, make her see he was innocent. Get her to call off the police. What else could he do now?

He quickened his pace.

78

April gripped the steering wheel tightly enough to turn her knuckles white and choked back tears as she drove home. How could Sam have abused her like that? She'd trusted him and he'd turned against her when she needed him. Worse, Carlee was dead and it felt like her fault.

Broad Street turned into Old York Road as April crossed the county line. The left turn for Briar Hill approached, but she kept going. The nearest liquor store was a few blocks straight ahead.

Fuck sobriety.

She bought a bottle of Chardonnay – already chilled – so she wouldn't have to wait for it to cool in her fridge. Or have time to change her mind. She pulled into her space in the parking garage, locked her car and walked to the elevator. Images from the apartment flooded her head – Carlee's lifeless body. The smell of death. The angry neighbors.

Angry Sam.

Impervious to her inner turmoil, Boris and Natasha rushed April as soon as she opened the door. She crouched and gave them a few perfunctory pats. Standing and inching forward carefully, to avoid stepping on the cats, she made her way to the kitchen and set the wine bottle on the countertop.

Where had she hidden the corkscrew?

She opened the drawer where she normally kept it and rooted through the utensils, while the cats meowed insistently. No corkscrew. She'd stashed it somewhere else – out of sight, out of mind. She tried to remember where.

Boris leapt up onto the countertop and rubbed his nose against her face.

"C'mon," she muttered. "Not now." She averted her face, but he butted the side of her head, purring.

"Damn it, Boris!" She lifted the cat and put him back on the floor. He meowed in protest and Natasha joined the chorus. April saw their empty food bowls.

"Okay, okay." Maybe if she fed them, they'd leave her alone. She refilled their water bowl and quickly opened a can of cat food. Why was the stupid can opener so easy to find? She put the kitty turkey and giblets into two bowls for Boris and Natasha, who immediately began lapping at the gravy.

The corkscrew.

Damn! Where had she put it? Hell, it had only been a week.

A pang of guilt hit her. A week, and already she was relapsing. Maybe she really was an alcoholic, not merely someone who'd been careless about her drinking. She yanked open the silverware drawer. No corkscrew.

Even as her mouth puckered in anticipation of that first glorious sip of cold wine, bitter thoughts streamed through her mind. If only she'd tried harder to convince Carlee to sign herself into the hospital. She might still be alive.

Where the hell was the damned corkscrew?

She opened another drawer, grabbing whisks and spatulas and throwing them onto the countertop. An oven thermometer rolled onto the floor with a clatter that startled the cats.

The doorbell rang and April froze.

She considered ignoring it, but the ringing was followed by insistent knocking. Muttering a curse, she slammed the drawer closed, to a chorus of rattling utensils, and went to the door. She looked through the peephole and caught her breath.

April undid the safety chain and faced Sam.

"I wanted to make sure you got home okay," he said.

She stood at the doorway, not moving back to let him in. "Why wouldn't I?"

"You had a shock. I was worried about you." His face looked pinched and a deep furrow sat between his brows.

"You don't have to worry, Detective. I'm fine." She started to close the door, but he put out a hand and held it open.

"April." His face was tight with concern. "You're not fine, we're not. Can I come in and talk to you, please?"

The distress in his voice made her step back from the door. A hot wave of embarrassment hit her as her sideways glance took in the chaos in the kitchen and the bottle of wine she'd left sitting in plain sight on the countertop. Quickly backing away from the doorway, she motioned him in.

"Let's go into the living room." She tried to walk nonchalantly, wondering if he could read the tension in her shoulders. She made a point of sitting in the chair, instead of on the sofa, so he couldn't sit beside her. She was having enough difficulty controlling her emotions without the possibility of Sam's touch.

He stopped in the middle of the room, stood and rubbed at his hair. Its mangled condition suggested he'd been worrying it for a while. He stared so intently at the rug that she wondered if she'd dropped something there. When he looked up, his troubled eyes locked onto hers.

"I really lost it with you, back there at the apartment."

"I'd say so." She was too angry to let the pain in his voice move her.

He held up a hand to silence her and came a step closer. "No, the thing is, you don't know how out of character that is for me." He gave a short, bitter laugh. "Mr. Control."

She narrowed her eyes. "So for me you made an exception?"

"You don't understand." He looked back at the floor for a moment, struggling for words, before raising his eyes back to hers. "You – the feelings I've had since I met you – it is exceptional."

She caught her breath. "Sam – " He cut her off before she could go on.

"I freaked this afternoon because you put yourself in danger." His eyes were full of regret. "The last thing I wanted to do was bully you like that. I'd like to explain if you'll let me."

She nodded mutely. As a therapist, she recognized Sam's need to unburden himself. As a woman, she hung on his every word.

He came over and sat on the sofa beside her chair. He exhaled a deep breath. "See, I was married."

"Me, too." She shrugged. "The divorce rate is around forty per cent."

"No." He looked away. "It wasn't divorce."

April felt a pang in her chest. "She died?"

He nodded.

"How long?"

"Three years ago."

"I'm so sorry." She ached to reach over and touch him, but instinct told her it wasn't the time yet. The distress in his face told her there was worse to come. "What happened?"

Sam rubbed his forehead. "More than anything, Toni wanted children. She had two miscarriages." He sighed. "We did in vitro. We had a son."

April felt a sense of dread.

"He died after three days, of a congenital heart defect." His voice was a monotone.

"Oh, no," she murmured.

Sam stood and walked over to the balcony doors, staring out. As April started to get out of her chair, he sensed her motion and held up a hand to stop her approach.

"Toni was depressed. She saw a shrink, who gave her all kinds of pills – for post-partum depression, for sleep." He shook his head. "Maybe if she'd had therapy, with someone like you…" His voice trailed off. "But she didn't." His right hand clenched into a fist. "And I coped by throwing myself into my work. Fucking clueless!" He pounded the heel of his fist against the balcony door, rattling the glass.

She couldn't sit by anymore. "Sam, " She rose from the chair and started toward him.

"I came home and found her." His voice caught. "The paramedics were too late. She took so many pills." A sob broke from his throat. "I failed her!" He wept soundlessly, the shaking of his shoulders the only indication of his grief.

Tears filling her own eyes, April approached and stood behind him. When he didn't move away, she tentatively placed a hand on his shoulder.

"Have you ever considered that maybe she failed you?" she asked softly. Her own audacity amazed her. She wasn't his therapist. Or his lover – although maybe she wanted to be.

His sobbing became audible. Her arms encircled his waist, as if of their own accord, and she rested her head against his back. After a few moments, he inhaled and let out a deep sigh.

"I'm sorry," she murmured. "I had no idea you'd been through anything like that."

"Not something I tend to talk about." He fumbled in his breast pocket for his handkerchief, blew his nose. "Some tough cop, huh?"

She raised her head and leaned over to look at his face. "I happen to think that strong and vulnerable is an awesome combination. Thanks for trusting me with both sides of you."

He sighed again and covered April's hands, locked around his waist, with his own. "So much for Mr. Control."

She tightened her embrace. "I'm liking Mr. Accessible."

He turned and took her in his arms. "I swear I'm not going to let anything happen to you."

They clung to each other as if that could make it so.

79

"I should get going," Sam murmured, his breath warm against April's cheek. "I told the crime scene technician I'd be right back and I don't want him to leave Carlee's apartment without telling me what else he found."

She pulled back from his embrace and met his eyes. She could happily drown in those dark pools. "You okay?"

"Better than I've been for a long time." He gave her a wry smile. "You gonna send me a bill?"

She smoothed his hair, trying to undo some of the mess he'd made of it. "Nah, professional courtesy." They walked to the door and saw his gaze travel to the kitchen, where utensils lay strewn about and the unopened wine bottle sat on the counter.

"Did I interrupt happy hour?"

"Oh." Embarrassed, April realized she'd forgotten all about the wine. "Do me a favor?"

He smiled. "Name it."

She retrieved the bottle. "Would you mind taking this with you?"

He raised an eyebrow.

"It's just... " She hesitated. "I don't want to drink for another three weeks, and it would be better to have it out of here."

"Sure." He took the wine from her. "We'll have it then."

"Great." She was grateful that he wasn't asking questions. "So what happens now?" She went to the pantry closet for a bag and handed it to him. "About Carlee, I mean."

"See what the forensics show." Sam bagged the wine bottle. "Try to track down Kit."

She stifled a yawn as exhaustion began to catch up with her. "Sorry."

"Hey, you've had a rough day. Take it easy tonight, huh? No more adventures for now."

She nodded. "Okay."

He leaned in and kissed her. "Holler if you need me."

She kissed him back. "Maybe I already do," she murmured. "You sure you have to go?"

He made a soft sound, between a moan and a growl, and pulled her closer. "You're dangerous. I'd better get out of here while I still can."

She smiled. "Rain check, then?"

"Absolutely." He kissed her more slowly this time, then stepped back and gave her a seductive smile. "Probably be more like a monsoon."

Sam left, and the warm glow of April's emotions went with him. The day's events crashed down on her, leaving her weary. Mechanically, she started cleaning up the kitchen, returning the scattered utensils to their drawers. When she put away the meat thermometer, the missing corkscrew lay in plain sight. She shook her head. Her Higher Power must be watching over her, she thought, half joking and half wondering. She poured herself a glass of cold water, quenching her thirst, but not her worries. Thoughts of Carlee tainted each swallow with guilt and remorse. Why hadn't she done more to protect her?

April wondered about Kit – could he have reappeared in Carlee's life, even killed her? He was a mystery man. Denise had told her he'd been nicknamed for a writer, like Shakespeare.

April couldn't think of any writers named Kit. Kit Carson? Was he a writer? He'd been some Wild West hero, she thought. Nothing to do with Shakespeare.

April visualized Carlee's patient record, the chart she'd left on her desk. She had started to look through it right before Denise came in and interrupted her. Something in it had bothered her. But what?

Her tiredness evaporated. She wanted another look at that chart. Maybe there was information about Kit, something that could help Sam identify him. At the very least, she could find Carlee's date of birth, making it easier to track down her birth certificate and get her mother's maiden name. Kit's last name.

April glanced at the kitchen clock – a few minutes past six. She could be back at Praxis in half an hour. Sam's voice echoed in her head – no more adventures tonight. She'd promised him.

She heard the ring of her cellphone, coming from the purse she'd left hanging from the knob of the pantry door. She hurried over and pulled out the phone, noticing with surprise that the call was from an extension at Franklin.

"Hello?"

"April? It's Chris Willis."

"Chris!" She was surprised he'd called her cell. It was to be used only in emergencies. "What is it?" she asked. "Is something wrong?" What else could go wrong today?

"I'm sorry. I tried you at Praxis but I guess you'd left for the day. It's been so crazy here I lost track of the time. The reason I called – this is kind of embarrassing." Chris sounded sheepish.

"What is it?"

"Some of the pages from the chart of your patient, Carlee, got separated from the rest. Maybe one of the staff here was checking something. I don't know." He laughed nervously.

That made no sense to her. Why would the ER staff remove pages from a Praxis chart?

"Anyway," Chris continued, "I thought I could drop them off at Praxis when I leave, and wondered whether the cleaning man or anyone might still be there to let me in."

April frowned. "My staff have probably gone by now, but the cleaning guy might still be wrapping up. What's the urgency? Can't it wait until tomorrow?"

"I – guess so." He hesitated. "It's just – " She heard the rustling of paper. "I thought some of this information might be important. Because of what you told me about her brother."

He'd piqued her interest. "Why? What's on the pages you found?"

"It's a family history."

April inhaled sharply. That's what had struck her about the chart! Something missing from the hospitalization summary. She hurried to the closet for her leather jacket as she spoke. "Actually, Chris, I was on my way over to finish up some paperwork. I can meet you there in half an hour, if that's okay."

"Perfect."

80

It was nearly dark and Felipe, already anxious and hungry, was now getting cold, as well. The light coming from the Praxis storefront windows held him outside on the sidewalk, like a lighthouse drawing a small boat through stormy waters. He'd stood there for maybe an hour. As long as the light was on, Dr. April might still be inside. He had to convince her he hadn't killed Carlee. Felipe wasn't about to budge until that light went off and Dr. Simon walked out of the building.

He had no place else to go.

Finally, the lights at Praxis went out. Felipe approached the doorway, watching for Dr. April. Instead, a tall black guy wearing jeans and a do-rag walked out, turning to lock up behind him. Felipe stopped short. Who the fuck was that?

"Evening." The man eyed Felipe.

"Uh." Felipe stood there, filled with uncertainty. "Uh, is anyone else still in there?" Dumb question. What idiot would be sitting there in the dark?

"What'choo want, man?"

"Nothing." Felipe turned and started off down the street. Half a block away, in front of the parking lot next to Praxis, he stopped and looked back. The man in the do-rag was preparing to cross Vine Street. Felipe sighed with relief. The last thing he needed was someone else to be suspicious of him.

The sound of a passing car made Felipe glance over at the parking lot. It was nearly empty at this hour, but now he saw a small, yellow car pull in. And he recognized the driver.

Ψ

April made the drive to Praxis in a record twenty-three minutes. The papers Chris claimed he had might help her identify Kit. And maybe Chris could explain why his staff had held onto them in the first place, instead of leaving them in Carlee's chart, where they belonged.

She parked her yellow Mini in the lot next to Praxis and walked out to the street, fumbling in her purse for her work key ring. She didn't see Felipe until he stepped out of the shadows and grabbed her arm.

April yelled, but there were no other pedestrians around. All the activity was across Vine Street on the hospital side.

"Let go of me!" She tried to jerk free of Felipe's hold.

"I gotta talk to you!" He tightened his grip on her arm. "I din' kill her!"

"Then what were you doing there? Why did you run?"

He tugged at her arm. "Listen! I can explain – "

"Let. Me. Go!" She wrenched free of his grasp.

"Wait!" Felipe cried.

April didn't. Maneuvering around him, she ran toward the traffic light at the corner, hoping to get the attention of people crossing Vine Street. But in the fading light she stumbled over a crack in the pavement – one she could have sidestepped in daylight. She fell to the ground.

In an instant, Felipe loomed over her.

Ψ

Who the hell was this guy, Kit? Sam drove back to the crime scene at Carlee's apartment, playing the question out in his head, until an idea came to him. He pulled out his phone, speed-dialing his partner's cell.

"What up, bro?" Justin sounded buzzy, like he'd been drinking coffee all day.

"I need you to work your computer magic. You in the office?"

"Unfortunately."

"Good. I want you to track down a birth record," Sam said.

"Piece of cake." Justin liked these puzzles. "Who'm I looking for?"

"Name is Randall, first name, Carlee, spelled with two 'e's, born here in Philadelphia, some time in 1978."

"What are you looking for? The exact date?"

"No," Sam replied. "Her mother's maiden name."

Ψ

"Hey, you! Stop!"

Still on the ground, April looked up at the sound of a familiar voice and rapidly approaching footsteps. Over Felipe's shoulder, she saw Chris Willis racing toward them.

"Chris! Help me!" she shouted.

He sped to her side and Felipe sprinted off. Small and fleet, he was a half block away by the time Chris reached her.

He helped her to her feet. "Are you all right? Hey, you're bleeding."

Cradling her stinging right hand, April examined a gouge on the heel of her palm. She'd scraped it against the pavement, trying to break her fall.

"I'm okay. Just a cut."

Chris inspected her hand and clucked his tongue. "Nasty, though." He nodded toward the entrance to Praxis. "You have a first aid kit inside?"

"Yes, but – " she turned back in the direction Felipe had gone. "We can't let him get away!"

"Ah-ah, doctor's orders." He steered her toward Praxis. "He won't get far."

"Wait!" April stopped in her tracks. "The key! I must have dropped it when – "

"Got it." Chris bent to retrieve her key ring from the pavement. He put a hand on April's shoulder, guiding her forward. "I'll get the door and we'll go in and take care of that hand."

Ψ

Sam's phone rang as he pulled up to Carlee's apartment. He checked the display – Justin.

"That was fast!" he said. "What've you got?"

"First, repeat after me: 'I owe you one, partner.'"

"All right, all right, your next beer is on me." Sam stifled his impatience. "The mother's maiden name – did you get it?"

Justin chuckled. "Does the Pope wear a funny hat?"

"Justin! The name?"

"Willis."

"Holy shit!"

"Something wrong? Sam?"

He ended the call and immediately dialed another. He had to reach April right away.

81

Chris Willis used April's key to unlock the storefront entrance to Praxis. "After you." He stepped aside and motioned April into the empty building ahead of him.

"Thanks." She flipped on the lights and immediately opened her bag, looking for her cellphone. "I'm calling the police. I don't want Felipe to get away." She groped for the phone. "You don't realize how dangerous he is."

She looked up when she heard the click of the entrance door lock.

"Can't be too careful around here at night." Chris slipped her key ring into his pants pocket as he walked toward her.

"My keys!"

He took hold of April's injured hand. "Let me take a look at that scrape in here, where it's light enough to see."

Why did he pocket her keys? Probably he was just distracted, April told herself. But as she watched Chris examine her hand, she noticed he wasn't carrying a brief case, an envelope or anything that might contain the papers from Carlee's chart. Something felt wrong.

"Not too bad." He peered at the scrape. "A little disinfectant and a bandage and you'll be good to go."

"Great." April started to pull away. She needed to get out her phone, call the police, better yet, Sam. But Chris didn't release her hand. What did he want?

"I'll just go for the first aid –" She looked down at his hand clasping hers. She saw the scar.

Kit.

Carlee said she'd cut a crescent-shaped scar into her brother's hand. Like the one April was staring at. She'd never noticed it before, but suddenly the riddle was solved. 'Kit,' a nickname for Christopher Marlowe. Or Chris Willis.

Act normal, she told herself, as her stomach clenched in fear. Don't let him see that you know. "It's back there." She motioned toward the hallway with her head. "The first aid kit. Want me to get it?"

Chris stared at her, his eyes cold. His teeth bared in a jack-o-lantern smile. "No, let's go back there together." He tightened his grip on her right hand.

April's heart sank. She hadn't fooled him. If she could just get to her phone. "Yeah, okay." She slipped her left hand into her open purse. "But maybe I should go wash off this cut before – " Her hand closed on the cellphone. "Before you – "

With a sudden movement, Chris yanked April forward, stepped back and flipped off the lights. "We need some privacy now." He reached for her phone. "I'll take that."

April pulled her arm back.

"The phone. Now!"

Still gripping her right hand, Chris spun April around and twisted her arm up behind her back. She cried out in pain, but managed to keep the phone from his grasp. He pulled her arm up higher, reaching for the phone. She couldn't keep it away from him.

But maybe she could still send a distress signal.

Stepping backwards to decrease her resistance against his hold, April cocked her left arm. With a guttural cry, she threw the phone as hard as she could, hurling it at the glass façade of the Praxis entrance. She prayed the glass would shatter and catch the attention of someone – anyone – outside.

Her phone hit with a loud crack, but the glass held. The phone fell to the floor and broke into pieces.

Chris swung her around to face him, his features twisted in fury. "That was very, very cute!" He accompanied the last word with a backhand slap to April's face. She screamed in shock and pain, tears springing to her eyes. She would have sunk to the floor, but he yanked her roughly to her feet.

"Let me make it clear why you shouldn't try anything stupid like that again." He twisted her arm back behind her until she feared it would snap. He used his left hand to pin her arm in place, and reached back to the waistband of his pants with his right. "I'm afraid I didn't bring the family history I took from my sister's chart. But I've got something better." The knife he pulled out had a black handle and a jagged blade that looked deadly.

And familiar.

"Like my new knife?" He pressed the point to April's cheek. "Much too dangerous to let Tyrell keep, don't you agree?"

She froze.

"Waste not, want not, right?" He shifted the blade to her throat. "Now keep quiet and do as I say."

Ψ

"C'mon, c'mon, pick up." Parked in front of Carlee's apartment, Sam muttered with impatience as he listened to April's cellphone ring. After a single ring, it cut off. Cursing, he hit redial. This time he got a canned message that the user he'd reached was out of service. No voicemail option.

"Damn!" He pounded the steering wheel, then took a deep breath to steady himself. It could be nothing. Her battery might be dead. He'd told her to take it easy. Maybe she was resting and turned off the phone. There was no reason to believe April was in danger tonight.

But Sam's gut told him otherwise.

He restarted his car and pulled out of the space in front of Carlee's building, tires screeching. He was going back to April's apartment to check on her. He flipped on his scanner as he drove away.

82

"Let's go." Holding the knife at April's throat, Chris maneuvered her down the dark hallway of Praxis to the first group room. He pushed her through the doorway. "Turn on the light."

She flipped the switch, illuminating the group-sized tables and stackable chairs that furnished the windowless interior room.

Chris snickered. "Well, speaking of Tyrell! Here we are back at the scene of my legendary showdown with him." He gestured toward a row of metal closets lining the back wall. "What's in those closets?"

"Worksheets," April said. "Craft supplies." *He's grandiose,* she thought. *Full of himself.*

"Any tape?"

"Huh?"

"You know, scotch tape, masking tape," Chris said impatiently.

"I think so." She curbed an automatic impulse to nod, in deference to the knife against her neck.

Chris pushed her toward the closets. "Get it out." He followed, holding her arm pinned behind her and the knife at her throat.

With her free hand, April opened the door to the middle closet, revealing an assortment of art supplies. The light reflected off a pair of scissors with workably pointed tips. She eyed them with longing.

Chris pushed the knifepoint into her throat. "Don't even think about the scissors."

A sharp prick at her neck made her wonder if he'd drawn blood.

Slowly and deliberately, she reached in and picked up a roll of masking tape. She started to hand it back to Chris, but instead of taking it, he kicked away one of the chairs from the nearest table.

"Sit!" He steered her to the chair, releasing her arm, but keeping the knife pointed at her face. He pushed her down into the chair.

Pins and needles tingled up and down April's arm as the circulation came back. She wanted to rub it, but didn't dare risk a move that might provoke Chris.

He nodded at the masking tape in her hand. "Tape your ankles together." Awkwardly, she complied, her scraped wrist stinging as she worked.

"Two more wraps, and tighter."

She continued unrolling the tape and binding her ankles.

"All right. Now put your arms out behind your back."

Holding the roll of tape, April extended her arms behind her. Chris stepped back, keeping the blade at her throat. He grabbed both of her slender wrists with one hand. Transferring the knife to his teeth, he used both hands to secure April's outstretched arms with several tight wraps. She winced as the tape pulled at her scrape. The pins and needles in her arm became a dull ache as both arms were immobilized. Her cheek throbbed where Chris had hit her. She didn't think he'd fractured any bones, but she had so much adrenalin pumping through her system that she probably wouldn't feel it if he had. While he bound her wrists, April flexed her ankles. A little give in the wrapping, but not much. At least it wasn't duct tape.

Finished, Chris grunted with satisfaction at his handiwork. She tried to keep her expression impassive as she met his gaze. She wanted to spit at him. She felt like a trussed turkey. As if to underscore her helplessness, he turned her chair to face the table and calmly sat on the tabletop. Smiling, he tossed aside the roll of tape.

"This is more like it." He toyed with the knife. "If I have to, I'll gag you." He poked at the tape roll with his weapon. "But it will be very uncomfortable for you, and won't do much for our conversation. Will it?"

April felt a glimmer of hope. If he wanted to talk, maybe he wouldn't kill her. At least, not right away. Grandiose as he sounded, perhaps Chris wanted to brag.

"I won't scream, if that's what you mean," she said.

"Wise decision."

"You're Kit. Carlee's half-brother. Or, you were."

"Aren't you the smart one? I knew you'd catch on. That's why I invited you on this date tonight." He grinned. "Did you read about me in that family history, before I shredded it?"

"No, I missed that." She pointed her chin at his hand. "I recognized your scar."

He lifted his hand. "Did Carlee tell you how I got it?"

"She told me a lot of things." April swallowed. Where was this going? All she knew was that she had to keep Chris talking.

Ψ

Sam made a right onto Broad Street and picked up speed, heading for April's apartment in Jenkintown. His scanner produced a steady stream of police calls, the usual nightly litany of burglaries, traffic accidents and domestic violence.

Then he heard the report of a suspected assault in progress at a familiar Vine Street address. He pulled a U-turn on Broad, to a cacophony of blaring horns and angry shouts, and sped back toward Center City.

83

Bound and helpless in her chair, while Chris gloated over her, April felt like Scheherazade in The Arabian Nights. Could she stave off her own execution as the wily queen managed to do for 1000 nights? April had no mesmerizing tales to buy her life for even one night. Only her wits and therapeutic skills. She prayed they'd be enough.

"So my sister told you things." Chris's smile mocked her. "You were her therapist, knew her secrets. He laughed bitterly. "And you think you know all about it, right?"

He wanted her to understand, April realized. If he only meant to kill her, she'd be dead by now, not arranged as his captive audience. She might not have stories to tell, but Chris did. His story might be all he had left.

"I'm sure there's a lot I don't appreciate," she said. "Why don't you tell me?"

"How much do you already know?" He stuck the blade into the table.

Where to start? She needed to engage him, buy time. "Well," she stalled, "I wouldn't want to violate patient confidentiality."

He laughed and pulled up the knife to scratch a check mark into the tabletop. "Aren't you the conscientious little professional? But you're forgetting – Carlee signed a release for you to talk to me."

"A release to talk to the ER staff," April said mildly. "Which she didn't know her brother directed. Hardly informed consent."

Chris pointed the knife at her face and she felt a rush of fear. "Carlee's dead. Her confidentiality privileges died with her."

April nodded. She had to stay calm. "Guess you're right about that." She tried to swallow, her mouth dry. "Here's one thing I think I know. You were at her apartment today, weren't you?"

He carved another check mark next to the first. "Correct."

She made eye contact. "You didn't go there to hurt her, did you?"

Silently, he carved a heart around the two check marks. Grief twisted his features. "I loved her." A trace of the hurt child he'd once been flickered across his face. He pointed the knife into the tabletop, balancing it there with his forefinger on the handle.

At least it wasn't in her face now.

"When you told me about her," he said "that she was here, in Praxis, I could hardly believe it. After all those years, it was like a sign. I knew it was time for us to be together again." He frowned, as if pulled from a daydream. "You said she was afraid of me. I couldn't let that stand. I had to see her and try to make it right between us."

"So you went to her apartment?"

He nodded, rotating the knife on its axis. "At first she wouldn't let me in. But I kept talking to her, through the door. I promised I wouldn't hurt her, told her I was a doctor now. That seeing each other could help us both heal."

"And you persuaded her to let you in?"

"Yes." His eyes widened, wonder transforming his face. "She was even more beautiful than I remembered. Fragile, but so brave."

"Yes, she was." April's eyes welled as she remembered Carlee.

Chris stood, glowering, as if her tears had provoked him. Leaving the knife stuck in the table, he paced around April, who eyed the blade with longing.

He grabbed her chair and shook it. "Easy to sit in judgment of me, is it?"

April kept silent, her heart pounding. In the distance a car horn blared, a reminder of the world outside that now seemed so far away.

"We grew up in hell." Chris's voice was flat.

"She talked about it. A nightmare."

"Hah!" he barked bitterly. "You don't know the half of it." He walked over and pulled the knife out of the tabletop.

Her stomach knotted. "Tell me."

"You want the whole story?" He came closer, knife raised. "You comfortable?" His voice dripped with sarcasm. "Sure it's not too warm in here for you?"

April shook her head frantically. "No, I'm –"

"Let's loosen your jacket." She gasped as he slashed open the buttonholes of her favorite leather jacket. "There. That's better."

Despite her terror, a flash of anger burned in her chest. She hoped she could use it.

"So, did Carlee tell you about our mother?"

"She sounded seriously depressed," April replied.

"That's your diagnosis, Doctor?"

"You were in a better position to make that assessment. Was she?"

"Oh yes." He rattled off the psychiatric diagnostic code.

"Major depression, recurrent and severe." April nodded, translating.

"Beyond recurrent. More like continuous. Most days she couldn't get out of bed, let alone take care of two children." He grimaced. "It hurt to look at her."

"So she couldn't protect you – from your stepfather, I mean." April noticed the perspiration on Chris's brow. The room wasn't that warm. He'd cut open her jacket, but she hadn't been the one feeling the heat.

"Ah! My stepfather. What did Carlee have to say about him?"

"He was abusive," she ventured.

"Abusive! Yes." He leaned in close, almost in April's face. "Did she mention that he used to come home late, stinking drunk? That he liked to use his belt on us?"

She lowered her gaze. "Yes."

He nodded, put his mouth to April's ear. "Did she tell you he'd make one of us watch while he beat the other one?"

"No," she whispered, sickened.

Chris stepped back, examining the knife. "I swear to God, I don't know which was worse, getting the beating or watching." He regarded April with detachment. "So she didn't tell you that part?"

"No."

He perched on the table, studying the blade again. "Of course, things started to change a bit as I got older." He looked up at April and smiled. "Things become stimulating," he winked, "to a growing boy."

She inhaled sharply.

"Watching got kind of exciting. When he'd pull down her little panties, and –"

April turned away in disgust. Carlee had been violated in so many ways.

In a flash, he was on top of her, grabbing her shoulders and shaking her. "Self righteous bitch!" He slapped her. "Should we talk about your sex life?" He leered at her. "You doing that cop?"

He leaned in close enough for her to smell his sour breath. "He use his cuffs on you yet?"

April took a deep breath, fighting to stem her panic. Her face throbbed. She had to defuse this. Chris was destabilizing, his emotions shifting from moment to moment. He was dangerous. "I'm sorry." She met his eyes. "You and Carlee were both victims."

He nodded. "And my mother!"

"Yes."

"All his victims," Chris thundered.

"Your stepfather's, yes."

"Him?" Chris looked at her with scorn. "He was a maggot, feeding on a carcass!" He shook his head. "The one who set the whole rotten thing into motion was my real father – by abandoning my mother and me."

"Your real father?" April mentally reviewed the scant history from Carlee's records, but recalled nothing about the man who'd fathered Kit.

He chuckled. "Haven't figured out that part, have you?"

As she stared at Chris, April had a sense of *déjà vu* and realized who else's face she was seeing. Her eyes widened in shock. "Lowell Morgenstern!" Her jaw dropped as the rest of it came to her. "You killed him!"

His smile was triumphant. "Yes, I did. It was ridiculously easy to steal some Botox from dermatology. I dispensed justice to my eminent, illegitimate father."

"Justice?" April blurted out. She, too, had been illegitimate and abandoned by her biological father. Perhaps the experience had damaged her, but she'd never contemplated vengeance.

"That's right, justice. For my mother!" Chris brandished his knife, as if making a toast, then drove the blade into the table to scratch another check mark. "He used her and threw her away like a piece of garbage!" His voice became louder. "Along with me!" He waved the knife in the air again. "For the years of misery he caused."

Another check mark, etched even deeper this time. April hoped she'd live to order a new table.

"And for God only knows how many other women he trashed!" Chris slashed wildly at the marks he'd made, as if trying to obliterate them. "Look what he did to Sandra!" He was screaming now, spittle forming at the corners of his mouth. "Used her, humiliated her! That was the final straw. All those victims, and what did he get? Awards, accolades, power!" With an animal grunt, Chris stabbed the knife into the table. He exhaled, his expression turning steely. "It had to stop." A half smile curled his lips. "So I stopped it."

April tried to concentrate her reeling thoughts. Chris was unraveling. How much longer before he snapped?

"Tell me," she said, "how did it happen that you were here – I mean, at Franklin? Did he know –"

"Who I was?" He laughed bitterly. "The son-of-a-bitch was too wrapped up in himself to realize who he hired to run his psych ER. The height of arrogance, right?"

"But did you know?"

"Who he was? Of course. That's why I came to Franklin. To look him in the eye." His face wrinkled with disgust. "I even entertained the idea that he might –" Another sharp laugh. "Acknowledge me. But he was just…fucking…oblivious." He snorted in contempt.

April stared. With his face twisted in that expression of arrogance, Chris's resemblance to Morgenstern was unmistakable. No wonder Tyrell was so receptive when Chris came into this room to talk him down! She had missed it. Everyone had.

Fear froze her stomach and parched her mouth, but she managed to rasp: "So you – you ended the evil?"

He smiled, bowed theatrically, and pulled the knife out of the table.

More grandiosity, she thought. Did she dare push further? "And Carlee?" she asked tentatively.

The smile vanished. "I thought she'd be glad I killed him." His eyes welled.

He fingered the knife, absently, his gaze out of focus, perhaps back with Carlee. As though she were still alive.

His emotions were bouncing all over the place, April thought. No telling what he might do next.

Chris wiped his eyes with the back of his hand, child-like. "But she looked at me like I was a – a monster! She was going to call the police." He sounded petulant, a boy who'd been denied a promised treat. Perhaps she could use that.

April recognized the sudden click of the front door unlocking. She froze. Chris didn't react. Was he too distracted to hear it?

"I put my arms around her, like I used to." He sounded far away, as if in a reverie. "Not to hurt her, but to comfort her, reassure her." He looked at April, his expression bewildered. "But she started screaming. The pillow – it was just there. I never wanted to hurt her. Why?" His eyes implored her. "Why would she fight me like that?"

My God, were those footsteps coming down the hall? Keep him occupied, April willed herself. Keep him engaged.

"Kit," she said softly.

He gazed at her, as if drawn by her use of his childhood name.

That was it! She had to appeal to the little boy. "Your poor sister had no choice. Morgenstern hypnotized her, as part of his research."

Chris gaped. "What do you mean?"

The footsteps came closer. Soft, like someone on tip-toe.

Focus on me, on me, she silently willed Chris. "He gave her a post-hypnotic suggestion to make her keep seeing him, depend on him. She couldn't have tolerated anyone taking him away – not even you."

"No!" His cry of anguish dissolved into rage. "That bastard!" he roared, tightening his grip on the knife. "He stole her from me!"

"Police, Willis," a voice called out from the doorway. "Drop the knife and put up your hands."

84

April couldn't believe her ears. "Sam!" Tears of relief filled her eyes.

"April!" He stood in the doorway. "Are you all right?"

"I'm –"

In the blink of an eye, Chris grabbed her with his free hand, yanking her from the chair. Her hands caught behind her, April felt like her shoulders were being wrenched from their sockets. She screamed in pain as Chris kicked away the chair and thrust her in front of him. His free arm locked around her neck and he pointed the knife at her throat.

"Willis!" Sam yelled. "Let her go!" His gun was already drawn. He glared at Chris, and April could read Sam's anger in the set of his jaw.

"It's Dr. Willis! You're not giving the orders here."

Crushed against his body, April could smell the man's fear. "Chris," she murmured, "please don't hurt me."

"Think about it, Dr. Willis." Sam's voice dropped to a quieter level. "There's no way for you to get out of here."

Chris flicked at April's hair with the knife. "But she's the one you've got to worry about, isn't she? One step closer and she dies."

"And then what?" Sam kept his tone level, but April saw worry flicker across his face at Chris's threat.

"Please, Kit," she begged. "No more killing." The blade at her throat wavered – or had she imagined it? She reminded herself to keep talking to the frightened little boy.

"Look, I won't come in," Sam proposed. "I'll stand right here, and we can talk about what to do. All right?"

More footsteps came from down the hallway. Without taking his eyes off Chris, Sam held up a hand to stop their advance.

Chris tightened his hold on April's neck. "Don't come in here!"

Sam raised one hand in a gesture of surrender. "No one's coming in." He lowered the gun in his other hand. "Let's talk about you coming out."

"You and your men leave the building," Chris said, "and maybe I will."

April remembered the emergency exit at the end of the hallway. Did Chris know about it? Was that his escape plan?

"We're not leaving, Dr. Willis," Sam said evenly. "This will work out better for you if you let her go."

"Don't act like I'm stupid, Detective. She's my insurance."

"But if you kill her, the policy expires."

Chris chuckled. "True, but the coverage includes injury, too."

He pressed the knife to April's cheek. Her heart raced.

"I could flick out an eye, or ruin her pretty face."

"No!" Sam took a step forward.

Chris pressed the knife harder and a trickle of blood ran down April's cheek. A small whimper escaped her lips.

Sam froze and clenched the handle of his gun. "Willis," he growled. "I'm warning you..."

"I know!" Chris sounded gleeful. "How about a lock of this lovely red hair?" His hand shot up from April's neck and he grabbed a handful of her hair, pulling it taut.

"No!" she cried.

Swiftly, he sliced off a hank and tossed it onto the table in front of them. "A little souvenir for you, Detective."

The sight of her hair strewn across the table was horrifying – a violation. April was helpless. With her ankles bound, she couldn't even stand unless Chris held her up. His grip on her neck made it hard to breathe. Her eyes telegraphed a plea to Sam, and she saw rage and frustration in his.

"That's enough, Willis." Sam's gaze locked on April's. She tried to draw strength from it.

"You and your men get out of here, Perone." Chris's tone was icy. "Or the next thing I'll cut off is her little finger."

Panic accelerated April's heartbeat and she fought to keep from hyperventilating.

"You'd have to look away from me to do it." Sam raised his gun. "I can shoot faster than you can cut."

Chris pulled harder against her neck. "Don't be so sure. In med school they teach you where the major arteries are."

His words made April reel with nausea and fear. It was a stalemate, and her life hung in the balance. Was there something she could do? Any words to reach Chris? She couldn't go on dangling from his grasp, like a useless rag doll. She had to take a chance.

Talk to the little boy.

"I know how much you loved her, Kit," she whispered. His sudden intake of breath encouraged her. "She wouldn't have wanted this for you."

"Fuck do you know?" he muttered in her ear.

"Carlee adored you. You were her hero."

His grip eased slightly. His next breath rasped.

"I know you didn't mean to hurt her, Kit. It was an accident."

"They won't believe us!" His voice rose higher, childlike.

"I'll help you. You won't be alone. They'll – "

"Dr. Willis –" Sam fell silent as April mouthed: "No."

"Why is that cop here?" Chris whined. He gripped her neck tighter. "Are you with him?" He hissed the question into her ear.

"With him?" April's thoughts whirled. Was he jealous? Confused? Did he think she was Carlee? The blade tightened against her neck. She struggled to keep her breathing steady. "Please, Kit," she murmured. "Please don't make the detective kill you."

He made a mewling sound and the blade pulled away from her throat. A moment later, the grip on April's neck released.

Sam let out a sigh of relief. "That's right, Dr. Willis, now –"

A grunt, and something warm and wet sprayed against the back of April's head. Blood splattered the table. She gasped. So much blood.

With a groan, Chris dropped to the floor behind her.

"Hey!" Sam was already in the room. "On your feet! Hands in the air!"

April stumbled forward. She leaned over and twisted to the side, dropping onto the table. Sam rushed toward her, gun raised.

Time slowed. She didn't know if seconds or minutes passed before Sam crouched beside her, his hand clutching her shoulder, his face filled with concern.

"I'm okay." She managed a weak smile.

A quick squeeze of her shoulder and he stood. He pointed his gun at Chris, who lay in a pool of blood on the floor.

"He's down!" Sam's shout brought two officers running in from the hall. "Call the paramedics."

One of the officers reached for his radio.

"Where's the knife?" asked the other.

Sam lowered his gun. "In his neck." He knelt, checking for a pulse, then sighed and shook his head. "Guess he did know where to cut."

85

"Keep that ice pack on your cheek," the paramedic instructed, as he tied off the gauze bandage he'd applied to April's scraped hand. "There. How's that?"

"Better, thanks." She sat perched on a table in the group room while he attended to her.

He nodded, putting supplies back into his kit. He pointed at her hand. "You'll want to put a rubber glove on that when you wash all the blood out of your hair."

"What's left of it." April fingered the ragged locks hanging from one side of her head and frowned. She leaned against Sam, who stood beside her. "I'm a mess," she lamented.

"Hey!" He put an arm around her, despite the dried blood encrusting her jacket. "Nothing a shower and a good hairdresser can't fix." He studied her. "I'm trying to picture you with short hair."

"Please!" April made a face.

They turned to watch as the other paramedics carried out the body of Chris Willis. Quickly as they'd arrived after the 911 call, they'd been too late. His severed carotid had bled out in minutes.

Sam pulled up a chair and sat, facing April. He rubbed his chin reflectively. "I can't get over how you reeled him in like that. If you decide to become a hostage negotiator, let me know. The police could use you."

She chuckled, which she found a whole lot easier to do without an arm locked around her neck anymore. "It helped having a guy with a gun around as backup. Say," she added, "is that what they call Good Cop, Bad Cop?"

"Wise guy."

Her expression sobered. "I think he wanted to tell me what he did, and that's the reason I'm still alive." She shuddered and her hand involuntarily went to up her throat.

Sam reached for her hand and clasped it in his. "So he needed to confess to you about killing Carlee?"

She blew out a breath. "Killing them both – Morgenstern and Carlee."

"What?"

She quickly filled him in on the sordid history Chris had related to her.

"Wow!" Sam shook his head. "The ultimate dysfunctional family. But I still don't understand why he killed Carlee."

She pondered for a moment. "I suspect he was wracked with guilt about molesting her and coped by projecting all of his dark stuff onto Morgenstern. Every terrible thing that happened became his fault. Murdering his biological father was more than vengeance for Chris. It was an act of purification, a way to wipe out all the wrongs of his past."

"And he expected Carlee to congratulate him?" Sam's eyes narrowed with skepticism.

"It's crazy, but yes, I think he did. When Chris found out she was here, he took it as a sign. But then, when he went to her and told her what he'd done, she was horrified. Remember, Carlee was deeply attached to Morgenstern because of the hypnotic suggestion he gave her."

"So Willis lost it and killed her?"

"Pretty much." April nodded. "Then he unraveled. I don't know whether he abducted me to keep me from exposing him or to forgive him. Maybe both." Her eyes widened. "Or maybe he wanted to die. He had no burning cause to live for anymore."

"Huh! Suicide by cop I've heard of. Suicide by psychologist, that's new." Sam shrugged. "Anyway, it makes sense that he'd have the medical knowledge to plant the Botox in Morgenstern's nasal spray, and –"

"Sam!" April suddenly sat upright. "I just realized – how did you know I was here?"

"I was worried about you. My scanner was on. When I heard the dispatcher put out a call to this address –"

"But – who made the call to the police?"

"Oh! Thanks for reminding me." He motioned to one of the officers.

"Yes, Detective?" the man asked.

"Is he still out there? Could you bring him in?"

The officer nodded and walked out. April stared at Sam in bewilderment, which turned to amazement a moment later, when Felipe Diaz cautiously entered. He hesitated at the doorway, looking around. His mouth formed a perfect "O" as he took in the state of the room.

"Felipe!" April cried. "You called the police?"

He nodded. "When that man ran over, outside, I recognized him. He was hanging around Carlee's building this morning when I left." He frowned. "I could tell he didn't belong there. He looked like a bad man. After you fell and he chased me away, I – I was afraid for you."

A lump filled April's throat.

"So I came back," Felipe concluded. "A light went on in here, then off. Then something crashed into the glass –"

"My cellphone!" April exclaimed. "He tried to take it, so I threw it."

"Smart move," Sam commented.

"Si," Felipe agreed. "So I looked in and saw him hit you and pull out a knife. I went to call the police, but I had to go across to the hospital to find a pay phone."

April hopped off the table and rushed over to him. "Felipe! You saved my life." She felt an impulse to hug him. Instead, she extended her hand.

He shook it. "S'okay." He looked away in embarrassment. The hug would have been too much.

"Muchas gracias, Felipe." Her eyes brimmed.

He stood up straighter and met her gaze. *"El gusto es mio."*

86

Felipe left Praxis, after promising to return tomorrow so April could free him from Morgenstern's post-hypnotic suggestion. Her savior deserved respite from his compulsions. Also, April thought, a lot of kittens might be better off. As Felipe waved and walked out, she yawned and stretched. Her wrists, elbows and shoulders were stiff from being tied behind her.

"C'mon, let's get you home." Sam took off his jacket, nodding at the blood-encrusted one April still wore. "Take that thing off and put this on. It's chilly out there."

She pulled off the tan leather jacket she'd once loved and wrinkled her nose at its condition. "Yuck!" She crumpled it into a ball and threw it on the floor.

"Here." Sam draped his jacket over her shoulders.

A faint trace of his scent enveloped her and she felt like purring.

"Let's go," he said.

"My car is next door." She looked at her bandaged hand.

"And it can stay there tonight." He took her by the elbow and led her to the door.

April hadn't expected to walk out of the room alive. "But won't they tow it?" she asked. "Or give me a ticket?"

"Trust me. I've got it covered."

It was a good thing Sam drove. April dozed off in the passenger seat on the ride home. She woke to Sam's hand on her shoulder.

"Huh?" She looked around, bleary-eyed. "Where are we?"

"Home. Yours." He smiled.

The look on his face stirred something inside her. She marveled that desire could follow so soon after a brush with death. Although April had read about that instinct, now her very being taught her the truth of it. She felt a powerful yearning for Sam's touch, a longing to surrender to the tide of passion rising within her.

"It's good to be alive," she whispered.

Sam kissed her, his lips gentle against hers. "Amen," he said. "Come on."

They took the elevator up to her apartment. Boris and Natasha greeted her with typical feline enthusiasm. Cats are always ready to celebrate life. April felt a sudden pang, thinking of what might have become of them had the evening turned out differently. She knelt to pet them, savoring the feel of their fur and the sound of their purring.

Sam lifted his jacket from her shoulders. "I'll bet you'd like to go get cleaned up. How about I make you a cup of tea?"

She grinned up at him. "Wow! A guy who cooks."

He gave her a look of mock reproach. "I'll have you know I make a mean lasagna."

"That's more than I can say." She stood. "Tea would be great. There's some herbal stuff in the cabinet." And no wine in the refrigerator, which was okay. She didn't need it.

But she knew what she did need tonight.

She reached up and fingered the back of her head, feeling the dried blood matting her hair. Not too sexy. "I think I will go take a quick shower."

"Sure." He nodded. "Take your time. I'll get the tea."

"Okay." She turned, then looked back over her shoulder at him. "Just help yourself to anything you want."

He arched an eyebrow. "There's an offer I can't refuse."

She decided to make the shower a brief one.

Ten minutes later she rejoined him in the kitchen, her towel-dried hair still damp, skin bare under a turquoise terrycloth robe.

He handed her a mug of hot tea. "You look a lot more comfortable."

She took the mug. "You, too." He'd taken off his gun holster and his tie. A hint of soft brown hair peeked out from his open collar. The sight induced a fluttering sensation in April's belly. She took a sip of tea.

He reached over to run his fingers through her wet, ragged hair. "Anything else I can do for you?" He smiled. "Stay and tuck you in?"

She put down the mug and edged closer. She opened a button on his shirt. "I'd like that, Detective." She ran a finger through soft chest hair, heat radiating down her thighs. "But I'm afraid I'm too wired to sleep."

She opened the next button. "And I have to go in tomorrow and hypnotize those other Pacifil subjects."

She pulled his shirt tail out of his pants, and he drew a swift breath.

"You know," she continued, "to remove Morgenstern's post-hypnotic suggestion."

He pulled her close and kissed her. Her hands traveled up under his shirt, feeling the taut muscles of his back.

"I think you should plan on sleeping in tomorrow," he said.

Strong arms encircled her. The hardness at the front of his pants wasn't his gun, and April felt her own answering wetness. She pressed herself against him.

Sam moaned softly. "If you're so bent on doing hypnosis, you can practice on me." His lips grazed her neck. "I'm already pretty well under your spell."

"Mmmm. In that case…" She raised her lips to his ear. "Let me give you a suggestion." She whispered it, then gently nibbled his earlobe for emphasis.

The next kiss was deeper, longer. His hands were warm on the turquoise terrycloth, exploring, caressing.

Untying.

His voice was husky. "That does sound entrancing."

The robe slipped to the floor.

Atlanta, Wednesday, 10-27

Epilogue

In the psychiatrist's tastefully contemporary office, two men stood and shook hands, sealing the verbal agreement they'd just reached. Freddy Kurtz, pharmaceutical rep from Basel Aniline Farbenfabrik, was a happy man this morning. He'd salvaged the Phase Two Pacifil study, after the tragic death of his buddy, Lowell Morgenstern.

"Dr. Martin," he said, smiling. "It's been a pleasure. On behalf of BAFF, we look forward to a fruitful collaboration."

"As do I, Mr. Kurtz." The psychiatrist nodded. "You'll have the full resources of Stanton Medical's behavioral health programs behind this project."

"Your idea of beginning the Pacifil trials with inpatients, then following them to the outpatient programs, will certainly help ensure drug compliance."

"Oh, we'll make it work, Mr. Kurtz. Our continuity of care is top-notch. You won't have a problem with subjects dropping out or falling through the cracks."

"Please! Call me Freddy," the rep insisted.

Dr. Gerald Martin clapped a hand onto Freddy's shoulder as he walked him to the door.

Freddy turned to smile at his new primary investigator. "So, then," he said. "We'll get that check for the start-up costs in the mail to you by the end of the week. And I'll personally e-mail you Dr. Morgenstern's hypnosis protocols." Freddy winked. "Which, as we agreed, will remain our little secret. Right?"

The psychiatrist nodded. "I understand."

Freddy shook his hand once more. "Go celebrate tonight. I predict Pacifil will be the next wonder drug!"

Acknowledgements

Many people kept me afloat through successive drafts of this novel. Thanks to my psychologist colleagues, Sharon Feeney, Ph.D., Psy.D., Glenda Insabella, Ph.D. and Randy Simon, Ph.D., and Maureen Fitzpatrick for their comments and suggestions. The dynamic duo of June Zagury and Captain (Ret.) Mike Zagury gave generous input on psychiatric emergency and police procedures, respectively.

Special thanks to my niece and social media consultant, Hannah Forman, who lovingly eased me out of my cave and into the online world that any author must inhabit these days. I'm grateful to Sage Adderley for superb technical and publicity support and to Bradley Knox for the sensational cover design.

This book would have remained unfit for human consumption without the astute critiques and warm camaraderie I've enjoyed from my fellow members of New Providence Writers. Finally, to my husband, Dan Hansburg, thanks for all your listening, ideas, encouragement and support in ways both large and small.

CPSIA information can be obtained
at www.ICGtesting.com
Printed in the USA
FFOW04n1403290914
7657FF